The Expansion

Christoph Martin

Clink
Street

London | New York

Published by Clink Street Publishing 2017

Copyright © 2017

First edition.

ISBN: 978-1-911525-29-5 paperback
978-1-911525-30-1 ebook

"Be subtle, even to the point of formlessness. Be mysterious, even to the point of soundlessness. Thereby, you can be the director of the opponent's fate."

—Sun Tzu, *The Art of War*

Prologue

Prologue, I

Burns Estate, Surrey, England
January, 1993

She'd always been beautiful.

Even as a young woman, before the diamonds and designer handbags. Before she discarded the snug, high-street polyester and invited him to dress her slowly—lovingly—in silk.

As he fought his way toward her that winter's night, through the crush of champagne glasses and dinner suits, he recognized in his wife's eyes the same, potent attention that had drawn him—and so many others—toward her, all those years ago.

Because Helen Burns saw people—she really *saw* them.

Just as she'd seen him. And his estate.

Her canny ability to smell opportunity had been the reason his already impressive holdings and assets had exploded beyond mere wealth into the realm of fortunes: theirs, and those of the souls fated to stray into her orbit.

"My love, you'll never believe whose path I crossed last night. It was meant to be …!"

Edward Burns felt the stab of pain in his chest.

"Ed, what is it? Is something wrong?" She must have seen him, because now she was beside him.

"We need to get out of here!" He gripped her arm.

She pulled back. "What?"

"Helen, if we don't go now—"

"What are you talking about? We can't leave in the middle of our own party—"

"They've arrested Garcia!"

"*Rupert* Garcia …?"

She froze.

Slowly, she turned her head. Her gaze travelled over the glassy twinkle of Christmas lights and the swirling theatre of laughter and faces, as though seeing it all for the first time.

She looked back at him.

"Shit!"

And he saw the set of her jaw.

"We need to take care of this, Ed," she hissed. "*Now!*"

She waved the head of their household staff over, issued instructions and—within moments—they were away: through the marble foyer of their home, onto the gravel swing drive, past mistletoe and ivy that clothed the stone columns, and out onto the frosty grounds of the Burns estate.

By the time the skids of their Robinson R44 helicopter were lifting into the night, she had called their lawyer.

"*We're on the way to London,*" she'd said, as she strapped herself in.

The heli's rotor blades roared, shoveling icy air. They gained altitude fast.

Expertly, Ed took the craft above the tree line.

"I've made arrangements for Max." He spoke into the lip microphone.

"What arrangements?" Her voice was in his headset.

"He'll come back to England next week to live with Alan—"

"With *Alan?!* Are you crazy? I'm not having my son on a housing estate! Do you know what those places are like—?"

"*Enough*, Helen! You're not listening! It's *over!* We don't get to choose any more. There's a warrant for our arrest." He looked at the well of blackness he knew to be the Surrey forests below, and his stomach lurched. Perhaps there was another way …?

"But this is *us*, Ed: me and you. We'll pull through, like we always do."

"Except it isn't just us this time, is it? It's everybody else you convinced to buy into Rupert's bloody scheme! All of our friends, Helen!"

"I wasn't to know—"

"No!" He cut her off. "You knew exactly what you were doing." He turned to her, and an emptiness began to steal over him. "Everything I did, I did it for you. I always loved you so much. I still do."

She said nothing.

"But everything we have … It wasn't enough. It was never enough."

Still, she remained silent, and Ed turned away.

They had reached a flying altitude of three thousand feet.

His fingers found what they were searching for: the smooth, plastic sheath that guarded the engine's idle shut-off valve.

It would only take a moment.

Numb, he turned to his wife. She had covered her lips with her hand, and he heard a sob. In the darkness, the diamonds at her throat had lost their fire.

"It's the best way. I can't let them put you in jail," he said. "Max will be able to make a clean start. One day, I hope he'll forgive me—"

"*No!*" she shrieked, swiveling frantically in her seat. One hand was on the window pane, and her eyes were on the ground, far below them: on the freckled lights of their receding home.

With all his remaining strength, Edward Burns reached for his wife. He drew her toward him, and he hugged her tightly.

Then he pulled the valve.

As the engine died, she fought the cage of his arms.

But it was only a moment.

Then the canopy tore away, slain with disembodied metal

blades, and the torque threw them, spinning, pitching, toward the ground.

Edward Burns felt nothing as his skull split open.

Prologue, II

Zuoz, Swiss Alps

Dragging his suitcase over icy cobblestones, sixteen-year-old Max Burns stumbled toward the stone water trough that sat at the top of the rise. The old fountain had frozen over months ago, although Max knew nobody would have need of it until late spring, when the valley thawed.

His classmate, Godfredo Roco, had abandoned his own bag on a nearby snowdrift, and was settling himself on the edge of the stone basin.

Godfredo was classically good looking despite an impressive bruise that marred his left eye socket, and he carried a fat and expensive cigar between gloved fingers. He had helped himself to several cigars from his father's collection with the express intention of saving them for his birthday, although—after a few too many slugs from the smuggled schnapps bottle on the four-hour trip from Zürich to Zuoz that evening—he'd stepped off the train and announced, "Fuck it. Now's as good a time as any." And promptly lit one up.

Max now plonked himself alongside his friend, and slid off his knitted beanie. He ran a hand through his blond, perpetually tousled hair, and surveyed the village below. Its narrow, stone streets had been laid hundreds of years before the first growl of a motor, and snow lay thickly on neat, fairy-tale rooftops. Twinkling Christmas lights delineated eaves and chimneys, and wisps of wood smoke hung low in the valley.

Max pointed to the highest mountain peak. He squinted along the length of his arm.

"I reckon I was about *that* high in the helicopter last week," he slurred. His words were slow and deliberate, thanks to the schnapps and the icy air on his lips.

"Should've seen my dad's face, Fredo!" he said. He dropped his arm to his lap and turned to his friend. "Sort of like he was shit-scared that I was up there in the heli all by myself for the first time … But also really, really bloody proud."

Sighing, he flung an arm over Godfredo's shoulder. "I bloody love that, you know? I bloody love *him*." He hiccupped. "Always pushing me to do big stuff." He hiccupped again, stumbling over his words. He laughed. "'Scuse me."

There was no response but a pulsing orange glow as Godfredo sucked repeatedly on the cigar.

Max released his friend and punched him playfully on the arm.

"You should ask your dad to get you some flying lessons," he said, recalling the rush of adrenalin as he watched the grounds of their English country estate drop away below him. "Seriously, Fredo, you'd love it. You've got one hand on the cyclic …" He closed his eyes. "You pull on the collective—"

"Jesus!" Godfredo cut him off. "Can you imagine my dad spending a nice Sunday afternoon watching me go up in a fucking helicopter?" His tone wasn't bitter, although—as he turned—Max saw his friend's smile was forced.

He tried to imagine Godfredo's larger-than-life father, Paco Roco, doing anything recreational with his son.

At least, anything that didn't involve hordes of hot women on yachts.

Or hollering his head off at horses on the racetrack.

"Okay, maybe not—"

"You fucking got that right!" Godfredo's laugh was brittle. He held out the cigar. "Here, *hermano*." He often addressed Max this way, and his voice carried a rich lilt and a trace of his Argentinian-Spanish mother tongue, despite having lived in England with his father for going on a decade.

Max took the cigar and inspected the label.

"You know, Fredo, if I wasn't so sodding drunk right now, I'd call up your dad."

"Yeah?" Godfredo was looking out across the valley.

"Yeah. I bloody would. And I'd tell him he's gotta stop hitting you."

Immediately, Godfredo turned to look at Max. "He doesn't mean it."

Max shook his head. "Dude, face it. Your dad's a complete asshole."

He didn't see the punch coming until Godfredo's fist collided with his stomach.

Immediately, he doubled over in pain.

The cigar dropped, its embers scattering like shooting stars.

Godfredo was on his feet. He pointed at Max with one finger. "*I* get to say he's an asshole. *You* don't."

In a second, the two boys were fighting, all right hooks and headlocks. They writhed, their limbs entangled, landing heavily on icy snow.

Godfredo wrenched himself from Max's hold and dived for his suitcase.

Slowly, Max lifted his head. He watched as Godfredo strode away and—just as quickly—swung around and strode back.

He stood within arm's reach, his lips pressed together.

"You know, sometimes I fucking hate my dad. More than life itself." He paused. "But he's the only one I've got. So … yeah."

Before Max could apologize, Godfredo had set off, alone, up the last, steep stretch of road toward the Alpine boarding school.

As Max approached the cluster of stuccoed, salmon buildings that comprised the exclusive school grounds, he glanced up. The ever-reliable clock on the squat bell tower told him it was close to midnight.

Trudging through fresh snow, he followed Godfredo's tracks past the solitary fir tree that stood at the center of the courtyard. Its branches were laden with snow and silver Christmas baubles.

He hauled his suitcase into the building.

The foyer was warm and brightly lit, and still smelled of the evening's meal: doubtless roasted meat and vegetables. For those who'd arrived back at school on time.

He stamped his feet to rid his boots of snow and kept his head down, hoping above all hope that he could slip by while the housemistress was dealing with Godfredo: his friend was masterful at hiding his inebriation, which came in handy in the face of the school's zero tolerance policy.

"Sorry'm a bit late," he mumbled, glancing up, briefly.

He stopped walking.

Godfredo was staring at him. The housemistress was staring at him. And the receptionist's door stood open.

"What's going on?"

Max turned to see a large man by the office door. He wore a flimsy trench coat—surely not enough for the ravages of an alpine winter. His huge, no-name, nylon sneakers were ill fitting and heavily worn.

Max recognized him immediately.

"Uncle Alan?" He looked from his uncle to the house master. "I don't understand."

Alan stepped forward, twisting a red-and-white English soccer scarf in his enormous fists.

"'Fraid there's some bad news from home, lad. It's your parents."

Max felt his stomach lurch.

"There was an accident," Alan continued. "They didn't survive the crash. They passed on." He placed a heavy hand on Max's shoulder.

"They … what?"

"They died, lad." Alan's deep voice was gentle. "I'm real sorry. We tried to reach you, but we—"

"No." Max cut him off. He shook his head. "There must be a mistake. I saw them just … only …" He started to take off his jacket and looked at Godfredo, trying to think how long they'd spent in Godfredo's vacation apartment on the Bahnhofstrasse in Zürich. "What was it, Fredo? Two days ago?" He waited for confirmation, but his friend's face was stricken.

"Leave your coat on, Max," the housemistress said. "It's best if you go now. Your uncle will drive you to Zürich."

"But we just came from there."

"Yes, yes, you did," she said, her tone affirming. She turned to Alan and lowered her voice. "The mountain pass is open, it's quite safe to travel at night, but I'd suggest you leave now if you want to get on the early flight. When did you say the funeral was?"

Max turned to Godfredo as a wave of sickness washed over him.

Godfredo stepped quickly toward him. "You're okay, *hermano*," he said. "You'll be okay."

Dumbly, Max nodded.

"I'll come over in a couple of days," Godfredo said. "I'll be there. I promise." He hugged him hard.

When he stumbled out into the night once more, Max felt nothing.

His only thought was of the frozen water fountain above the village.

The feel of ice-cold stone, and of water molecules changing shape as they expand in the pipes. And how he wouldn't be there to see the valley soften and come alive in spring.

Part One

Chapter One

London, England
November, 2008

Through the darkness and driving sleet, Max Burns could see the glow of the Land Rover's red taillights as it sat, idling, by the curb.

Running, he dodged pedestrians and puddles until he reached the passenger side. He pulled the door handle and dived into the front seat.

"Sorry I'm late," he said. "I ran into Professor Moyle as I was leaving the auditorium."

Sarah smiled and leaned in to collect a kiss on her cheek.

"Ugh! You're all wet!" she said. She wore a Burberry scarf and she smelled good.

Max put his leather bag at his feet and began stripping off his sodden, down jacket. "God, it's cold out there."

Sarah gave the wheel a confident spin and steered the car into the flow of traffic toward the edge of campus.

"So how does it feel, Dr. Burns? Was it terribly sad giving the very last lecture of your university career?" She flashed him a triumphant smile.

Max gave a dry laugh. "Hardly. 'Megascale project best practices' and 'trust-based collaboration' …? You can imagine the glassy-eyed effect I managed to induce. Teaching is …" He laughed again and shook his head. "Well, let's just say I'm doing the students a favor in moving toward private enterprise."

They passed the perimeter of the university grounds, and Max watched as the stately buildings that had been his professional home base for the past five years receded.

He turned to Sarah. "We've been invited to dinner tonight."

"Tonight?"

"Yes. Moyle has organized a sort of farewell do."

"That sounds fun. Fairly short notice, though."

Max merely nodded, ignoring the trace of disapproval in her tone; over the years, he had learned that Sarah—and indeed the whole Beauvoir family—required at least two weeks' notice for social engagements. They did not appreciate last minute surprises.

Perhaps because he was silent, Sarah turned to him, briefly. "Is something wrong?"

"Of course not," he said.

"So why aren't you smiling, then?"

Max ran a hand through his hair. "The Panama Canal is being expanded."

"So?" Sarah's gaze flicked to the rear vision mirror.

"Moyle wants to put together a team and submit a bid."

"For the expansion? Wow. That's ambitious." She pulled up at a traffic light, indicator on, and turned to him.

"Yes," he said, nodding. "It is."

For a moment, Max thought of his long-time colleague Alexandra Wong, and he wondered if Moyle had told her yet. It had been quite some time since the two of them had worked together on a project, and this one would be right up her street.

A flicker of concern crossed Sarah's face. "Wait. You're not considering …?" Her voice trailed off and she turned away. She put a couple of fingers to her forehead, as though warding off one of her migraines. But when she turned to him, her expression was fierce. "You have already signed a contract with my father. And yet Moyle is still trying to get his hooks into you?"

A horn honked behind them, and Sarah threw the car into gear with force.

"But then again," she snapped, as they lurched forward,

"it doesn't surprise me. In fact, I expect it's no coincidence that they announce the expansion of the Panama Canal and—gosh!—all of a sudden, the esteemed Professor Moyle decides tonight would be a good night to honor your departure—"

"Sarah, please." Max cut her off. "I'm a geomatic engineer, for God's sake. It's logical and completely understandable that if an incredible opportunity like this were to come his way that he would think of me to be part of his team."

She didn't respond. The windshield wipers sped up a notch to combat a fresh downpour.

They had arrived at the street they lived on, and Sarah pulled the car into a parking space out front of their terrace house.

"I know you're upset," Max said, as Sarah reached for her handbag from the seat behind them. "But I would really appreciate it if you would join me tonight."

She paused, her bag in her hand, and pulled out her umbrella. "I don't think so," she said. "I don't feel the need to step into an arena with Moyle."

The car door slammed.

Sighing, Max gathered his jacket under his arm and watched her run toward the house.

Chapter Two

London, England

"Hellooo!" A woman's voice shredded the Baroque string music that played quietly in Professor Moyle's small apartment.

Max caught the familiar flash of a red trench coat as the professor waved Alexandra Wong in. Her coat clung to her slight frame, and her usually sleek, black tresses were tangled and dripping.

"Oh my God! Rosemary!" Alex said with glee, as she walked ahead of the professor into the room. "It smells like a full roast dinner!" She closed her eyes and inhaled, a smile on her lips. "Delicious!"

Max, wine in hand, was standing alongside the generous island counter that divided the kitchen from the living room.

"And hello to you, too, Alex," he said, laughing.

Moyle's flat was modern, and bookshelves lined every inch of wall except in the kitchen, where—Max had recently learned—Moyle's defiant refusal to dispose of any books had resulted in a curious repurposing of his tomes: a pallet-load of hardcover books that looked to be relics from last century were stacked neatly and had been secured with long metal bolts to form the solid base of a rustic, timber-topped kitchen counter. A similar stack of books formed the base of a glass-topped coffee table in the center of the living area.

"So did he tell you?!" Alex asked. She stood next to Max, and tipped her head towards the professor, who had resumed his position behind the kitchen counter and was now chopping carrot with robotic precision.

"I did." Moyle's tone was haughty. "Please remove your wet items, Alexandra."

She obediently took off her coat and hung it over the back of one of the nearby dining chairs.

Moyle placed his knife on the counter. "Would a hanger by the front door not be a more appropriate choice for your attire?" he asked.

As Alex picked up her coat, Max poured her a glass of red wine from a chipped and finger-smudged crystal decanter.

"So are you on board?" Alex returned and took the glass.

"On board?" Max looked at the professor, who appeared to be closely inspecting the page of a recipe book. He forced himself to suppress the feeling that Sarah may have been right: this was not a farewell dinner.

"The Panamanian government is going to open the tender process on Monday," Alex said, interrupting his thoughts. She beamed at him.

"So soon?"

"I know, right?" She jumped up and down slightly, her face animated. "We'd need to get a team together to register our interest, then we have six months to submit our bid, and we'd need to—"

"Come, come," Moyle interjected. "Let's not put the cart before the horse. We'll wait until Gian arrives."

"Gian's also coming tonight …?"

"Yes," Alex said. "We can't submit our bid without a software whiz."

"Our bid …?" Max stopped. He started laughing, and shook his head. "This is starting to look less like a farewell party and more like a welcome party, isn't it?"

Moyle smiled. "Would that be so wrong?"

"You know I've already signed a contract with the Beauvoir Group. Two months ago. I can't just walk away from that."

"Shit a brick, Max!" Alex exploded. "Don't you get it?! It's the Panama Canal!"

Max held up his hands in a gesture that he hoped was distancing. "I'm sorry. I'd love to join you, you know I would, but—"

"Max." Moyle placed the knife beside the chopping board once more. "The decision is yours. However, consider this: you know the story of the canal." He tipped his chin down and looked at Max over the top of his glasses. "You know what a beast it was to build!"

Max frowned, as though to say, 'don't insult me.' He had written his Ph.D. thesis on the Suez Canal and, in the process, done extensive research on the Panama Canal: the French-initiated behemoth that ultimately became America's triumphant engineering debut on the world stage.

Moyle continued, his tone sober. "Even if you weren't to make it past the bidding process, it's still a chance to get your gray matter around one of the biggest engineering challenges in the world." He looked at Alex and Max in turn. "And the two of you …" He clamped his lips shut for a moment. "Well, I'm far too old and tired to take on something of this magnitude myself, but you two have a real shot." He paused. "You won't be able to do it alone. We'd still need to pull together a first-class team, including local experts from Panama—"

The doorbell chimed once more, and Moyle excused himself, making his way to the front hall.

"Great," Alex hissed, her voice dripping with sarcasm. "You walk away … and there goes my opportunity to work on something really epic."

Max turned to her. "Alex, you can partner up with anyone you like. You're the senior lecturer in this department. And I know Moyle will support you, whatever you do."

"No, Max. It won't work without you." She pointed to where the professor was now helping Gian Tarocco with his coat. Her expression was bitter. "He won't back me if I'm on my own. He said as much. Because,"—she air-quoted with her fingers—"'Your work is a thousand times better when you work with Burns.'"

"Alex, you of all people know how excited I am about the news," Max said. "It's an engineer's dream. The chance I've been waiting for. But I have to consider Sarah."

"Burns!" Gian Tarocco strode across the room toward Max, a huge smile on his face. "So you're joining the team!" He was already equipped with a cold bottle of beer.

Chapter Three

Wolverhampton, England

"Francisco Roco! Are you still chasing women from Madrid to Mallorca?"

"Who's this?"

Paco Roco put down his pen and sat back in his leather chair. It wasn't so unusual to hear someone call him by his full name, but this caller seemed to know him better than that. He put his feet up on the large oak desk.

"It's someone who can whip your sorry ass at blackjack!"

In an instant, Paco was on his feet, causing the small dog—a black-and-white Boston Terrier—under his chair to startle.

"Well fuck me! If it isn't the long-lost Prince of Panama himself!" he said. "How are you, my old friend?"

He strode across to the French windows, his smile broad, and opened the room to the tediously gray English day.

The dog followed him onto the terrace.

"No such thing as royalty in politics, Paco. We take our gloves off before we get in the ring."

Paco roared with laughter. "Gloves? When did you ever wear gloves?! You love getting your hands dirty!"

Hearing his old friend's voice, he was reminded of the sweltering heat and the hustle of Madrid where the two of them had met, working a short stint alongside each other during the upswing of the southern European housing bubble. It had led to far bigger collaborations when they had together expanded operations into South America.

There was another laugh. "*Those were the days! But I can't complain. I've done alright in Panama.*"

"Oh yeah?"

"*Even my flatracers are coming through for me.*"

"You're still playing the field?"

"*Of course! I have a great trainer.*" There was a pause. "*Say, Paco, you want to come meet him?*"

Immediately, Paco felt the familiar rush of adrenaline.

"Talk to me," he said, all business; he knew subtext when he heard it. "What do you need? I know you didn't call to talk about horses." He slid the dog to the side with his foot and leaned forward to rest an elbow on the stone balustrade.

"*I have a ... Let's call it a retirement plan.*"

"Holy mother. You're talking about the goddamn Panama Canal, aren't you? I saw the news."

His friend laughed.

"You sly bastard! So are you personally overseeing the whole process?"

"*Yes. That's why I'm calling. So, you're interested, then?*"

"My friend, I'm in construction. You say, 'Concrete'; I say, 'How much?'"

And all of a sudden, Paco felt good. He hadn't felt this good in a long time.

But he'd been in business too long to think it would be that simple.

"What's the caveat?" he asked.

"*We do it my way.*"

Paco pursed his lips.

Fucker thinks he can push me around, he thought. *Well, he didn't get to where he is now without me.*

"Are you thinking of leaving politics, then?" he asked innocently. "Is everything alright? How's Rosa?"

There was a brief silence.

Paco knew he had him.

"*She's okay. If you like the cancer-wig look.*"

Paco winced, as an uninvited image of his own, dying mother flashed before his eyes: her skin gray and deflated. Her dry, spider-veined hands no longer able to respond to touch.

Still. There it was: his insurance. Who knows how long Rosa herself had on this earth, but a bit of extra financial liquidity would certainly ease her passage to the infinite beyond.

"I'm sorry to hear that," Paco said, in a much better mood. "Let's talk in person. I can be in Panama mid-week. I'll send Godfredo over right away—he can leave tomorrow. You and me, we can talk details when I get there."

"Perfect. I'll get my man Fuentes to meet him at the airport."

Paco ended the call and replaced the receiver on the desk in front of him.

Resting his hands on his chest, he breathed deeply. He leaned down and picked up the dog.

"You hear that? This is gonna be the big one," he said to the small creature. "The one that saves Paco Roco's bacon."

He sat the creature on his desk between two framed photographs: Starlight Starbright and Running Hot, both of them still yearlings, but on track to become his best flatracers.

"What'm I gonna do with my horses if I go to Panama, eh?" He cocked his head to one side. The dog followed suit, wagging its tail. "What's Godfredo gonna do without his lapdog?"

The dog quivered with unspent energy.

"Godfredo!" he bellowed, and the dog skittered off the table. "Pack your bags! And while you're at it, find your fucking dog a new home!"

Chapter Four

Obarrio, Panama City

A spectacular sunset had started to creep across the sky as Godfredo Roco stuffed papers in his briefcase. The driver—Fuentes—took the corner sharply as he navigated the early evening traffic.

"Jesus!" Godfredo laughed. "You get your driver's license from a Hollywood stuntman?"

Fuentes grinned and expertly pulled the car to a standstill, narrowly avoiding a collision at the traffic lights.

Not for the first time that day Godfredo thanked his lucky stars he'd agreed to have a driver. Panama's streets were a war zone. At every intersection, your balls were on the line, and honking loudly and long was the *lingua franca*. Godfredo was used to running his own schedule, and considered himself a natural talent behind the wheel—he owned two Bugattis and a sweet, vintage Corvette back in England—but when he saw the state of the Panamanian roads, with their great, mismatched concrete slabs and traffic snarls, he was glad he hadn't subjected a custom, low-suspension ride to these conditions. Or his ass, for that matter.

He checked his watch, and scooped up his briefcase and jacket.

The Marriott Hotel and its adjoining casino commanded most of the real estate on the street.

Directly across from it stood a row of run-down buildings. A small tavern was set back a little from the main thoroughfare, its denuded vines and flickering, green neon lighting tubes incongruous in the face of its shiny, moneyed neighbor.

As he alighted from the car, Godfredo cast an eye in its direction, half expecting to spot his father seated on the patio among scantily clad waitresses; throwing back a quick drink, perhaps. The bar, however, with its mirrored splash-backs, was empty, save for a couple of high-heeled women resting their elbows on bench tops.

Turning his attention to the upcoming meeting, Godfredo entered the spacious foyer of the hotel, and made his way to the lounge.

Paco was seated in a low, black leather sofa at one of the glass-topped coffee tables. His eyes were on a document in front of him.

"You're wearing glasses!" Godfredo said. His father must've been blind as a bat if he'd bothered to go to the trouble of getting glasses.

"You're late." Paco didn't look up as Godfredo sat opposite, instead indicating the beer bottle that sat, untouched, on the other side of the table.

Godfredo helped himself, pouring the liquid into a tall glass.

"We have a big-ass task ahead," Paco continued.

Godfredo smiled. "You think?" he joked. "Even Fuentes was doling out advice about managing Panama's water supply." He paused. "Who does he work for, exactly? He knows an awful lot about the canal."

Paco finally looked up. He took off his glasses. Ignoring Godfredo's questioning, he asked, "Did you go over the material?"

Godfredo pulled the sheaf from his briefcase. "Yes. It says here ninety percent of Panama's drinking water comes from the Chagres River—"

"*I've* read the documents," Paco cut in. "I was asking if *you'd* read them."

Nonplussed, Godfredo continued: "Yes, and you don't have to be a rocket scientist to see it's all about the water management." He exhaled as he leafed through the papers.

"Bridges and urban waterways are one thing, but this is a whole fucking wetlands ecosystem."

"You got some names for me? Hydrographers?"

"Nope." He shook his head. "Not yet."

"Godfredo, you think this is a fucking holiday?"

"Dad, relax. I got all the blueprints, submitted the expression of interest, and now I'm five feet deep in eco-fucking-flora-and-fauna documents. I haven't had time to look for megascale hydrogeologists."

Paco grunted. He leaned back in his chair. "Alright. I've got few ideas, I'll make some calls. I know a couple of Dutch guys." He paused. "What about that kid you went to school with in Switzerland?"

Godfredo drew a blank. He shook his head.

"The one whose dad got screwed over by Rupert Garcia. What happened to him?"

"Max Burns? He left."

"I know that. I'm asking: what did he study? Didn't he do engineering? Something about Egypt?"

"You're right." Godfredo sat forward, tapping the table as he trawled his memory. "I remember he did his thesis on the Suez Canal. He studied in London. I haven't seen him for fucking ever. I think he's teaching now. He might know someone."

"So what are you waiting for? Get in contact with him."

Godfredo wrote '*Max Burns*' on the cover of the dossier in his hand, as a reminder. He tossed it onto the table, leaned back in his chair and took a long draught of beer. He pointed to the documents that lay on the table in front of Paco. "And just so you know, I want fifty–fifty on the profits for this one," he said.

Paco froze, his beer half way to his mouth. He looked at Godfredo. "Fifty–fifty?" He started laughing.

Godfredo recognized the laugh: he was about to be shot down in flames.

To his surprise, however, Paco started nodding slowly,

and there was a look of approval on his face. "Fifty–fifty," he repeated. "*Now* you're thinking like a Roco."

Paco's laugh exploded once more. Then he wiped his mouth with the back of his hand.

"No," he said. He stood up and pointed at Godfredo. "You don't get to tell me how it works." He straightened his jacket. "I'll tell you how much you get, once we're through."

As he entered his apartment on the top floor of the hotel, Godfredo started loosening his top buttons.

"Asshole," he said. "One more *fucking* carrot …"—he ripped off his tie—"*dangling* … in front of my face."

He pulled the tie free from the collars of his shirt, scrunched it into a ball and sent it, missile-like, toward the window. It unraveled mid-air, landing on a fresh display of tropical foliage and bright orange blooms. The room had been tidied immaculately—except for Sofia's pink G-string, which had been placed, neatly folded, at the center of the headrest on one of the armchairs, like some absurdist antimacassar.

Godfredo checked his watch. He might have time to see her tonight.

He looked out the floor-to-ceiling window: the Atlantic tide was well on its way out, revealing extensive mud flats below, and a horizon that was invisible behind the haze of a storm out at sea.

Across the bay, to the right, beyond the old Spanish domes and façades of Panama's Old Town—the *Casco Viejo*—about fifteen massive cargo ships sat, anchored, awaiting their turn to pass through the canal. As he watched, the foremost ship inched toward the estuary, where it would make its way north, through the first two sets of locks. Each passage came in at around two hundred thousand dollars—no credit, no checks—amounting to two billion dollars in revenue each year that was desperately needed to keep the Canal Authority and the country afloat.

The thought of it—the pure scale of it—was enough to make Godfredo's heart-rate escalate. It would require more dredgers, more basalt, more earth movers and cranes than he'd seen on any one project before, ever. Tens of thousands of laborers would have to be on the payroll.

He walked swiftly to the refrigerator and twisted the top off a bottle of beer.

What if they really could submit the winning design? What if they won the whole goddamn project?

Yes. Godfredo nodded, setting his jaw. He could smell the money. And the chance to be Paco's equal in a very, very big game.

As long as they could nail the right team.

Max Burns.

Godfredo laughed.

Of all the people to crop up on the radar after all these years!

Max Burns was the only one of his boarding school friends who'd ever been able to match him drink-for-drink on the rare weekends they'd escaped the school confines. Many times, they'd taken the train together to Paco's bachelor pad on the Bahnhofstrasse in Zürich; that's where they taught themselves to play blackjack.

Max had also been the only friend who'd had the temerity—or perhaps cared enough—to outright confront him one night about the bruises he'd acquired during the school holidays.

"Your dad's a complete asshole." Max's exact words.

Godfredo's smile faded at the memory of that night—at the memory of his seething anger toward Max, the sound of his own fist striking his best friend's jaw, and the two of them locked together in a brawl. Falling hard onto the ice, when they ought to have been making their way up the snowy road to the alpine boarding school with their suitcases. His own blood staining the front of his jacket.

That night was the very same night Max's strange uncle,

Alan, had shown up in the boarding school foyer, clutching a scarf and wearing a thin mackintosh raincoat. The night Max first heard his parents had gone down in a fatal helicopter accident.

How quickly lives can change.

Godfredo pushed the image of Max's stricken face from his mind, and moved across to the table. He opened the laptop.

"Okay, Max Burns," he said as he typed into the search engine. "Where are you now?"

Chapter Five

Hippodrome Race Track, Panama City, Panama

It was early for alcohol—well before lunchtime—but Godfredo was parched after spending two hours or more in the heat, waiting for the so-called 'urgent' meeting with his father.

On the television screen above the bar, an aerial view of Miraflores—the southernmost set of the Panama Canal locks—cut away to a shot of the mules: motorized engines that ran on tracks, moving steadily alongside a hulking vessel from the People's Republic of China. It was loaded with shipping containers.

"*The canal used to belong to the United States until the 1970s, didn't it?*" came the interviewer's voice, as they switched back to a two-way interview with a reporter in Panama.

Godfredo tapped the bar impatiently and watched the waitress as she meticulously unfolded two tiny paper cocktail umbrellas. She had a good rack underneath that white button-up. But they all did, those Colombian girls.

"*Not 'belong', exactly,*" came the reporter's response. Godfredo looked back at the screen. "*The US took over custodianship until 1999—the 'millennium change', as it's called. That's when the canal was handed back to the Panamanians on the proviso that the US retain—and I quote from Wikipedia here—'the permanent right to defend the canal from any threat that might interfere with its continued neutral service to ships of all nations.'*"

"*The Torrijos–Carter treaties, right?*"

"Exactly. Signed back in 1977, between US President Jimmy Carter and General Omar Torrijos. So even though the US gave away control of the canal, they still have the contractual right to step in, with military force if necessary."

"I expect there'll be more than a few scientists with something to say about the ecological impact of expanding the canal. Have you observed much opposition to the project, there in Panama?"

The waitress placed the drinks, complete with their tiny paper umbrellas, on the bar. As Godfredo pulled out his wallet, he kept his eye on the screen.

"There's surprisingly little opposition here on the ground. The Panamanian government have been very transparent about their plans to design, construct and operate in compliance with the environmental regulations of the Republic of Panama, as well as being in line with international guidelines such as the Equator Principles, which essentially outline criteria for sustainable development."

"And what about the Smithsonian Tropical Research Institute? They're deeply embedded in the region, aren't they? They're an American institute … What do they have to say about it?"

"Yes, American researchers have been in the canal's region since the turn of last century, but they've always had a very good working relationship with the Canal Administration and the Panamanian government. Interestingly, most of the opposition seems to be coming from the members of congress over in the US …"

Godfredo paused, bank note in hand.

"… There has always been opposition, ever since the Torrijos-Carter treaties were first proposed. Many Americans to this day still don't understand how their government could have given away such a huge asset. So, ever since the treaties were drawn up, the more vocal dissenters have focused on what they call a 'transcreation' issue, arguing that the Spanish version reads differently than the English version, and the difference in wording

more or less 'voids' the treaties ... But the larger issue seems to be that they still haven't been able to swallow the idea that they gave the canal back for free. After all, it's the most important waterway in the world."

"So we can assume the Americans will be putting in a bid for the expansion project, then?"

"They will. And we know that the Pittsburgh-based Siegel Group will be competing. I spoke with the American Ambassador in Panama, Larry Roebuck, earlier today ..."

Godfredo had heard enough. He handed the waitress a large note and told her to keep the change. He took the glasses and made his way to the door. They were already wet from condensation.

He was hit with a wave of heat once more as the door closed behind him.

Paco himself had been doing the rounds of the racecourse trainers since early that morning; he was even bringing in a vet later that week, with a view to purchasing another animal. Which Godfredo took to mean that he had every intention of staying in Panama—of winning this canal expansion project bid.

Sofia was sitting under the shell-shaped grandstand like some incredible, sexy Venus de Milo. She wore a broad-brimmed hat, and was leafing through a magazine. Several kids were kicking sticks around nearby.

"*Maracuja,*" he announced.

Sofia rewarded him with a smile. She liked the icy, sweet stuff. Passionfruit was her favorite.

As he handed her the drink, he saw Paco striding across the expanse toward him.

"Tell her to get lost," Paco called out. "I need to talk to you." He waved an arm in Sofia's direction.

Godfredo wasn't keen on being dissed in front of Sofia—regardless of their financial arrangement—but Sofia's facial expression gave no indication that she'd paid any attention to Paco's words; one long, smooth leg was crossed over the other, her foot tapping to an inaudible rhythm. Uncomplicated. Godfredo liked that.

He smiled, and said to her, "Give me half an hour."

"Sure, baby." She slipped the magazine into her bag and wandered off with her usual, casual gait. All the time in the world. She settled herself at a table out front of the bar.

"I don't like the shortlist," Paco said, stopping in front of Godfredo. He thrust a paper at him. He was slightly breathless, and his shirt was wet with sweat. His gold signet ring sat tight on his pinkie.

"What do you mean?" Godfredo took a moment to look at the paper.

"These guys?" Paco pointed to a couple of names on the list. "They aren't reliable. They worked on that big hotel that collapsed in Rome." He wiped his forehead with the back of his hand. "Christ, it's hot."

"That's the risk you take when you refuse to use your regular contractors," Godfredo retorted. His father smelled like he'd been with the horses all morning.

"What about the Burns kid?" Paco said.

"Max? I spoke to him last night."

"And?" Paco perked up visibly.

"He'd be perfect: he's a geomatic engineer now, and he knows a hydrogeologist who's won ass-loads of prizes, and even consulted on the Maasvlakte project in Rotterdam." Godfredo smiled ruefully.

"So? They sound perfect. What's the problem?"

"He says he can't take time out to come to Panama. He's signed up for some big-ticket job in London. Plus, he's getting married."

"Of course he can fucking do it. Strike a deal, offer him money, whatever he wants. It's only six months for the tender process. Just get him over here. It can't be that difficult."

"I can try, but I don't know if that will work."

"Time's ticking, and we need a reputable engineering team from a well-known university in the UK," Paco said.

"They don't have to be fucking Albert Einstein, but they need to be reputable. Nice and clean. That's all."

Godfredo squinted. "You just said 'reputable' twice in one sentence. Should that bother me?"

Paco looked at the sky. "Just get the fucking engineers, Godfredo. Is it so hard?" He flapped his fingers in a come-here gesture. "Gimme the drink."

Godfredo watched his father flick the tiny paper umbrella away like a mosquito before draining the glass.

Paco emitted a long sigh. "I tell you, if this doesn't work out …"

"What?" Godfredo said. "If what doesn't work out?"

Paco was silent for a moment. Eventually, he said, "Okay. Since you asked: our company is dead in the water if we don't get this project."

Godfredo gaped.

"You know the business we're in." Paco crushed ice between his teeth. "The Spanish market? Dead. And the British government are cancelling contracts and cutting building costs and subsidies all over the place. I still need to maintain staff back in the UK, in Madrid, São Paolo. We're running at a loss most of the time."

"How …?" Godfredo searched for words. "How can you be so relaxed about it?" He suddenly had the urge to look around him. As though they were being observed. "Do we have some reserves stashed away somewhere you're not telling me about?"

He couldn't understand how his father could keep his cool.

"It's business, Godfredo. You take your risks, sometimes it pays off, and sometimes you end up churning out fucking shopping malls and parking lots and cleaning up other people's screw-ups. Because mistakes in concrete aren't pretty." His laugh was coarse. "But this one … This one is different. This is our chance to play in the big league again." He paused. "I *build*. I've built some of the greatest bridges in Europe. I saved this company after your mother's idiot family drove it into the ground."

Yeah, and renamed it after yourself.

Godfredo considered his father's words for a moment. "So basically you're saying this is a last-ditch attempt to get a megadeal that will save your ass. And you're not worried?"

"No. And it will save your ass, too."

"I still don't understand. You're the one who says, 'work with people you've worked with before. Less risk,' you say. And here you are, asking me to pull in a team of engineers that I don't know from a can of paint."

Paco was silent.

"Jesus," Godfredo said. "You don't really care about the team, do you? You cut a deal. Who with?"

"You don't need to know."

"Dad!" Godfredo turned away from his father, walked a couple of directionless steps. "Fuck. I should have known. Not even you would take a risk on something this big unless you knew it was a walk-in." He turned and stared at his father: the asshole'd had some hair implants to disguise that balding spot since the last time he saw him. Subtle, but it was there if you looked.

"You still want to be able to drive your Bugatti?" Paco asked. "Or you want to end up in a London housing estate like your friend Max? Because that's what happens when your father loses everything, Godfredo. Remember?"

"That's not the point! We can still win this without any of your so-called '*assistance.*' We're better than that."

Paco gave a brittle laugh. "Okay, you believe that if you want. Like I said: *reputable.* It's all we need. And make sure they know they'll get a nice, fat remuneration if we win the bid." He thrust the empty glass back at Godfredo. He patted his chest and hip jacket pockets, and seemed to find what he was looking for. "I've got a meeting. Sort it out today."

Meeting? My ass. Godfredo knew what his father meant, and he suspected it wore a short skirt, and was in a tavern less than a stone's throw from the foyer of the Marriott Hotel.

Fucking bankrupt.

Godfredo paced alongside the racetrack, staring out at the small tractor as it inched along, combing the dark, river-silt surface of the track.

Pasting on a smile, he waved to Sofia and made his way back to the grandstand.

And Max ... What about Max?

The two of them hadn't seen each other or spoken for many years. Even now, they were only corresponding with text messages and emails.

But that's the way it had always been. Throughout their teenage years, every January—right around the time Max's parents had died—he had sent Max a postcard from his school in the tiny mountain village of Zuoz to London. At some point, later, they wrote an occasional email. Until the emails he sent to Max's free-service host started to bounce.

Godfredo never chased him up after that.

It would have been easy enough, but—really—what was there to say? *Just went parasailing in the Cayman Islands ... Just screwed the most beautiful woman I ever laid eyes on but I was too fucking gutless to call her the next day ... Just snorted my first line of coke.*

Godfredo kept his eyes firmly on the ground in front of him.

Well, be that as it may ... it was time to call his old friend.

He felt Sofia's cool hand on his arm.

"*Hola*, baby," he said. He pulled her to him, and planted a hand on one of her buttocks. "Let's go get us a boat, shall we? I'm in the mood for a party."

"You want me to call some of my friends?"

Godfredo nodded. "Ask them to clear their schedules for a few weeks. We might have us some visitors from England."

Chapter Six

London, England

When his cellphone rang, Max didn't recognize the number.

He picked up immediately; he had intended to clear out his university email account that day, but for the past two hours he'd been sidetracked on an email and its attachments from Godfredo Roco.

And now he hardly dared hope it might be his old friend on the line.

"*Hermano!*"

"Fredo!" Max leaned back in his chair and pushed his laptop to one side. "I'm so happy you called! It's great to hear your voice."

"*Same here, Max. Finally! It was about time, after so many years—*"

Max inclined his head. "Where are you? It sounds like a party!" The line wasn't great, and he could hear music and laughter in the background.

"*That's because it* is *a party! I'm on a yacht. And, Max ... the sun is shining, and it's just* beautiful! *You should be here!*"

Max could only smile at the unfettered joy in Godfredo's voice. "Fredo, you sound exactly the same as you did in school! And it looks like you haven't changed a bit!"

"*Yeah, well, I've got a bit more to show for myself than I did back then—*"

There was a crackle on the line, and his friend's voice dropped out.

"Hello?" Max jumped to his feet. "Fredo?" In an effort to get better cellphone coverage, he went directly to the front door, and out onto the steps of the terrace. "Fredo, can you hear me?"

The silence became gray noise, and then Godfredo's voice came down the line. *"Sorry, hermano, cellphone coverage isn't so great in the middle of the ocean. We're moored in the Pearl Islands, a few miles south of the Panama mainland. Did I mention how beautiful it is?!"*

Max laughed.

"Look, I won't take up all your time, I know you're busy, but I wanted to ask if you'd had chance to look at the files I sent through."

"Of course I did! And I didn't know your construction group had such an impressive profile these days. I didn't realize you guys were the ones who saved the Hemmingsgate Bridge."

"Yeah, the fucking Hemmingsgate! That was an animal of a job! We were almost done and fuck me if the river didn't shift course overnight. You should've seen Dad's face when he got the call."

"He freaked?"

"My dad?! Never!" Godfredo's tone was gleeful. *"He looked like a matador facing off a mad bull. That river didn't stand a chance!"* He paused. *"But about the email I sent you, Max, have you booked your flight yet?"*

Max grinned and hugged his free arm to his chest against the chill evening air. "Believe me, Fredo, if I could see a way to do it … It'd be a very different story if the timing wasn't so bad."

"Whoa, it sounds like a woman is squeezing your balls!"

Max laughed. "I wouldn't have put it exactly like that. But yes, it is to do with my fiancée."

There was a short pause. *"So what's she like?"*

"Sarah? She's great. She runs a lifestyle magazine here in London." Max ran a hand through his hair. "We've been together for nearly eight years, now."

"Holy cow! Eight years!"

"Yes. I'm starting the new job with her father's business at the end of the month. He's been very good to me over the years." Max paused. "I guess it's time to take that next step."

"*Dude! That's a great way to be buried alive at a very young age!*"

"Well, at least I'll be buried on solid ground."

Max turned to see Sarah's car pull up, out front of the house. He waved, and watched as she walked around the car and pulled a carry bag from the passenger side. He knew it would contain her favorite Thai soup: bean curd laksa, her Thursday night treat.

He turned away.

"I really appreciate you thinking of me, Fredo," he said. "I can't go to Panama myself. But I'll make some calls tomorrow and connect you with the head of the department, it's the least I can do."

"*Thanks, hermano.*" There was a pause. "*Shame. It would have been great to see the dream team on track again. So please send me some CVs, and make sure you tell them we will take care of the tender submission process and financials.*"

Max nodded. "Will do."

As he ended the call, Sarah reached the doorstep. He took the bag from her and opened the door. She offered her cheek, and he kissed it.

"Who was that?" she asked. She handed her coat to him.

"Godfredo. My old friend from school."

She kicked off her heels and took the bag of food once more. "Would you get some wine glasses, please, Max?"

"Of course." Max headed toward the sideboard and opened the cupboard door. He took a couple of glasses, and two linen napkins that were rolled inside silver serviette rings.

His phone buzzed.

He placed the glasses on the sideboard and flipped open the phone. It was a message from Godfredo: a photo taken from offshore—presumably from the yacht—of a pristine beach with a palm tree, in full, tropical sunlight.

Max snapped his phone closed and picked up the glasses. As he entered the dining room, Sarah looked up.

"So what did Godfredo want from you?"

Chapter Seven

London, England

Max sat in the car and stared at the bleak, concrete façades of the housing estate that had become his home at the age of sixteen. He'd driven over an hour to get there.

He gripped the steering wheel, as though forcing himself to turn it: to drive back across town to the safety and comfort of white terrace houses and tree-lined streets. Back to Sarah.

And yet.

He thumped the steering wheel.

Putting up the hood of his jacket, he stepped out of the warmth and strode across the denuded playground toward the closest building. The tree in the courtyard bore scars, and graffiti was etched into its trunk.

Max didn't bother locking the car; anyone who wanted to break in would do it, regardless. He'd done it himself once or twice, many years ago—broken into cars—although only under threat of physical injury from the local skinheads. Plus, he'd always made sure he wrote an apology note and placed it in the vehicle once they were well gone.

Those were the same skinheads who—less than a week after he moved onto the estate—had taken his father's golf iron out of his hands and wrapped it around a lamppost.

Max knocked on the door of the first in the row of flats and was immediately greeted with, "*Get inside, you!*"

As he went in, he saw the familiar, hulking figure of his uncle Alan in the kitchenette. An aluminum saucepan sat on one of the two electric coil elements, and Alan was applying butter thickly, methodically, to the topmost slice of a pile of toast. He was wearing an apron.

Smiling, Max looked around the tiny flat. It was a dive: no two ways about it. Despite Alan's best efforts, it smelled of abattoir—Alan's place of work—although Max had grown used to it over the years.

It had been his safe haven. His home, after he lost everything.

"I like what you've done with the place," he said, above the sound of the television.

Alan looked over his shoulder, and Max nodded toward the 2009 monthly calendar that was stuck to the door of the refrigerator. It was opened—prematurely—to the month of January, which featured a black-and-white, Hollywood movie still.

"*Maltese Falcon*," Alan said. "Sit down, then."

Max slung his jacket over the back of his usual armchair and sat down. It was always good to see his uncle.

Alan handed him a plate loaded with baked beans, bacon and toast, and Max took it gratefully; he hadn't realized how hungry he was until now.

Alan then furnished the makeshift coffee table with a fresh six-pack of beer and lowered himself into his own armchair. He settled his plate on his lap. "Could catch the overtime if we're lucky," he said. "Manchester and Spurs." He squinted at the TV screen and picked up the remote. He switched channels. "Beer?"

Max held out a hand. Alan pulled two beers free from the pack and handed one to him.

"Al, you know I've signed with the Beauvoirs?"

"Mm-hm?" Alan's mouth was now full. He chewed quickly and swallowed, his eyes still on the screen.

"And now I've been asked to be part of a different team on a really big project. A long way away from London."

"Where would that be, then?"

"Panama. But I really don't know what to do."

"No! Get outta there!" Alan yelled at the player on the television screen. He lowered his fork, shook his head and shoveled beans into his mouth. He looked at Max. "Panama. That's in the Pacific."

"Pacific on one side, Atlantic on the other."

Alan nodded. "You seen that movie: *South Pacific*?"

Max smiled and shook his head.

"A real old one, that is," Alan said. "Starts out in black-and-white and then half way though: *bam!* Technicolor!" He shook his head in apparent disbelief. "Never seen anything like it." For a moment, he seemed to have lost interest in the soccer game as he looked out the window.

He turned to Max. "I been saving for a cruise, did I tell you?"

"No, you didn't tell me." Max grinned, taken aback. He couldn't imagine how Alan could save any money on his minimum factory wages and he had never once accepted a penny from anyone. Even after Max had started working himself. "*Put it away. You'll need it someday,*" he'd said.

Alan now took a swig from his beer can. "Been wanting to do a cruise since I saw *Blue Hawaii*," he said.

"Then you should do it," Max said, delighted. "I don't think I've ever seen you anywhere except this room or the pub." He paused. "Would you be alright ... if I go to Panama?"

"Me? Gawd! Never you mind about me." Alan eyed Max as he chewed on a rasher of bacon. After a moment, he hit 'mute' on the remote. "So what's holding you back, lad?"

Max stopped chewing. "Sarah. And her father. I don't know how I'd face him."

Alan was quiet, his large fingers enveloping his beer can.

Max looked at him. "I don't want to be the guy who screws up everyone else's life because he can't face up to his responsibilities."

Immediately, Alan planted his beer on the arm rest.

"Lad, if you're talking about your father ..." He leaned

forward. "You'd do well to remember that your mother was no angel, neither. God rest her."

"What do you mean?"

Perhaps his expression belied his surprise at his uncle's words, because Alan continued, hurriedly: "Oh, don't get me wrong: I agree with you. It was bloody irresponsible. I could've spit chips when he topped himself with that ruddy helicopter." Alan's eyes were blazing. "He well knew what he was doin'. He knew it, and he took our Helen with him." His fist clenched tighter around his beer. "She may've been ashamed of me; of where she come from. But she was still my sister!"

Max felt the familiar ache of sorrow surfacing as he saw the blotches of red on his uncle's cheeks.

He looked at his beans and toast. He wasn't hungry any more.

Alan drew a deep breath. "Well, I was ready to blame everyone, wasn't I? Especially those rich folks your parents hobnobbed around with. Doing deals and buying up busi-nesses, and what-have-you." He shook his head. "But then I come home after my shift one mornin' and I see you snor-ing your head off on the chair right there, and I think to myself, 'Alan, that lad is the best thing to ever happen to your sorry carcass.' So if you're asking me about screwing up other people's lives …?" Alan sat back in his chair. "Ain't no such thing."

Max knew better than to hug his uncle.

"Thanks," he said, fighting back a grin. "You're not so bad yourself."

But Alan had already raised the volume on the television, nodding his silent acknowledgement.

Max stood. "Would you like some more toast?"

"Too right. I'll have a couple more." Alan mopped up the last of his dinner with his remaining half slice of toast. As he handed his plate to Max, he said, "I don't know nothin' about ladies and all that. I only know as long as you work the best you can, all the rest of it? It's just …" He fumbled for words. "It's just the rest of it."

Max smiled. "Got it." He took their plates to the kitchenette.

"And anyways," Alan raised his voice over the television. "If it gets too stinkin' hot for you over there, you've always got this place."

Not for the first time, Max was aware that if you only needed one person to have your back and that one person was Alan, you were without a doubt the luckiest bastard alive.

Chapter Eight

London, England

As he stood on the doorstep of the Beauvoir residence, Max looked along the uniform curve of the street. It was beautiful, even enveloped as it was in dank mist. The trees stood, evenly trimmed and skeletal, punctuating the regularity of the black, iron fence that ran the length of the sidewalk. In the glow of the streetlamps, the whitewashed façades of the Kensington terraces were cast a strange amber.

He had stood here on his own only once before: when he'd asked Henry Beauvoir for Sarah's hand in marriage. It had been Max's choice to approach him—it hadn't been a necessity—and Henry himself had found it amusing. But he'd also been impressed, Max could tell.

Thinking of Sarah, now, Max felt his heart sink. Their place had been dark when he arrived home earlier that evening. Sarah was no longer there, and he'd found a note: she was staying with a friend.

Bracing himself, Max pulled the old, iron knob and listened. Inside the Beauvoir residence, the doorbell chimed.

The door was opened, and Max was ushered in by the butler.

Shortly, Henry Beauvoir appeared. Even without a tie, Henry Beauvoir looked stately. This evening, he wore a crisp shirt, and his silver hair was combed back.

"Max." Henry held out his hand. His gaze was direct.

The handshake was brief.

"I apologize that it's so late," Max said, as he removed his jacket.

"Please," Henry said, ushering Max directly into the large front room. "Scotch?" He went ahead and poured, without waiting for a response.

Max took the glass he offered, but couldn't drink. "I expect you know why I'm here," he said. He turned the glass in his hand, unsure where to start. Henry Beauvoir was unsmiling.

"Regretfully, I cannot honor my contract with the Beauvoir Group."

Henry was silent.

"I have an opportunity I never imagined I'd have in my lifetime," Max continued. "And—"

Henry held up a hand. "You can stop there."

Max obliged.

Henry placed his glass on the table beside him. "I won't pretend I'm not greatly disappointed to hear this. I had hoped Sarah's impression of the situation was wrong."

"I'm sorry."

"Max, I didn't offer you this position in the Beauvoir Group as a favor. Or to ingratiate my daughter."

"I understand—"

"I haven't finished." Henry's voice boomed. "The fact is, you were far and away the best candidate we'd had in years. You are intelligent, and very talented." He paused. "However, I've also had time to consider this, and it's my view that anybody who embarks on a path without total commitment is not somebody with whom I wish to work. Nor entrust my business."

Max nodded silently. He looked at the older man. "I'm sorry. It wasn't my intention to hurt Sarah—"

"Enough!" Henry cut him off, his hand raised once more. "I understand and respect your reasons, Max. But beyond that—and I say this as a father—I don't ever want to see your face again. You are free to go." He paused, unsmiling. "Good night."

Chapter Nine

Smithsonian Tropical Research Institute, Panama

Karis Deen glanced out the window of the open plan office. She was alone. Across the courtyard, she could see the long, low building that had once been the old French hospital, but now comprised the Research Institute's housing quarters, where she'd been living for the past few months.

A smile crept across her lips: Dalisha—her roommate— was standing in the center of the courtyard below, in animated conversation with a man who wore a beard and dreadlocks.

Karis leaned across and pushed open the window.

"Dalisha!" she called out. "You're back already! How did it go?"

Dalisha looked up and waved. "I'm coming!"

Grinning, Karis sat back in her chair. It was the first day it hadn't rained in months—finally, the start of the dry season—and the Institute's gardens were swollen with lush foliage. Ripe mangoes lay in droves under massive, established trees, and vines hung heavily across building façades.

"You know what gets me? They really aren't concerned about the environmental impact. It's unbelievable."

Karis looked up as Dalisha stalked into the office. She and the rest of the postdocs and academics in the department had been out all afternoon at a meeting hosted by the Panama Canal Authority: the Panama Canal expansion project was making headlines in the scientific community, and the Smithsonian Tropical Research Institute was to play a large advisory role moving forwards. From where Karis sat, it looked like it would be an interesting development for Panama and the world, but she'd opted not to attend. She had to prioritize her time.

"Productive meeting, then?" Karis asked, with a smile.

"I don't know. I suppose so. It was a lot of talk." Dalisha ripped her canvas courier bag up and over her head and shoulders and threw it onto the desk in the far corner. "To be fair, the Canal Authority's presentation was comprehensive. They've done a lot of good work."

"I sense a 'but' …?"

"You can bet they're all funded by big-ass capitalist traders with one goal: to get the freaking canal expanded as fast and as big as possible. Never mind if it's inconvenient for humans or nature." Dalisha's eyes blazed. "We have a duty to keep an eye on this one! Those guys think global warming is a hoax; we can't let them rape the world over and over again!"

"Now there's the Dalisha I know!" Karis laughed.

Dalisha kicked off her shoes and flopped onto the small sofa by the door. "You know, I've got half a mind to talk to the Director about starting some kind of think tank—"

Karis grinned. "Attagirl, Dalisha! You want me to have a word with them? They might take it from someone who knows about dinosaur teeth."

Dalisha gave a short laugh, then sighed. "If it were only that simple." With her socked feet, she pushed dirty mugs and random, photocopied papers to the side of the coffee table. She leaned back, running her hands over her tightly-woven, black hair. "It's just depressing. We'll have to start moving our equipment off the Mothership next year."

"Off of Barro Colorado?" Karis frowned. "Why?"

Dalisha and her coworkers jokingly referred to the island of Barro Colorado as the Mothership, for all the unique bodies of long-term, ecological study that had been borne from its existence over the years. The island—once the tip of a mountain—stood in the flooded wetlands at the heart of the great waterway. It had become the Institute's primary research station in 1923, due to its enforced isolation after the Americans dammed the Chagres River to form Gatún Lake.

Dalisha looked at Karis. "Having a whole new set of locks for the canal means they'll need more water. So that means the entire wetlands' water levels will most likely have to be raised up to a meter. Or more, if their engineers don't know what they're doing." She sat forward, head in her hands. "That's another four hundred hectares of forest that'll be drowned in water!" She looked at Karis woefully. "Tell me bigger isn't always better!"

Karis fought back a smile. "Bigger is …" She paused. "Well, let's just say that sometimes, when things are already in progress, it's best to, you know, go with the flow. Just until you work out how you can—"

"Get to the point, Deen. Can't I just blow them all up? *Boom!* Problem solved."

Karis laughed. "That's definitely one approach."

Dalisha stood up with a groan. "I need beer. You want one?"

Karis nodded. "Please."

Still wearing her socks, Dalisha left the room. A moment later, she poked her head back in, around the doorframe. "By the way, I forgot to tell you, your brother called this morning. He wants you to call him back."

"Okay, thanks." Karis maintained a poker face.

He called the landline?

She'd call back later. When there were fewer people around.

In a moment, Dalisha was back and proffering Karis a brown bottle. "I didn't know you had a brother." She took a long swig of her drink.

"Yeah." Karis nodded. Without pause, she added, "He's having trouble with his business."

"How so?"

"He was supposed to take over the family business when Dad died, but our mom's been blocking the legal process …" She let her voice trail off. "You don't want to hear this. It's boring family stuff." She held up her beer. "Here's to Barro Colorado."

"Ah! Someone's singing my tune!" The Director of the Smithsonian Tropical Institute's voice boomed, and he strode into the office brandishing a bottle. He was followed by eight other people, all of them with Friday afternoon drinks in hand.

"Right!" the Director announced, good-naturedly. "Let's hear it, everyone: impressions from today's meeting …"

Karis leaned back on her desk and watched Dalisha as she launched into a postmortem of the afternoon's activities. For a moment, she felt a prickle of envy. It was hard not to warm to Dalisha's fire and authenticity; I would be nice to have that kind of freedom. To not have to come up with a story about a brother who does not exist. To not have to lie.

Part Two

Chapter Ten

Tocumen International Airport, Panama
January, 2009

As he moved with the throng of passengers along the gate, Max saw the familiar figure of his old friend.

"Godfredo! Finally!"

"Max fucking Burns! Welcome to Panama!"

The two embraced, then held each other at arm's length for a moment.

Godfredo's broad smile was exactly the same, with the addition of a small chip in the corner of one of his front teeth. He wore a stylish designer shirt, a pair of aviator sunglasses hanging from the breast pocket.

Clapping Max on the back, Godfredo laughed heartily. He ushered Max away from the crowd, through a side door, where a VIP-service concierge in a brown suit and collared shirt swooped in behind them.

Numerous ground staff nodded and waved in their direction.

"It's good to see you, Fredo." Max said. "And I see you have it all wrapped up here." He laughed.

"Of course! I'm a Roco! What did you expect?!"

They bypassed the queues of passengers that snaked back almost to the arrival gates, and continued toward the immigration counter, where an officer waved them forward. She was seated behind a monitor and a fingerprint scanner, her curly, black hair pulled back into a tidy ponytail. She held out her hand, looked at the three of them one by one, took Max's passport and started processing it.

The concierge, who had been standing beside Max, sidled

up to her desk. "*Te ha gustado el libro que te di, Madalena?*" he asked, timidly.

She ignored him.

"What did he say to her?" Max asked.

"Never mind," Godfredo whispered cheerfully. He turned and leant on her desk with one elbow, and continued to chat to her in Spanish. He was rewarded with a stern look as she handed back the passport.

She turned to Max. "*Disfrute su estadía en Panamá.* Enjoy your stay in Panama."

"Thank you. *Gracias,*" Max ventured.

As they took his luggage off the carousel, Max was acutely aware that his English, German and rudimentary French were going to be of very little use here.

Godfredo moved toward a single side door. The concierge followed with his suitcases.

"He said something about reading?" Max asked.

Godfredo nodded. "Poor Eduardo. He's been trying to get her to go out with him for about eight months. I suggested he give her a romantic book, because it's a nice, safe thing to give a woman. So, what do you think he gives her? *The Story of O.*"

"And what's that one about?"

"Bondage. And a girl who wants to be her boyfriend's sex slave." Godfredo started laughing.

"Oh dear. That doesn't sound like a good start."

"Nope." Godfredo opened the door at the end of the corridor and immediately they were hit with a wave of humid heat. "Especially because the Panamanian girls … they've gotta approve of you and trust you, or it's over before it's begun." Godfredo stopped walking and turned to Eduardo. "*Gracias, amigo.*" He put some dollar notes in Eduardo's hand and patted him on the shoulder. "Next time, try before you buy, eh? That's my philosophy."

Eduardo nodded. "*Gracias, Señor Godfredo.*"

The two of them watched as Eduardo meandered back

toward the terminal, waving to one of the baggage handlers, stopping to chat to several random passers-by. He looked up at the clouds, then headed over a man in a bright orange vest, who had a large dog on a leash. Both men lit up a cigarette.

"Blimey." Max turned to Godfredo, laughing. "I guess I'm used to people in London walking in straight lines."

"Yeah." Godfredo's expression was one of pure glee. "But this is Panama. It's like the land of the fucking Lotus-eaters. You're gonna love it!"

"What do you know about Lotus-eaters?" Max teased. "You never even opened a book when we studied it in school."

"Fuck-all." Godfredo grinned. "I saw it in a movie." He beckoned Max to follow. "Come on. I'm gonna take you to the place that'll be your home for the next six months."

"Okay, great."

"I was gonna take you on the boat, but it takes too fucking long."

Godfredo pointed to a small, maroon helicopter that stood out by the hangar.

"A heli!" Max said.

Godfredo gave a cheeky smile, but it faded almost immediately. He stopped walking. "Oh, Jeez. I didn't even think. You're okay with helicopters, *hermano?*"

Max nodded. "Of course!" He smiled, knowing immediately that Godfredo was thinking of his parents: they'd gone down in a dragonfly heli—a distant relative of this one.

Godfredo didn't look convinced.

Max put a reassuring hand on his shoulder. "Don't worry, Fredo. It was a bloody long time ago."

In fact, he was surprised Godfredo had made the connection after so many years. But, then again, of all his school-friends, Godfredo was the only one who'd had the balls to come to the funeral. And—looking back—he knew it would have been torture trying to navigate the adults' pity-ing looks and whisperings without his friend's irreverence. And for that he was grateful.

"I guess we have some catching up to do," he said, grin-ning, as they approached the craft. "So who's flying?"

"Me, of course!" Godfredo's cheerful demeanor had returned. "You trust me?"

"That depends." Max teased. "When did you get your license?"

"I didn't. I just flew so many times that one day I decided to put my hands on the stick."

When Max's jaw dropped, Godfredo started laughing. "Relax, *hermano*, I have Carlos with me all the time. He's my safety pilot. He can save me from myself." He pointed to the heli, where—sure enough—a man sat on the right of the cockpit, in the pilot's seat.

They loaded the suitcase into the craft, and Godfredo took the copilot's seat. He looked over his shoulder. "Are you buckled in?"

Carlos's Spanish was fast as he negotiated with air traffic control.

The chopper took off, and they started moving slowly across the tarmac to the east.

Finally, they were away: lifting quickly to escape the low altitude—the dead man's zone—and up and out across the stretch of city toward the Bay of Panama.

Max looked behind the craft—down, toward the great canal as it receded into the haze—and, as the shallow mud flats made way for open waters, felt a sense of relief to be away from the heaviness of London's gray skies.

"You going to tell me where we're headed, exactly?" He spoke into the lip mic.

Godfredo turned again and grinned. "No. But I can promise you, you've never seen anything like it!"

Chapter Eleven

US Embassy, Clayton, Panama

Ambassador Larry Roebuck was tall, his hair tending to silver-gray, and he knew he cut a good figure. He usually wore the top two buttons of his short-sleeved, collared shirt undone, although today he'd added a tie for the occasion.

He looked at the group that was gathered in the largest of the American embassy's private loungerooms. He had no idea what they'd be thinking; he hadn't met this particular type of professional before—engineers. Geomatics and hydraulics. *The ultimate breed of educated man*, his grandfather would have said.

Roebuck was skeptical: it rarely paid dividends to listen to others' definitions of greatness.

Well, no matter. All in good time. He looked forward to picking some brains over dinner that night.

"Welcome, welcome!" he exclaimed loudly, congenially—mostly to gain command of the room. He delivered one of the smiles that had won him the seat of Governor in Illinois, back in '92. "You all look like you haven't seen the sun for months!"

"It's January. It was blizzarding in Pennsylvania when we left." The man who spoke wore a gray business shirt. He was stone-faced, and there were large sweat patches under each arm.

For a moment, Roebuck was taken aback. It had been quite some time since the people around him had not been willing to play along in the game of social niceties, and it occurred to him that life in Panama may have been a little too comfortable.

He recovered himself, and smiled good-humoredly. The man, John Siegel, Junior, was in fact the most senior of the Siegel Group—the American engineering team. They'd spoken on the phone last week. *"Make no mistake, we plan to win,"* Siegel had said, and Roebuck had been pleased: it was always good to meet someone with ambitions.

And yet, looking at John Junior as he stood in front of him that morning, Roebuck was underwhelmed.

He couldn't put his finger on it.

Still, these engineers were the best America had to offer, and Roebuck was willing to concede that—between them—they must pack a punch. Despite their scratchy demeanor.

Roebuck smiled. He relished a challenge.

As he delivered his memorized speech, he made mental notes: *the hi-top sneakers is the dogsbody; the skirt is head of IT; the navy suit-pants and Italian leather shoes is the financial guy ...* He named them individually, welcoming each of them, to be sure they felt acknowledged.

Duly, they seemed impressed.

"And, may I say, on a personal note, what an honor it is for me to meet the Siegel Group today. You do our country proud." Roebuck nodded, as his audience murmured their appreciation.

He looked around the room. "As you know, this canal has a long and checkered history, and we—the Americans—have been here every step of the way, from the time we took over from the French back in the 1920s, until we handed the canal back to the Panamanian people less than a decade ago." He paused. "This is nothing less than the opportunity of a lifetime. An opportunity to contribute and make our mark in history, and to continue the long and fruitful relationship between our great countries: Panama and the United States of America."

He paused, watching his audience. Gauging.

There were nods and smiles.

Roebuck was pleased: they seemed like a committed bunch.

He continued. "Of course our government can't assist you in the work, but I can wholeheartedly guarantee that we at the embassy will do anything we can to help make your stay more comfortable." He smiled. "And wouldn't it be a day to remember if an American consortium won this bid?!"

Glasses were raised, and Roebuck acknowledged the approving faces with his own, raised glass.

Once back in his office, Roebuck took off his shirt.

He selected a freshly dry-cleaned one from the hangers by the door, and moved across to the window.

As he worked on the buttons with his fingers, he observed the grounds of the entire American Embassy compound as it stretched down the gently sloping hillside suburb of Clayton. Less than a kilometer away, as the crow flies, lay the Panama Canal itself, the Miraflores locks hidden behind a long, lean ribbon of lush vegetation, parallel with the horizon.

Every few hours, a new protrusion of massive steel superstructure and brightly painted shipping containers carved its way slowly—glacially—through the illusion of endless, tropical green. A reminder, perhaps, that outside this idyll, the world's traders were inching ever forwards.

The lights on the phone on Roebuck's desk started flashing.

"Summers?" he hollered.

The phone was still flashing.

He strode to the door of his office.

"Summers!" he called out again, and looked across the hall. But his assistant appeared not to be at his desk.

He frowned: this wasn't the first time Summers had dropped the ball. Roebuck had caught him only last week practicing his golf swing in the office. Which was understandable, of course: Summers was a young man, and Panama was the only place in the world you could play golf almost 360 days a year, thanks to its down-to-the-minute predictable, tropical weather.

If it had been a Friday, he'd have had no qualms about Summers taking the afternoon off—nobody in their right mind worked on a Friday afternoon. At least, no member of Panama City's business and diplomatic echelons.

But it wasn't Friday. It was Monday. And he was due at a dinner shortly with the senior members of the Siegel team and the Director of the Smithsonian Tropical Institute. He'd need his official car.

He strode back to his desk and reached for the telephone receiver. He punched a button with his forefinger.

"Roebuck," he said.

"Hola, Larry. It's me."

He knew the voice.

"Lord, it's about time," Roebuck said. "I was starting to wonder if you'd fallen off the face of the earth." He walked around his desk so as to have a view of the door. "Problem?"

"No, quite the contrary. Looks like there's a lot of international interest. It's going to be big!"

"Great news." Roebuck paused. "That's it, then?"

"Yes."

"Excellent. So don't call me again."

He hung up and turned to look out his window. He could hear children in the nearby playground, and a chorus of tropical birds.

It was nothing short of delightful.

Yes, Panama sure beat the pants off any other place he'd lived—or even visited—before. By comparison, this country was a frontier; an outpost. And outposts often offered more opportunities than one would expect. Opportunities to make a real difference.

And that's exactly why he'd taken the job.

"Sir? Sir!"

Summers arrived in his doorway, short of breath. "Sorry, Sir. I had to get taxis organized for the Siegel team."

"All it takes is a bit of communication," Roebuck said, coolly. "And then we're all clear on who's doing what."

"Yes, Sir. Of course. Your car is waiting. Your wife will meet you at the gate."

As he shrugged on his jacket, Roebuck thought briefly of John Siegel, Junior.

And now he was sure of what had been bugging him: the man had no presence. And, Lord knows, a man who doesn't inhabit his own skin is a risk.

A timely reminder that the linchpin isn't always at the apex of the pyramid.

Chapter Twelve

Contadora, Pearl Islands, Bay of Panama

As the helicopter lost altitude, Max saw the deep azure of the Pacific give way to shallower waters. Luxury yachts of all sizes were clustered periodically along the shoreline, and a short runway, running north to south, neatly dissected the tiny island, whose lush landscape was now taking shape.

Even as Max watched, the sun started to dip toward the horizon, casting the already orange sky blood red.

"Contadora Island, my friend!" Godfredo spoke into the lip-mic as he turned to look at Max from the cockpit. "Welcome to Paradise!" The last rays of light caught the side of his face, and he gave a broad smile.

"This is where we're staying?" Max asked.

"Yep."

Sprawling sandstone villas could now be seen amid lush vegetation and the fiery pinks and whites of bougainvillea, fronting slender beaches.

"I dunno, Fredo," Max teased. "Looks like it's going to be rough down there."

"You don't know the half of it!" Godfredo laughed. "The island is a lot of fun." Max eyed the arc of a broad and serene sandy cove. "What happens on Contadora stays on Contadora!"

Max opted to assume his friend was referring to the physical security an island would afford.

In fact, it hadn't occurred to him that there might be any security issues, but Godfredo—as had been his tendency, even at school—was always accounting for all possible outcomes. And Max was reminded of the very reason his friend had been made captain of the ice hockey team all those years ago: a surprise to those who didn't know that his blasé and in some ways superficial attitude masked a strategic mind.

As Godfredo expertly brought the heli down on a purpose-built landing pad in the grounds of one of the villas, Max knew he was in good hands.

"So tell me, Fredo," he said, as they unloaded their bags from the helicopter. "How did you organize this?"

Godfredo waved a dismissive hand. "Dad knows people," he said.

"He sure does," Max murmured, impressed, his gaze resting on the façade of a villa nearby. He looked at Godfredo. "And there'll be enough office space for all of us …?" He glanced around again. "Somewhere around here?"

Godfredo laughed. "Relax, *hermano*. I'll show you around later. There's another villa behind those trees there." He paused to look at Max. "Unless you want to go check the inventory now?"

Max knew he was being teased.

It was as they approached the main building that he heard music and the sound of raucous laughter. An older woman in a maid's uniform—gray dress with white apron—was carrying long, bamboo garden torches and standing them in brackets along the garden paths. As she reached up to light one, she smiled. "*Hola, Señor Godfredo!*" The flame danced in the gentle sea breeze and Godfredo greeted her with a wave and a few lines of Spanish.

He turned to Max. "We're just in time, *hermano!* This way!" His pace quickened.

"You sure I don't need to get my bags?" Max looked tentatively over his shoulder to the helicopter. There was still daylight enough for him to see that his bags sat abandoned on the outer perimeter of the helipad and the pilot was nowhere to be seen.

"Yep, the staff will bring them."

"Okay." Max jogged to catch up with his friend, who had disappeared up a small path. On either side were palm trees and brightly flowering shrubs. "Wait up!"

In a matter of moments, Max emerged from the trees to see a large man taking a run-up toward a turquoise swimming pool, and Godfredo standing poolside, his arms open wide. Plush, five-seater sofas and an assortment of cane chairs were arranged around the pool. Most of them were occupied by guests in little more than swimwear.

"Max!" Godfredo crowed. "Welcome to your home for the next six months!"

A moment later, as the running man's substantial body bombed the water, the two friends were drenched.

Having removed his shoes and replaced his wet clothing with a dry t-shirt and shorts, Max left his villa. There was no lock on the door and, briefly, he wondered where they were going to set up their office: to house all the equipment required to complete the job. Much of it was expensive, and had to be shipped in especially. Max only hoped Godfredo had this under control.

As he returned to the pool, he could see the party was in full swing. Music was pumping, and people were spilling from the villa into the well-kept garden that separated the main building from several more smaller houses.

As he passed a jacuzzi, Max scanned the faces for Godfredo. He nodded politely to two women in scanty bikinis. They slid, golden-limbed and giggling, into the effervescent water.

On the far side of the pool was a long, laden buffet table, and Max saw his friend.

Godfredo was helping himself to a bowl of long, coarsely cut white chips that Max knew to be *yucca*.

"What are we celebrating?" he said, as he approached.

Godfredo looked up and waved over a waiter. "You, of course!"

Max laughed. "No, really. What's the event?" He took the glass of champagne that was thrust into his hand.

"It's the warm-up," Godfredo said. "We'll have a proper party when your colleagues arrive."

"A proper party, eh?" Max smiled, unsure what to say. He had to admit, this wasn't exactly where he'd envisaged he'd be on his first evening in Panama.

"You're not from around here, are you?" A woman standing at Godfredo's side spoke softly. She put out her hand in the manner of someone who expected it not to be shaken, but kissed. Max obliged.

"Max," he said. "I'm pleased to meet you."

"My name's Sofia." She held his gaze while she put out her other hand, palm up, to Godfredo. Godfredo placed on it a small plate, piled with something orange, flattened, also fried. She offered the plate to Max. "You like *patacones?*"

Godfredo laughed. "Don't ask him! He wouldn't know a vegetable from a loaf of bread. He eats Marmite and baked beans!"

Sofia looked confused.

"Guilty as charged," Max said. "I'm English." When she smiled, he took a morsel from the plate she offered, and tasted it.

"They're plantains," Sofia said. "A type of banana. In Panama, we only eat them after they're cooked."

"And in Colombia?" Godfredo put his hand on the nape of her neck.

Sofia smiled and turned to look up at him. "You better watch out. Colombians eat anything."

Godfredo slapped her on the behind. *"Ve a buscar a sus amigas. Nos encontramos en el jacuzzi."*

She walked away, unhurried, the movement of her hips accentuating her tiny waist.

Fighting the urge to stare, Max turned to Godfredo. "And how long have you known Sofia?" he asked.

Godfredo pulled a cigar from his pocket. He held the

flame from his lighter at its tip and sucked. "Long enough to know she's worth every penny."

Max considered his friend's words. Slowly, he chewed on the remainder of the plantain; it wasn't sweet, but it wasn't unpleasant. He looked around, wondering how many of the women on that manicured, Bermuda grass were paid to be there.

But perhaps he shouldn't have been surprised at Godfredo's arrangement with Sofia: Godfredo had come back to school one year with stories of a trip to his father Paco's native Argentina, and how Paco had booked and paid for a woman to visit Godfredo one night. Max's jaw had hung open, in turn horrified and fascinated by Godfredo's apparent ease with the entire set-up.

"Hey, you remember the old bunker at school? Under the ice hockey field?" Godfredo interrupted his thoughts.

"Sure." Max cast his mind back. He remembered the bunker, because it had been the ice hockey team's change room in winter; a relic from the Second World War, buried under the alpine slopes.

"You remember how fat that door was?"

"Two feet of solid concrete."

"And you remember I got locked in there one night? I was supposed to be in detention, and if I didn't show, they were gonna expel me from school."

Max laughed. "I remember. I even ran to the village and threw clods of dirt at that girl's window to get her attention—what was her name—?"

"Susanne Testa."

"Susanne Testa! That's right! Because I thought you'd nicked off down to her house without permission."

"She was beautiful, though, wasn't she?"

Max laughed again. "I honestly don't remember! I just know I was the sucker who got in trouble when her dad couldn't find her. That man had the loudest bloody voice I've ever heard, and then some! I think the whole village could hear him."

"Yeah, well, it's probably good he never found out she was with me in the bunker all along."

"Yes. And may I remind you that you'd have both starved to death in there if I hadn't worked out where you were?"

Godfredo roared with laughter. "Good old Max! You always had my back!"

"Yes, I bloody did," Max said. "And you had mine, Fredo."

Spontaneously, Godfredo hugged Max. "I'm really happy you're here, *hermano*." He broke away and slapped Max on the shoulder. "We shouldn't have waited so long to get in touch again."

Watching his friend, now, as Godfredo followed Sofia toward the jacuzzi, Max smiled. It was good to see him again.

He downed another champagne, letting the mellifluous sea breeze wash over him, before another thought hit him.

Alexandra Wong.

Holy hell. What was she going to make of all this? Of Sofia?

He placed his glass on the table.

Chapter Thirteen

Contodora Island, Panama

DEAR MAX. GLAD YOU GOT THERE SAFE. YOUR NOT MISSING MUCH. PISSING WITH RAIN HERE. SARAH DROPPED OFF SOME BOXES FOR YOU. FROM ALAN.

The email had been in Max's inbox when he logged on early the next morning. It was all caps-lock.

Max knew Alan's dyslexia and his apparent lack of desire to conform to grammatical standards had always bothered his parents—Ed Burns, in particular, who'd cared deeply about apostrophes—but Max found his uncle's reliably dreadful spelling oddly reassuring. He'd spent many years as a teenager being handed scribbled shopping lists that included *tomatoe sauce, margerine, viniger,* and suchlike.

It wasn't until he'd responded to all his emails that Max realized there had been no word from Sarah.

But what had he expected? Her last correspondence—barely a week ago—had been definitive.

"Everyone's telling me I should be angry. But I'm just lost. Please don't contact me again."

Max closed the laptop, and padded across the apartment-style villa toward the door. He slipped on his shoes.

Outside, the morning was fresh. Already there was a slight breeze: a reminder that the wind and the elements keep a different timetable than the rhythms of humanity.

As he knocked on the broad, timber door of Godfredo's villa, he could hear various birdcalls and the sound of waves on the shore. Once more, his spirits lifted.

"*Door's open!*"

Max stepped inside.

"I told you, Dad, everything is under control." Godfredo was seated in front of a laptop, and he didn't look relaxed.

Max raised a hand in silent greeting.

Godfredo looked at him briefly.

"I gotta go, Max is here. I'll go through it with you later." He ended the call. "Fuck me." He shook his head and stood up. "Hey, *hermano*." He was wearing a short dressing-gown with someone else's initials on it. "You gave up early yesterday," he said. "Partying not your thing these days?"

"More like jetlag's not my thing."

"Fair enough. So there is room for improvement. You had breakfast yet?" He disappeared into the bedroom and reappeared wearing a lemon polo shirt and a pair of shorts. "I'll take you to the golf club."

"It's okay, Fredo. Thanks. I've had toast and coffee." He paused. "I thought we could go through some of my ideas together before you meet the team today. So you know where we're headed with this whole thing."

Godfredo looked at him with a blank expression.

"You know—the Panama Canal? My team …? Arriving in one hour …?" Max teased. "I guess you're still not a morning person."

Godfredo gave him a hug and laughed. "Screw you, Burns. It's way too early to be talking business."

As they walked back to the main villa, Max saw many guests had stopped and dropped right where they had been standing last night, and hadn't woken yet. Bodies were strewn around sofas and on lounge chairs by the pool. The large, pool-bombing man was asleep in the jacuzzi, head thrown back, mouth open.

Godfredo shook him, and he snorted loudly. "Jorge! Wake up! Time to go!" Godfredo snapped his fingers. "*Rápido!*"

The man smiled drunkenly and clambered out of the tub, leaving a sodden trail behind him.

Sofia appeared in the doorway to the main house, her long hair smooth and sleek in the morning sun. She looked composed and wide awake. She said something Max didn't understand, and Godfredo started laughing. He pointed to the woman that was asleep on a nearby cane lounge chair and turned to Sofia.

"*Despiértala. El ferry llega pronto.*"

Sofia stopped and shook her by the shoulder.

Max checked his watch.

"Can I do anything?" he asked. He knew he sounded tense, but the ferry was due shortly.

"No need," Godfredo said. He was pointing—apparently for Sofia's benefit—at a few girls asleep on the lawn. He turned to Max. "Don't worry, I said I'd organize everything, and I have."

"Sure." Max paused. "It's just … Alex is a bit particular. She'll want to know where the office is."

Godfredo looked at him, nonchalant. "And you think she'll be worried that she can't prepare properly for one of the biggest structural engineering jobs on the planet because she has to work on an insanely beautiful tropical island?"

Max ignored Godfredo's sarcasm, but his friend's attention seemed to have wandered: Sofia was now standing by his side.

Max tried not to look at her breasts, which were barely concealed by a hot-pink crocheted bikini top. She wore minuscule cut-off denim shorts that Sarah would have called 'barely a belt.'

"Should I go now?" Sofia smiled at Godfredo, tipping her head to one side.

Godfredo shook his head. "Get the girls to the pier. Throw everyone out as quick as you can so they don't miss the boat." He pointed at her. "But not you. You're not leaving. I need you to show the engineers to their rooms."

"Sure, baby." Sofia nodded, glancing at Max momentarily. "You know it will cost you more if I stay."

"Whatever." Godfredo tapped his ostentatious wristwatch to indicate that time was ticking on. Sofia obediently disappeared.

Max wasn't sure whether to laugh or cry. "So I guess it's not too early to discuss *that* kind of business," he said, and for a moment wondered if he was crazy to be leaving the control of so many dynamics in Godfredo's hands. He knew Godfredo could pull strings when he had to—he only hoped the strings weren't solely attached to a pink bikini.

"Come on, *hermano*." Godfredo waved impatiently for Max to follow him. "What are you waiting for? Let's go see the office."

They stopped in front of a long building with a thatched roof that could have been a spa or resort clubroom. Godfredo pulled a set of keys from his pocket.

"We don't usually lock stuff up around here, but this one's different." With a flourish, he swung the door open, and held it to one side so Max could pass. "You wanted an office?"

As he stepped inside, Max's mouth fell open.

"You sneaky bastard!"

The room was enormous, with ten or so large workspaces, two monitors on each desk—as requested. Vast, floor-to-ceiling windows gave an incredible, uninterrupted view across the sparkling Pacific Ocean.

"You can pay me back later," Godfredo said.

"It's perfect! Thanks, Fredo. Although I'm almost sure we won't need so many desks." Max turned to his friend, laughing.

"You're not the only ones working here." Godfredo snorted. "You really think I'd leave it up to a bunch of English academic farts to sort this thing out? I've got six local experts on contract as well. They'll be coming in on the ferry tomorrow evening so you can all start work on Monday."

"Oh." Max smiled sheepishly. "Of course." Abashed, he was sorry he'd doubted his friend, that he'd made so many assumptions. And Alex would be thrilled to have the local know-how at her fingertips.

Godfredo pulled his phone from his pocket and glanced at the screen. He slapped Max on the back, seeming once more like his usual self. "Ferry's nearly here," he said.

Godfredo locked the door behind them, and the two of them headed across the lawns toward the northern entry to the property.

"I received details of the other bidding parties this morning," Godfredo said. "Final list will be in the news on Monday, I suspect."

"Let me guess ... Americans, Japanese?"

"Yep. And Germany."

"China?"

"Don't know yet. But I bet they'll be a tough competitor. Chinese companies already control the ports at both ends of the canal, so they've built up a lot of know-how here." Godfredo stopped in front of a golf buggy and swung himself into the driver's seat.

Max climbed in, and the tiny vehicle took off, its striped, canvas awning flapping as they whizzed down the drive and through the main gates.

The day was clear, and the ocean a deep turquoise as they made their way toward the shoreline.

Godfredo pulled up alongside the small cove in a parking bay, within twenty feet of the beach, where a cluster of last night's partygoers stood in a huddle. A few lay on the white sand.

On board the sturdy yacht, Max could see Alex, along with Gian Tarocco—their systems optimization engineer—watching as the craft's bow came to rest on the beach. Alex was still tightly bound up in her red trench coat, despite the heat. She wore a trucker's cap pulled down low, and her eyes were on the shoreline, where Sofia herself was corralling girls in sarongs and bikinis toward the waterfront.

Godfredo stepped out of the buggy. "So let's go meet your precious Alex and show her how it's done on Contadora." He readjusted his sunglasses. "Plus, I need lunch. I've got the mother of all hangovers. Sofia is one goddamn kinky—"

"Okay, dude!" Max cut him off, laughing. "You're unbelievable."

He followed his friend toward the pier.

"Who is this ... *person*? And why are we following her?" Alex's voice was a strained whisper. It bore a trace of anxiety.

Max slowed his pace a little. Tarocco was keeping up, but Alex's ballerina shoes didn't look ideal for beach walking, slipping from time to time, losing traction on the fine, white sand. She had finally shed her red trench coat and now carried it above her, in lieu of an umbrella.

Max looked at Sofia, walking with her usual easy gait ahead of them, her long hair cascading down her back. He was fairly sure she could hear Alex's comments.

"Sofia," Max called out.

Sofia turned. Her breasts were even more magnificent in full, coastal sunlight. He felt like offering her his t-shirt.

"*Si, Señor Max?*"

"Sofia, these are my colleagues, Dr. Gian Tarocco, and Dr. Alexandra Wong." He looked at Alex. "And this is Sofia. She's an employee of Godfredo Roco."

Sofia held out her hand. "*Doctora Alexandra*," she said, by way of a greeting. "*Doctor Gian.*"

Alex's mouth was hanging open. She managed a strangled, "Hello."

Tarocco was mute, his eyes wide.

As Sofia started walking again, Alex turned to Max. She gripped his arm. "And what about our bags? Moyle lent me some of his drafting equipment. And it's *expensive*."

Max nodded. "Don't worry. Godfredo's bringing them

all in the buggy. They'll probably all be in your room by now."

"How do you know?"

"As far as I can tell, Alex, ninety-nine percent of the people staying on this island couldn't give a damn about our equipment. It's not going anywhere; believe me."

Alex's face conveyed her incomprehension.

Sofia turned to them again, this time holding out a bronzed arm to indicate the villa to their right. "Welcome," she said, and started making her way toward it.

The villa looked just as impressive from the seafront, Max had to admit. He turned to Alex. "Please don't jump to conclusions," he said, with a wry smile. "Godfredo's outdone himself with the office set-up. It's more than I could have hoped for. Trust me."

Alex nodded slowly. Her face relaxed. "I'm sure it's fine, Max," she said. "I'm looking forward to getting started."

Max smiled again. "Me too. It's good to have you here."

As they walked into the villa, he held his breath, hoping only that the dregs of last night's party had been sent on their way ... and that the ones who remained were wearing more than bikinis.

Chapter Fourteen

Smithsonian Tropical Institute, Panama
March, 2009

As Karis Deen walked the long hallway of the residence building that was her temporary home, she heard her cell-phone ringing.

Pulling the phone out of her bag, she cast a look around her.

The place was quiet: very few people were on this part of the premises at lunchtime.

"Sir?" she spoke into the phone.

"Are you free to talk?"

"I am." She stopped and unlocked one of the doors, and stepped inside. She closed the door behind her.

"This is purely information: we'll be pulling you out in August."

"That's early." She threw her bag on the bed under the window and opened the sash; the room was automatically air-conditioned and, as usual, it was too cold.

"Yes. A couple months earlier than we thought."

"Any particular reason?"

"Training."

"For …?"

"A new facility. I was only able to recommend five of my reports. And you're one of them."

Karis waited, but there was no information forthcoming. "Can you send me some more details?"

"No. It's highly classified. All I know is that you'll be picked up at Dulles. You'll be sent flight details. That's all I can give you right now."

"Okay."

"You'll get a full briefing once you get there—"

There was a crash and the door flew open.

Karis snapped the phone shut.

Dalisha was standing in the doorway holding an enormous plate of fried rice. Her mouth was full, and she had papers jammed under one arm, against her body.

"Far out," Karis said. "Don't you ever knock?"

"Don't hafta," Dalisha mumbled, through food. She swallowed. "It's my room too, you big princess." She attempted to drop the papers on the bed, but they slid out and across the floor. Rolling her eyes, she ignored them and sat herself on the second bed, which was in the corner of the room furthest from the window. She started shoveling more food into her mouth. "You had lunch yet?" she asked. "Meeting starts in ten."

Karis shook her head; one of the younger scientists at the Institute had organized a round-table discussion with the express purpose of coming up with a media and blogging strategy to inform the public about each new phase of the expansion project, and its impact on the environment. Karis had quickly observed that the guy was inexperienced and disorganized. He may have had good intentions, but she knew from her own experience that a message is only ever as effective as the people who carry it.

"You invited the Director to this meeting?" Karis started removing her shoes.

Dalisha, her mouth full again, frowned. "No. He says as long as we're not doing it under the Institute's name, we have every right to say what we think." She chewed silently for a moment, observing Karis. "Don't you care what's going on? Imagine what's going to happen once they start digging. This is huge!"

"Of course I care. But I have to call my brother back in fifteen minutes. That was him on the phone just now."

"Oh." That seemed to satisfy Dalisha for the moment. "Is he okay?"

Karis nodded. "He wants me to go back home, to Iowa."

"But you told him 'no'?"

"I told him I'd call him back."

"That's too bad." Dalisha looked concerned. "Can I help?"

Karis opened her mouth to respond, but wasn't sure what to say.

"Well, let me know." Dalisha put the plate on her bed and made her way to the door. "Catch you later," she said, and was gone.

Karis looked at the empty doorframe.

It was at times like this that she knew she was on thin ice. The constant need to draw on and invent stories that held no meaning: stories about a brother or a mother, or some family dynamic or other. Because who was she to know what it was like to have a flesh-and-blood family waiting for you at Christmas or Thanksgiving? To have a proper home?

She lay back and let warm air roll into the room and over her face, glad she'd pulled her bed across to the window.

The dense, tropical heat of this country didn't bother her.

Being shut in a cold room did.

Chapter Fifteen

Contadora, Pearl Islands, Bay of Panama
April, 2009

Godfredo had been awake for some time, but opted not to get out of bed in favor of a few more minutes listening to the waves lapping the beach outside his window.

It wasn't a crime to enjoy doing absolutely nothing after a long, hot night with the boundlessly energetic Sofia.

This morning, he'd requested she stay on longer. She'd declined this time, although—surprisingly—she had seemed genuinely sorry.

"I can't, baby. I gotta go put out some fires."

She'd been talking about her other job at New Horizons, which was a peculiarly Panamanian establishment also known as a push-button, a place where love hungry couples could rent rooms by the hour. She was one of the managers.

Godfredo knew the place, because he'd unexpectedly had to take a detour past it one afternoon, when Sofia had been called in to deal with a middle-aged couple who'd rented a room to get away from their kids and then refused to pay for their drinks.

As he waited out front for her, he'd become increasingly impatient, not aided by the fact that when she finally emerged from the front office, she seemed to be in no particular hurry, apparently languishing in the unconcealed stares of punters as they cruised along the motel-style strip in their cars.

"Why the fuck do you waste your time with this place?" he'd asked her, irritated, as she slipped back into the car. "Who gives a shit about a mom and pop who won't pay for a bowl of olives? I can think of way better uses of your time." He watched as she put on her seatbelt, seemingly nonplussed.

"Seriously, Sofia," he said. "I pay you enough to retire tomorrow and never lift a finger again."

"You do, baby," she'd said, turning to him with a smile. "But I like lifting my finger."

Thinking of her now, as he lay on the bed—of her incredible breasts, of their weight in his hands—Godfredo felt blood pulse in his groin.

The door to the villa flew open.

"Get up!"

"Jesus H. Christ!" Godfredo, fumbling, pulled on his trousers, and reached for his belt. "You said you were coming after lunch."

Paco looked around the room with a mock-curious expression. "What, no lapdog?"

"She's not a dog."

Paco's laugh boomed. "Okay, whatever you say." He became serious. "When're you going to get that set of numbers to me?"

"Settle down, I've nearly finished the first budget. Did you fly in just now with the heli?" Godfredo hoped to slow his father's trajectory a little with small talk.

Paco wasn't buying it. "Of course I flew in. You think I got out of bed at four o'clock to swim from the mainland?"

Godfredo reached for his shirt, and couldn't help smiling: there was no circumstance imaginable under which Paco would get up at four a.m. to see anyone, least of all his son. The exception being if there was a problem with one of his stupid racehorses over at the Hippodrome.

"Where's the team? Not still in bed, I hope." Paco's eyes were scanning the room.

"Eating breakfast maybe?"

"No."

"Okay …" Godfredo reached for his phone and dialed.

"Max? Where are you guys?" He paused. "Okay, I'll be there in five. Or less. With Dad." He ended the call and looked at his father. "Your slaves are in the office."

"Then what are you waiting for?"

"Well, a bit of fucking warning would've been nice."

Godfredo slipped on his shoes, tucking in his shirt as they walked.

The only thing that took the edge off his own indignation at being found still in bed at nine a.m. with a boner the size of the Matterhorn was that Paco couldn't argue with the fact that the work was indeed getting done.

"I heard Burns is keeping them all on their toes," Paco said. His pace was quick.

"That's what we're paying him for."

"He goes jogging every morning." Paco seemed to find this amusing. "You might wanna take some tips from him."

Godfredo grit his teeth. "I do my bit. Just not at six fucking a.m."

"What's the hydrogeologist like?"

"Wong?" Godfredo turned to Paco. "She's a pedantic smart-ass robot. And she hates alcohol." He opened the door to the main office. "She's on the mainland today with the surveying guys, thank Christ. You can go visit her if you like."

Paco snorted. "In your dreams."

Max, to his credit, gave no indication that he was taken off guard by Paco's visit, and ushered them to the center of the room, where architectural drawings were displayed on large LCD screens along each wall.

"We're just working on how we're going to communicate the designs for the presentation," he said.

The office now looked like a hi-tech museum exhibit, with a graphic interface presented on a large screen and several monitors spanning the southern wall. The local Panamanian ecologists had set themselves up in a cluster of workstations on the eastern wall.

"Looks good," Paco said, as his eyes swept the array of blueprints on the floor and finally came to rest on the large screen. "But what's gonna make it special?"

"The water-saving percentages."

Paco looked at the ceiling, and clasped his hands together, feigning prayer. "Hallelujah!" He looked at Max again. "How much?"

"Sixty percent."

"*Sixty?*" Paco's jaw dropped. He looked at Godfredo.

Godfredo nodded. "Max's idea uses gravity, not pumps, and it makes the overall running costs really low. Plus, the ecologists will love it." He grinned at Max.

"Please take a look at the map," Max said, pointing to the map on the wall. "The original idea was to put a dam here, and thus create a third lake. But this area here is now inhabited by one of the indigenous tribes, who moved in about a decade ago."

"So move them."

Godfredo shook his head. "Relocating them would add on millions to the overall cost. Anyway, there's no need any more."

"Brilliant!" Paco boomed. "So what can you show me? You've got a package you're working on?"

"It's just a mock-up ..." Max turned to Tarocco. "Gian?"

Tarocco bashed his keyboard for a bit and the big screen came to life with a smooth, rotating representation of the three-tiered water basins.

"There'll be a voiceover, like, you know ..." Tarocco cleared his throat and adopted a deep, Hollywood block-buster voice. "*Bigger than the five-step Trigorges Dam in China, and yet sixty percent of Panama's life-giving water, every step of the way, is retained. After three full cycles, the water is released, and a fresh intake is initiated, making these gravity-driven water pipes the largest lock footprint—and the most efficient lock system—in the world.*"

Max laughed as Tarocco dragged out the last word for maximum effect.

"Enjoying our five seconds of fame, are we?" he teased. He turned back to Paco. "We don't think the other teams will come up with anywhere near as high a reutilization rate."

"Well, I gotta say … that's quite something!" Paco nodded silently at each person in the room. "I'm very, very impressed." He looked at Max. "Can I take a copy of these blueprints with me? And I'd like an update every week."

"Yes, of course," Max nodded. He rifled through papers on a nearby desk and pulled out some sheets. He rolled them up and handed them to Paco.

Paco pumped his hand for what seemed like an age. "Well done, son. Well done."

Chapter Sixteen

Contadora, Pearl Islands, Bay of Panama

"*Well done, son.*"

Paco's words echoed in Godfredo's head.

When had Paco goddamn Roco ever called anyone his son?

Godfredo felt a familiar, rising anger. Really, he had no idea what went on in his father's head.

He bit his tongue, determined not to say a word until they were out of earshot of the villa that housed the consortium's office.

Before he could open his mouth, however, Paco stopped walking and turned to him.

"Godfredo."

"No, Dad, you listen to me—"

Paco put a hand on Godfredo's shoulder, and—force of habit—Godfredo stopped talking immediately.

"Good job." Paco said.

"Huh?"

"That's good work you did there. You pulled an impressive team together."

"Oh. Right." Godfredo wasn't sure what to say.

Paco offered him a cigarette, and then the lighter. "I'm giving you credit for this now, but it's crucial—for both of us—that Max feels he's responsible for any successes we might encounter."

"What?" Godfredo squinted as he lit the cigarette. He handed the lighter back to his father. "What do you mean?"

"It's just good business. Good psychology. You make someone *feel* responsible …"—Paco took a long drag of his own cigarette and exhaled—"… and they don't question you when you *hold* them responsible."

"Come on," Godfredo shook his head, incredulous, and looked away. "You don't seriously think we're gonna need to do that, do you? We're on a winner here, Dad. You saw the designs. Max is a fucking genius."

Paco pointed his cigarette at Godfredo. "That kind of thinking is gonna get us in trouble."

"No it won't."

"You're a Roco," Paco barked. "My blood." He stared hard at Godfredo. "If the Americans or the Chinese want to win this contract, believe me, kid, they'll find a way." He jabbed at Godfredo once more with his cigarette. "You better do what I say. And keep your fucking opinion to yourself." He paused. "There's a race on this afternoon. I'm going back to the mainland. Send me those figures as soon as you can."

Paco flicked his cigarette into a bed of flowers under a nearby palm tree and, with that, strode away.

Godfredo stood alone on the grass expanse for some time after Paco left.

For a moment, he had the sense that maybe—just maybe—his father had a point. Who was he to doubt that his father, in his own way, had their best interests at heart?

As he smoked the rest of his cigarette, he paced.

He didn't hear Sofia until she was standing at his elbow.

She wore a sheer, halter-neck top and a pair of long black pants: wide-legged and silky, with a delicious slit up the side of each leg. She carried her overnight bag, clearly poised to say her farewells before catching the next ferry.

"What?" It was more of a statement than a question.

Sofia put a hand on his arm. "Baby, I saw you talking with Señor Paco."

Godfredo ground his cigarette butt under the toe of his shoe. "So you're spying on us now?"

"Of course not. That's not my line of business."

He sighed. "Shame."

"Yeah." She gave him a consoling look. "What do you mean?"

"I could use some information."

"Who from?" She put her bag on the ground at her feet.

Godfredo laughed. "You're serious?"

Sofia shrugged. "My business model can be flexible." She treated him to one of her genuine smiles.

Godfredo nodded slowly. "Okay." He considered her for a moment. "Do you have any idea what we're doing here? Me and Max?"

Sofia shrugged again, in her usual nonchalant fashion, yet, when she spoke, she was direct. "The Panama Canal expansion. You're putting in a bid. And that's why you brought in Max and Alexandra."

"Right." He cast a brief look around them, lest they had an audience, but the garden was quiet. "Now I'm thinking it might be good to get as much information about our competitors as we can."

"Sure, baby." She nodded. "Can you give me a few names? At least, as a starting point."

"We don't know exactly who's submitting. But you can definitely start with the Americans and the Chinese. Maybe the Germans."

"Okay. What do you need?"

"Numbers. Budgets. Blueprints. Anything you can get your hands on."

"Okay, I'll see what I can do." She looked at him with a slow smile. "But it's going to cost extra."

Godfredo laughed. "How much?"

"Triple my hourly rate."

"Triple?!" Godfredo baulked. Never mind the doe-eyed simplicity act: this woman knew what she wanted. "Double," he countered.

She was silent for a moment, her lips pressed together.

Finally, she nodded. "Okay." She held out one French-manicured hand, and he shook it.

"If you find out something," he said, "I want no record. No paper trail, no messages. You come directly to me."

"Okay."

Impulsively, he started laughing. "I can't wait to hear how you … acquire the information!"

"Yeah." Sofia sighed. "Me too. I imagine it's gonna require an extra skillset." She picked up her bag. "So if you want to hear about that part of it, you'll need to pay me triple."

"Holy Toledo, you drive a hard bargain!" Godfredo said. "Okay. Triple. But it better be a good story."

She smiled and, teetering on tiptoes, kissed him on the cheek.

Godfredo grunted. Transfixed, he watched her as she walked, unhurried, down the path.

"And it's only because you're good at negotiating!" he called after her.

She turned and blew him a kiss.

Chapter Seventeen

American Embassy, Clayton, Panama

"Enter!" Larry Roebuck looked up and replaced the receiver. "Dr. Siegel. Have a seat. Leave the door open." He raised his voice a notch. "Summers! Coffee!" He made a vague hand movement to indicate it was safe to close the door now.

John Siegel Junior obediently closed the door.

Roebuck came around from behind the desk and stood in front of one of his Chippendale chairs. "Please have a seat."

Siegel stretched his lips slightly, and Roebuck presumed it to be a smile.

"I'll get to the point, Dr. Siegel. Can I call you John?"

Siegel gave a curt nod as he sat on the baby blue velvet sofa.

"John, a set of blueprints has arrived on my desk."

"Blueprints?"

"Yes. I'm no expert, but it looks like a design for a set of locks. I was hoping you could clarify."

"They're not from me." Siegel was already defensive, but Roebuck had been expecting this.

"Then perhaps you can take a look?" He handed Siegel a manila envelope. It was addressed to 'The Ambassador.'

Siegel paused for a moment, and Roebuck saw a shadow of doubt in his expression.

Roebuck waited.

"Okay, I'll take a look." Siegel opened the envelope, and Roebuck watched his frown go from one of concentration to one of concern as he pored over the scanned pages, turning them ninety degrees occasionally, to read the notes.

Finally, he looked up. "And this came in the post?"

"Somebody dropped it in our mailbox."

"Who?"

"That's where I was hoping you could help."

"Is there more?"

Roebuck shook his head.

Siegel laid the envelope's contents on the coffee table in front of him. "We have a problem."

"What do you mean?"

"First of all, I shouldn't be looking at this."

"Whyever not?"

"I can't see their whole design," Siegel said, tapping the papers, in front of him, "but it's enough for me to know that this is part of a bidding plan for the expansion of the Panama Canal."

"What?!"

"For me to be looking at this …" He looked very concerned. "It's in direct contravention of the rules."

"Oh gosh, I am so sorry to put you in this position!" Roebuck said. "If I'd known—"

"It's alright." Siegel said. "What's done is done." He was silent for a moment.

Roebuck waited.

"What worries me more …" Siegel seemed to stop himself.

"Go on."

"What worries me is that whoever did this is very, very good." He grimaced, and rubbed his forehead. "I shouldn't have seen it." After a moment, Siegel looked at Roebuck. "Sir, I'd like to show this to my team, but I don't think that would be wise."

"Agreed, agreed," Roebuck said hurriedly. "Let's contain it for now." He stood up and scooped the envelope off the table. "I'm so sorry to have bothered you."

But Siegel remained seated.

"John?" Roebuck looked at him.

Siegel sighed. "Whichever team this is—and I have my theories—their technical rating is going to be extremely high."

"Well, I expect the standards would be—"

"I'm afraid it has serious consequences for us."

"For …?"

"For the United States. For our submission."

"How so?" Roebuck sat once more, and looked at Siegel intently.

"Sir, you understand there are two parts to the bidding?"

Roebuck nodded. "The technical and the financial."

"Yes. And if we can't beat this design for the technical part of the challenge—which unfortunately I now see as a distinct possibility—we have no option but to come in with a very low bid for the financial part."

"This design is that good? But now that you've seen these prints, can you not adjust your technical proposal?"

Siegel shook his head. "Impossible. We are too close to deadline. It would take months to change our concept at this stage."

He sighed. "We had roughly five-point-five billion as our best-case scenario," he said, almost to himself. "If we went down to five billion, or four-point-eight …?" He stood up and sat down again. He shook his head. "No, that's madness. We wouldn't make a cent. We might even run at a loss."

Roebuck exhaled slowly. "Okay. So what would be a good figure? What would be unbeatable?"

Siegel shook his head. "I don't know." He paused. "Do you have *any* idea who sent you these plans?"

"No!" Roebuck held up his hands. "But if you're suggesting we could try and get more information, you know I can't get involved."

Siegel nodded. "Then we need to bid low."

"How low?"

"Five billion."

"*Five* billion?" Roebuck's eyebrows shot up. "What was your original figure, again?"

"Five-point-five. But, look, we can still make it worth our while if we request some kind of financial support from Washington."

Roebuck now increased the distance between them, very slightly. He shook his head, warily. "I'm afraid that's not a possibility, John. You know the tender regulations. The nearest thing would be perhaps some tax credit—"

"Sir, with all due respect, I don't think you understand the seriousness of this situation."

Roebuck now allowed himself to show indignation at the tone Siegel was taking. "I'm sorry, Dr. Siegel, but that's the way these things work. You know that. The US government can't be seen to be—"

"No." Siegel stood up once more. He pointed at Roebuck with his forefinger, his gray eyes unflinching. He looked hot and he looked flustered. "Contact Washington," he demanded. "I think you'll find this project carries a bit more weight than you realize."

As Summers appeared in the doorway, bearing a tray of coffee cups, Siegel added, "Let me know the minute you hear anything."

He pushed past Summers and was gone.

Chapter Eighteen

Marriott Hotel, Obarrio, Panama City

Paco was perched on the arm of the sofa in his hotel suite, with the phone to his ear. He checked his watch for the third time.

"Francisco?"

Paco jumped to his feet. "Jesus. You took your time."

"Apologies. My job at the canal isn't getting any less busy these days. As you can well imagine." His friend's laugh came down the line.

"We're close to deadline and I haven't received a price yet."

"I know, I know. But I have no control over that."

"Well, you better do something." Paco started pacing. "Find a way to speed it up."

"The minute I get confirmation, I'll let you know. What I can tell you is that it looks like the Americans will run a low number."

"I need more than that."

"And you'll get it. Just be patient." There was a pause. *"Say, what's your team like? Did they enjoy my beach house on Contadora?"*

Paco smiled, and gave a short laugh. "That's the good news; they had a blast. And the result is much better than we could have hoped for."

"Excellent, excellent."

"So, tell me, who is your source for the numbers?"

"It's safer for you not to know."

"Fair enough. But I've got one last question: is this guy working for you? Or are you working for him?"

"*How do you know it's a man?!*" His laugh exploded down the line. "*Ah, Francisco. The old Francisco. Always trying to be in control.*"

The line went dead.

Chapter Nineteen

CLASSIFIED BY: Roebuck, Ambassador; REASON:
1.4(B), (D)
April 9, 2009

1. (C) On the morning of April 9 an anonymous
envelope arrived addressed to 'Ambassador
Roebuck, the Ambassador of the United States.'
It contained an incomplete copy of engineering
blueprints for a Panama Canal expansion
submission. The source of this information is
unknown, and an investigation is underway.

2. (C) The Ambassador subsequently requested
an immediate meeting with expert engineer,
John Siegel Jr (head of Siegel US engineering
consortium) to verify the nature of these
documents. He confirmed that they did not
belong to the US team, and he concluded they
were plans for the Panama Canal expansion,
leaked from another competitor. He was
extremely concerned that the quality of this
submission might be far above that of the
current US technical proposal. Accordingly,
he has requested the Ambassador enquire
about government subsidy. The Ambassador
advised against this, due to strict submission
regulations.

Chapter Twenty

American Embassy, Clayton, Panama

"Ambassador Roebuck, were you out of your mind?"

"Madam Secretary." Roebuck swung his office chair so he could greet Rebecca Eisenhower, the US Secretary of State, via a video call.

"First of all: John Siegel should never have seen those documents!" Eisenhower's face was incredulous.

"Ma'am, it was an honest mistake. I'm not an expert, I assumed they were the original canal blueprints."

"Where did they come from?"

"We're not sure yet."

"Okay, but let me get this straight … John Siegel thinks—based on these anonymous plans—that the United States might be out of the game? How does that work?"

"Ma'am, if those documents are to be believed—and John Siegel says they're the real deal—then this other engineering team have a very, very strong technical proposal, and it's much too late in the day for Siegel's team to change their whole concept."

Eisenhower frowned. "How can this concept be so different from any of the others? Surely there are only 'x' number of permutations, given the parameters they're dealing with: big river, wetlands, existing canal—"

"Ma'am, I'm not the expert. But what I can tell you is that Siegel is very concerned. He believes the only way the United States can be competitive now is to offer a very, very low bidding price. Otherwise, the risk of losing is too high."

"Well, I've already spoken with the President and with

the Chairman of the Joint Chiefs of Staff and we are in agreement that we can't ignore this. Especially if it turns out those plans are part of a Chinese submission. We can't take the risk." She paused, leaning forward in her chair. "Look, I'm sure you're aware, Chinese influence and control of world trade has reached unprecedented levels."

Roebuck nodded soberly.

"We believe having a US team on the expansion would get us one step closer to having a bigger say in what happens to the canal in the future. At least, regain some level of influence."

"So what would you suggest, then?"

"Well, for a start, Siegel is right: we need to get creative about funding."

"Ma'am, government financial involvement is not permitted." Roebuck was emphatic.

"We can find a way around that. Tax credits, deferred payments; we have the means to make this work. I'll start the wheels in motion over here, and you speak to Siegel and find out how much help they need."

"Yes, Ma'am."

She pursed her lips and sat back in her chair. "If we don't win this one, I can tell you there are more than a few interested parties in Congress who'll make it their business to obstruct anything the party brings to the table in the future." She smiled wryly. "And I do not want to have to deal with the fallout of any world-record-breaking filibusters, regardless of how much I may agree with the sentiment."

"Of course, Ma'am."

Roebuck didn't bother to mention that it was precisely those 'interested parties' who had supported his Ambassadorship in the first place: the ones who—right from the beginning—had opposed the Torrijos–Carter Treaties that put the canal and its profits back into the hands of the Panamanians by the end of 1999.

"Keep me informed. In black-and-white, Larry. I need a paper trail."

"I shall, Madam Secretary. Give my best to the President."

Gently, he replaced the receiver in its cradle.

He hit the intercom button.

"Summers! Get John Siegel back in here as fast as you can."

Chapter Twenty-One

Contadora, Pearl Islands, Bay of Panama
May, 2009

Max opened the door of the villa that was his living quarters to see Alex Wong on the doorstep. Her face was shiny from the heat, her hair pulled away from her neck, and she was carrying a cheap, nylon lace fan she'd picked up on a trip to the mainland a few weeks ago.

"What happened to your face?"

But it wasn't just her face. It seemed like her entire body was covered in small red bites, some of them inflamed and weeping, others scabbing over.

Max beckoned her in. "For God's sake, take off your shoes," Max implored. "You make me feel hot and itchy just looking at you."

She stood in the hallway under the ceiling fan, but wouldn't go any further.

"If this is about all the unexpected visits from Paco, I apologize," he said. "I don't think he's trying to put pressure on us. I think it's his way of—"

"It's not that." She looked up, at the villa's ceiling, and when she breathed out, it was with a slight shudder. "How am I expected to keep on living and working in this environment?"

"Is it too luxurious for you?" he teased gently. He'd hoped to get a smile, but for one terrifying moment it looked as though she might be about to cry.

"I have *no privacy* whatsoever!" she blurted. "My room opens onto the beachfront, and there are constantly ... *women* there, wearing practically nothing. One of them even wandered inside, casual as you like, and helped herself to my hand cream."

Max noticed that her once crisp linen dress looked saggy, and her patent black pumps were now scuffed and dusty from weeks of wear and tear in the sand. She looked like she hadn't slept in days.

"This morning there was no breakfast *anywhere*. Not until *eleven o'clock!* That's lunchtime, Max. I don't know where a shop is, and I couldn't get those stupid, bloody golf buggies to work. I tried to find a shop by walking, but I got bitten by so many of those bloody *chitra* sandfly midge things—"

"Hey, Alex," Max interrupted her. "It's okay."

"No, it's really not okay." The tears were seeping now from the corners of her eyes. "Last night, I was kept awake nearly all night with the noise from *yet another* party. And on top of that, I'm lactose intolerant." She swallowed a sob. "There's no soy milk for my muesli."

"Oh, Alex, why didn't you say before? I'm so sorry. I'll get them to order some in."

She wiped her eyes. "It's really not that. I can live without muesli."

"Then …? Tell me what I can do."

"Max, this is the chance of a lifetime in my career, don't get me wrong, I know that. But …" she gulped. "I'm living with … with *prostitutes*." She wrung her hands together. "I'm an award-winning scientist! If my parents knew I was living like this …" She took a long, shuddering breath. "I could never, *ever* tell them. They would be so ashamed of me." She started sobbing.

"Oh, Alex, I'm so sorry." Max paused, trying to digest it all. "Okay. So I'll find out if you can switch rooms with one of the others, and I'll see if we can get you a refrigerator. We'll get ourselves some wheels first thing tomorrow morning, okay? And we'll make sure we just keep running our ship the way we're used to running it."

Alex's lips were pressed together but he could see her lower lip quivering. "I don't know if I can," she said. "I'm so tired. I'm getting less sleep than when Lucy was a newborn." Her voice cracked. "I miss her so much."

Max tried not to look too concerned, but he was. Alex rarely spoke about her daughter, and never about her parents: she was ferocious in her defense of her privacy, under normal circumstances. But he had to admit, this environment was a far cry from normal. A far cry from that which he'd observed to be Alex's usual, orderly life.

"Just give it a couple of days," he said, gently. "Godfredo's a good guy. He knows what he's doing. Even if it looks like utter chaos from time to time."

"Max, that's the thing: I don't think he *is* a good guy. You may have known him when he was a teenager, but …" Her voice trailed off and she shook her head. She wiped a tear that had dripped to her chin. "He doesn't like me. He's made that clear."

"Did something happen that I need to know about?"

"No, no, it's just … It's the whole package. He doesn't show up for meetings. He doesn't even start work until lunchtime. His work ethic … it's really messed up. I don't trust him."

Max frowned, and turned toward the beachfront.

Again, he wondered: had he been wrong in his assessment of his old friend?

He turned back to her. "I hear what you're saying, Alex, but he always delivers on time, and the figures seem to check out so far. You and me—we're used to working together. But, in reality, we live in a small, academic bubble, and it's easy to forget that's not the way everyone operates." He paused. "You want me to talk to him?"

"People don't change just because someone wants them to. If I could have done anything about it, I would have. But I can't …" She faltered momentarily, her voice breaking once more. "I can't deal with this level of unpredictability any more. I'm so tired."

As a fresh round of tears flowed, Max moved across to her and put an arm around her. "Come on. It's okay." He could feel the tension in her small frame. "We can do this. We're so close to the finish line." He paused. "I'd really hate to see you leave now."

She sniffed, wiping her nose on the back of her hand.

He stepped back once more and looked at her. "At this stage, we need all hands on deck if we're going to submit on time. So please stick it out, Alex. I'd really appreciate it."

After a pause, she said, "I'll give it a few more days. But only because you're asking me to." She wiped her nose again. "But if it doesn't improve, I'm leaving."

Max crossed the room and looked out at the Pacific Ocean.

He wondered what Alan would make of the view.

Sighing, he turned his mind to the issue at hand. In many ways, he could see Alex was right. They were at the mercy of Godfredo's unhurried approach to work. Yet Godfredo had organized the whole set-up on Contadora, and he'd been generous, too: small details had been taken care of, like good wines and interesting local delicacies that appeared daily alongside clearly written-up agendas. And—perhaps purely as a joke, but so what?—there was always a fresh loaf of sliced, white bread and a new can of baked beans in the kitchen storeroom, on a special shelf, labelled: *Max.*

He was reticent to believe Godfredo was as negligent as Alex made him out to be. If anything, he had observed his friend to be exactly as he had been all those years ago: reliable—but only if you looked hard enough. He'd certainly been smart enough to know that on an island with no bars or restaurants, the only thing you could do was relax … and do the work.

And, indeed, they'd powered through, focusing on and creating what was undeniably their best work to date. And now they were on the home run. With only a matter of weeks before they were to submit their bid, he crossed his fingers that Alex would be able to go the distance.

Chapter Twenty-Two

Casco Viejo, Panama City, Panama

Lunch was Larry Roebuck's favorite event. Especially when it was at the American Trade Hotel in Panama's Old Town.

The Hotel had been there since the early days of the Panama Canal and had recently been reopened, white-washed, and luxuriously refurbished in a way that nurtured its 1920s heritage. The splendid building could now be seen clearly, unimpeded by the heavy, hanging snarls of black telephone and electricity wires—most of them illegally connected—that still marred the rest of the city's streets. The Old Town had been a veritable construction site for almost two years as the streets were dug up to make way for the relocation of the cables. The effect, Roebuck believed, was worth it: better to remove these kinds of ugly complications from the public eye. Bury them underground.

As he made his way toward the foyer that day, Roebuck waved benevolently at a local man who was often to be seen out front. Rumor had it the man was an ex-gang member from before the area had been cleaned up.

Yes, there was certainly something about a building with a history. It drew in those who cared about its story: people who knew that the past held the key to the future.

Larry Roebuck was proud to be one of those people.

"Welcome, Mr. Ambassador!" He was greeted enthusiastically by the doorman, and cool air washed over him as he stepped into the foyer.

He was shown to his regular table, alongside a broad-leafed palm tree.

He scanned the room, making sure a warm smile was etched on his face as he greeted people in passing. The wonderful thing about dining alone—within arm's reach of numerous foreign embassies and Panama's own Presidential Palace—was that you never knew who might show up and take a seat in the chair opposite.

He was unprepared for today's visitor.

"Mr. Ambassador."

It was John Siegel Junior. He was carrying a briefcase, and he looked to be on his way out of the hotel.

"John! Good to see you!" Roebuck stood, delivering an expansive smile. "I'm looking forward to our meeting later today."

"Yes. However, seeing as I'm here ..."

But Roebuck had no intention of talking business over lunch.

"Let's leave all that until this afternoon, shall we?" Roebuck smiled and said nothing more.

Siegel didn't move. "That's fine. You can tell me now. Why not? It'll save us a meeting this afternoon." His face, as usual, was expressionless.

Roebuck marveled at the man's tunnel vision; his utter focus on information and efficiency. And he knew when he'd met a brick wall.

"Very well," he said. "Have a seat."

Siegel sat on the edge of the vacant chair.

Roebuck lowered his voice. "I've been tasked with informing you that you will have financial backup if you need it."

"What?" Siegel's expression became contorted. Roebuck assumed it was a kind of ecstatic smile.

"You've no doubt had time to think about it over the past few days," Roebuck continued. "So what do you think? What price will you be offering? I'll need to let Washington know."

Siegel had by now flushed a decent shade of red. "Yes, yes," he blustered. "We have been over the numbers. I must say, I'm—"

"And?" Roebuck interrupted, enjoying for a moment the fact that Siegel was off balance.

"Four billion."

"Sorry? Did you say *four* billion?"

All of a sudden, Roebuck was grateful for the general backdrop of noise: this wasn't a conversation that should have been held in public. He lowered his voice. "Are you sure?"

Siegel nodded. "My CFO and I are in agreement that without subsidy, we can go for five billion—*maybe*—and we might be in with a chance. But if the government could come up with a billion-dollar subsidy, we could secure it with four."

"That's more than two billion less than your original amount. It's an awfully big cut."

"Sir, you asked me what it would take, and I'm telling you." He could see Siegel was becoming agitated.

Roebuck now shifted in his seat. "John, I have to say, I'm uncomfortable about this."

"Of course you are. You're an ambassador, not a contractor."

Roebuck ignored his terse tone, and persisted: "It was risky enough taking it to Washington," he said, "but if you push it …?" He exhaled, and once more glanced around the restaurant. "It could be seen to be taking advantage of the government's good will."

Siegel frowned. "Like I said, we made the assessment. And, given the circumstances, we believe this is what it will take." He stood up, clutching his briefcase.

"And if one of the other consortia go lower?" Roebuck asked.

Amazingly, Siegel emitted a short laugh. "They won't. Nobody in their right mind would ever bid lower than that." He nodded to Roebuck, serious once more. "I told you the government would see the big picture."

Roebuck baulked, but restrained himself. "Indeed. And I

thank you for drawing it to my attention. I take it you won't need to meet with me this afternoon?"

Siegel shook his head. "I have everything I need."

"Very well," Roebuck said, as Siegel stood up. "And, John, if I may … I'd strongly urge you to make sure your own proposal and your documents are secure. As we now know, we cannot trust anybody."

Siegel simply nodded and walked directly toward the main entrance. Through the huge, floor-to-ceiling windows, he could be seen climbing into his car out front of the hotel.

Exhaling, Roebuck turned away. His gaze landed directly ahead of him, where a mural stretched the length of the wall above the bar. It depicted a long lane of aquamarine water and an art deco style cargo ship passing through.

For the first time in many months, Roebuck felt a niggling unease, and wondered if he'd perhaps bitten off more than he could chew.

He pushed it aside: if Siegel was nothing else, at least he was determined. You could only call that a strength. The right man for the job, without a doubt.

Chapter Twenty-Three

Obarrio, Panama City, Panama

Godfredo was impatient for Sofia to finish.

He looked up at the high ceiling with its wooden ceiling fan as it rotated, so slowly, and counted to ten.

Finally—*finally*—she swallowed.

She sat back with a long sigh.

"So?" Godfredo now thumped the table, causing the cutlery to jump. "I've been waiting long enough."

"Where do you want me to start?"

"You can start by telling me who's competing."

"Okay, I haven't found out anything about the Germans or the Japanese yet."

"But they're definitely entering?"

She nodded, and took another spoonful of strawberry mousse.

"And the Chinese?"

Her usually smooth forehead was now furrowed. "Baby, I don't think they're entering a bid. Unless they're working remotely or in some secret hideaway somewhere."

"What do you mean? Of course they're entering."

Sofia shrugged. "Panama City is a small town. I'd have been able to find out about it if they were, I'm sure of it."

Godfredo looked at her, exasperated. "Okay. Whatever you say." But he didn't believe it. There was no way on earth the Chinese wouldn't want to be in the game. Not when they already operated both the Atlantic and the Pacific ports at either end of the canal.

"So what did you actually find out?" he asked.

"Well, I met up with an American. He was nice. I liked him. He reminded me of one of my uncles in Colombia."

"Oh yeah? Come on, Sofia, what else?" Godfredo was fit to flip his lid: the woman told stories even slower than she walked.

"We went to a bar and we talked." Sofia leaned forward in her chair, put her elbows on the white table cloth and looked longingly at her empty dessert bowl.

"You talked?" Godfredo asked. "That's it? You didn't have to, you know, seduce him with chains and a whip? Break into his room at midnight with a flashlight?"

She looked at him impassively. "No, not really."

He sat back in his chair. "Okay. So give me the figures then." He didn't bother keeping his voice down: they were the last two lunchtime customers in the usually busy downtown restaurant, a few blocks from his hotel.

"Four billion."

"*Four* billion?" His laugh exploded. "You're so funny! That's hilarious!"

She tipped her head. "Godfredo, that's the figure."

"No. Can't be." Godfredo whistled through his teeth and leaned back in the cane chair. "The numbers *we* came up with are pretty fucking low. But *four billion?* That would be insane." He started laughing again, and looked at Sofia. "Maybe you should do less talking and more screwing. I think somebody's taking you for a ride."

"I don't think so." Sofia's expression remained pleasant, although he could see the flint in her eyes.

"So tell me: who is this mysterious client?"

"My business relies on confidentiality. You know that."

"Whatever." He'd had enough of noncompliance for the day. He signed the bill, and addressed Sofia as the waiter left. "I hope your little chat was discreet. I wouldn't want the Americans getting suspicious. Even if they were just spinning you a bunch of bullshit."

"Of course, baby."

He stood, and looked at her sideways. He shook his head. "Extra skills, my ass. Get your bag, Tiger. You're going back to Contadora. I don't want you let loose on the streets of Panama. At least, not until our bid is safely signed, sealed and delivered."

He watched her gather her jacket and her handbag: one of those ridiculous Gucci or Prada type affairs that matched her shoes.

"Four billion!" He started laughing again and helped her put on her jacket. "If we go any lower than four-and-a-half, all my profit will be gone. Every single fucking penny." He pulled her toward him so that her handbag was mashed between them. He kissed her neck. "We wouldn't want that, now, would we?"

"No, baby."

He slapped her on the buttock and the two of them made their way to where his driver was waiting with the car by the front entrance.

"Take her to the ferry," he instructed Fuentes.

His phone started ringing.

Sofia turned to him with a pout. "You're not coming with me?"

Godfredo shook his head as he took his phone from his pocket. "I got a few big meetings lined up. I'll be there in a few days."

He waved his hand briefly and answered the call. It was Paco.

"Dad, I'm on my way—"

"You see the news just now?"

"No, what?" Godfredo started moving up the street briskly.

"The Chinese aren't entering a bid for the canal expansion!"

"What?" Godfredo stopped walking.

"The Chinese aren't entering a bid! Fredo, this is the best fucking news I've had all year."

Immediately, Godfredo turned in his tracks. He scanned

the street. The car, along with Sofia, was just disappearing around the corner.

"Jesus. She was right," he murmured.

"*Who was right?*"

"Never mind. I'll see you in a couple minutes." Godfredo killed the call and moved fast up the street toward the hotel.

Chapter Twenty-Four

Contadora, Pearl Islands, Panama
June, 2009

"Where the bloody hell is Godfredo?!" Max added yet another box of paperwork to the pile that sat in the first of four golf buggies, and ran a hand through his hair.

He hadn't showered. For that matter, he hadn't slept. It was only twenty-four hours until they were due to submit their bid; they were to convene at the National Bank of Panama—*Banco Nacional*—along with all the other competing consortia to hand over the technical documents.

"Is it really a surprise to you that he's not here helping us?" Alex was struggling under the weight of two boxes. "Maybe it finally dawned on him that he was better off running a brothel, so he stayed on the mainland and—"

"Really?!" Max, irritated, cut her off. He had jogged across to help her, but now he stood looking at her; the urge to assist her had dissipated. "Alex, please. We're all tired. And this negative attitude really isn't helping."

Alex glared at him. "Whatever. Can you take one of the boxes?! I have to go. The plane leaves in fifteen minutes."

Max took both boxes, and loaded them into the second buggy.

When he returned, Alex was leaning down, holding her calves tightly. They were still covered in sandfly bites, many of them weeping and inflamed. "Argh!" She stood up, and strode in a tight circle. "Bloody *chitras*! They're driving me crazy!"

A group of men was approaching—the buggy drivers—and Max checked the boxes once more to be sure they were secured. He didn't want to hear that their months of work had fallen off the back of the buggy, only to be swept out to sea.

"You can take them now!" Max called out to the men. "*Gracias!*"

He turned back to Alex and hugged her tightly. "You did a fantastic job."

She nodded. "I'm sorry I can't stay for the submission."

Max shook his head. "I understand. You stuck it out till the end, and I'm really grateful for that. Call me when you get back."

She nodded. "Of course."

The men had started up the buggies and the first three were wending their way towards the road that led to the island's tiny runway, where the plane was waiting to receive the cargo.

The one remaining man had taken Alex's suitcase and was shoving it, on top of the boxes, into the final buggy.

"Hey! Be careful!" Alex moved hastily toward the tiny vehicle. She turned to Max and waved. "Fingers crossed!"

Max watched as the final buggy moved off.

"Wait! Alex! I have something for you!"

He swung around to see Sofia running towards him. She wore a long, green slip, and she was holding something in her hand, above her head.

The buggy slowed, and Alex hopped out, her face anxious. "I forgot something, didn't I?"

"This is for you." Sofia approached Alex, breathless. "I hope this will help with the pain." She thrust a small packet into her hand.

"I … er … that's very kind of you, Sofia." Alex looked at the package. She slid it into her handbag.

"I hope you have a good trip home." Sofia waved to the driver, and the two of them watched as the buggy took off once more.

Max turned to Sofia, puzzled.

"I didn't know you and Alexandra Wong were close."

Sofia shook her head as she walked toward him. "We weren't. I thought she could use some lotion. For her *chitra* bites," she said. She tipped her head to one side. "You look terrible."

"I don't doubt it." Max laughed.

As they started back toward the villa, Max felt her eyes on him. She smiled. "You are a really nice guy, Max," she said.

"That's very kind of you, Sofia—"

"Yes, but I'm not really sure if you like women."

Max started laughing. "Of course I do!"

She offered a short, "Hmm."

"What?" He looked at her. He had no idea where this was going.

"I'm not offended," she said. "I think it's sweet."

"What?"

"Well, you don't look at me like the other men on the island do."

"Right. I see."

"Shall I ask one of my friends to come over? You're staying in the *Casco Viejo* tonight, right? Perhaps a massage—?"

Max laughed loudly, shaking his head. "Don't worry, Sofia. I'm fine." He grinned. "Really. I'm all fine."

Chapter Twenty-Five

Banco Nacional, Panama City, Panama

Come on, Godfredo! Where are you?

Max looked out across the crowd that had gathered outside Panama's *Banco Nacional*. He held his cellphone to his ear: Alex was on the line from her home in London.

"No sign of him yet," he said.

"*Why am I not surprised?*"

Max ignored her tone and craned his neck to get a better view of the front entrance. A big screen and loudspeakers had been set up in the square outside. Beyond the Spanish-influenced bell towers and domes, seabirds circled and the sky was already heavy, promising the usual wet season storms.

Inside, where he stood, reporters and photographers were clustered around a lectern. Rows of seating were positioned in the center of the large, plush foyer, and members of the competing consortia were gradually working their way to the chairs.

Max knew he'd have to be sitting in one of those seats in the next few minutes—with or without Paco and Godfredo—because this was it. This was submission day. The day all teams were to hand over their boxes of technical documents, and deposit their financial proposals—in official, cream envelopes—into the highly secure vault of Panama's *Banco Nacional*, where they would be kept for several weeks while the technical submissions were assessed.

Except—so far—Max was the only senior member of the British consortium present. And Paco and Godfredo were supposed to be bringing the official envelope with their offering price.

He looked at his watch once more, as the Director of the *Banco Nacional* arrived with the Commissioner of the Panama Canal himself—José Gonzáles.

Together, they stood next to and inspected three rows of trolleys, on which sat fifty or more boxes: blueprints, plans and reports that comprised proof of the digital submissions from all the teams. The paperwork and hard copies were to be handed over purely for safekeeping: in order that nobody could tamper with their own—or others'—original technical plans.

"*No messages?*" Alex asked.

Max looked back out at the street. "They'll be here."

"*You hope.*" She scoffed. "*God, I can't even tell you how happy I am to be back—*"

"Wait! I see him! Gotta go, Alex. Talk later." Max killed the call, and kept his eyes on his friend's car as it turned the corner into the square.

As the car pulled up alongside the bank, Godfredo jumped out the passenger side. A young man who had been standing out front of the bank crossed the street and started chatting to Godfredo. Godfredo stopped, and laughed. He clapped him on the shoulder.

"Don't stop walking, Fredo!"

Max ran from the bank, out into the street, and toward his friend.

As he got closer, he recognized the man with Godfredo. It was Eduardo: the concierge who had greeted him at the airport, all those months ago.

Paco emerged from the far side of the car and, with a curt nod to Max, made a beeline for the bank's main entrance.

"Godfredo!" Max called, beckoning his friend.

Godfredo stopped chatting and waved. "Hey, Max!"

"Let's go!"

"One minute, *hermano*, I haven't seen Eduardo for weeks! You know Eduardo, right?"

"Fredo, where the hell have you been? They're starting the bloody ceremony—"

"Relax. We went to the wrong branch of the bank. That's all." Godfredo now started walking, following his father toward the main entrance. "Are you coming, or what?"

"The wrong …? Oh, come *on*, Godfredo. The National Bank has no other branches." Max threw his hands in the air. He jogged to catch up. Eduardo ran alongside, grinning.

As they reached the entrance, Godfredo flashed his ID and turned to Eduardo, bidding farewell in rapid Spanish. Eduardo waved cheerfully, and was soon lost in the crowd.

The security guard waved them past.

"You have the envelope?" Max asked.

"Dad has it, don't worry." Quickly, Godfredo scanned the room. "Eduardo was just telling me about a crazy gangster who just got released from prison. He used to live on the second floor of that big hotel around the corner—the American Trade Hotel—back when it was a gang squat. He says the guy had to dive out a second story window one day to escape being shot …" He pointed. "Dad's saved us some seats over there." He turned to Max. "The gangster guy got hit pretty bad, and now he can't move one side of his body." Godfredo limped a few steps, as if to show Max what he meant. "And his skull still moves if you press it here." He pushed at his forehead with one finger. "Freaky story, right?"

Max's mouth hung open. "And you're telling me this … *why?*"

"Because you love that kind of shit. You should thank me for enriching your boring little academic life." He pushed his way toward the free seats. Max followed.

As they sat down, Godfredo said, "Whoa. A lotta people here today. Where's Dr. Wong? Counting the seconds so she can tell me how late I am?"

"She's gone."

"As in: she left because she wants to make us feel bad that we're late?"

"As in: gone home. Back to England. Yesterday."

"Huh." Godfredo stopped. "Wow. She's actually gone?" He'd clearly not been expecting that answer.

Max reached deep for patience. "She's got a baby at home."

"What?!"

"Yes. I think she prefers to spend time with her."

Godfredo looked at him incredulously. "You're telling me someone was willing to screw her?" He threw back his head and laughed. "Well, at least that explains why I stopped getting twenty emails every morning complaining about faulty air conditioning and the terrible food. Did you know *hojaldras* are one hundred percent devoid of nutrition? They're basically powdered and fried dough. And you know how I know this? Wong. She wrote up a scientific analysis for me and left it on my desk." He sighed, grinning. "I think I'm gonna miss her—"

"*Ladies and gentlemen!*"

Max elbowed Godfredo and nodded toward the podium.

The bank manager was on her feet. "I give you ... the Commissioner of the Panama Canal ... José Gonzáles!"

Spontaneously, the crowd outside started cheering.

Grinning, Max looked at Godfredo. "Here we go!"

Gonzáles moved to the microphone. "On behalf of the people of Panama, I hereby accept the technical submissions for the expansion of the Panama Canal!"

There were more cheers, cameras flashed, and television crews followed the uniformed Panama Canal Administration staff as they wheeled the boxes of technical data into the bank's elevator.

On a large screen behind the podium, Max watched their progress as, one load after another, all the trolleys were taken to the vault under the bank.

The Commissioner looked to the room once more. "I now ask the consortium delegates to submit the second part of their bid: their financial proposals."

He turned to the bank manager, who stood by a plexiglass box at the side of the podium.

Silently, the first of the delegates walked to the front of the room and slid a cream envelope through the small letterbox slit at the top.

As the second delegate approached the box, a small hand movement from Paco caught Max's eye: Paco was beckoning him forward.

Uncertain, he looked at Godfredo, but Godfredo's eyes appeared to be on the bank manager's legs.

Max stood and joined Paco at the side of the room. "Something wrong?" he whispered.

Shaking his head, Paco placed the cream envelope in Max's hand.

"Paco, I—"

"You should be the one to represent the team."

"Are you sure?"

"I am. It's a big moment for CISCO. And we couldn't have done this without you." He nodded respectfully, and nudged him with his elbow. "Go. We're the last one."

Max turned and walked toward the box.

He slid the CISCO envelope in.

Spontaneously, the audience broke into applause, and got to their feet.

Once again, television crews followed, and all eyes were on the big screen behind the Commissioner as two armed security guards lifted the box and carried it to the vault.

As the vault door swung shut, the crowd outside the building erupted, and Commissioner Gonzáles's voice boomed, amplified and ricocheting across the room and the street.

"I now officially declare the submissions process for the expansion of the Panama Canal *closed!*"

Triumphant, Max turned to look for Godfredo, but he was lost in the crowd.

Part Three

Chapter Twenty-Six

Casco Viejo, Panama City, Panama
July, 2009

"Well, Max, me lad … Thought you might like to know I've done some research on the world wide web."

"You did? Where? At the library?"

"Yeah. They have one of them computers. So, I looked up the cruise last week. The one I told you about. 'Caribbean Cruises: Every ship carries the key to your dreams.'"

"Sounds good. Is it a big ship?"

"Yes, it looks enormous. Like it could fit half of Wembley Stadium."

"Fantastic! Did you look at any others?"

"I did. But this one's a beauty! It's got 'Cinema under the Stars.' That's a fancy name for watching a movie on the deck at night."

"Aha! Sounds perfect. Have you booked it?"

"Maybe next year … And when will you know if you're staying on in Panama?"

"Couple of weeks. You seriously wouldn't believe how much paperwork we had to submit for our entry. Boxes and boxes of the stuff!"

"Oh, Lord … Did I mention? Sarah sends her hellos."

"Sarah?"

"Aye, she called a couple of times. Askin' me how I'm doing on me own. I believe she's missing you."

"Oh. Did she say that?"

"No. But believe me, lad, in this world you don't have to say stuff to say stuff."

"Right. I hear you. Well, it was kind of her to check in

with you … Alan, I'm on my way to dinner now with a couple of the engineers, so I'll leave you in peace."

"*Right you are. Good luck, then, lad.*"

"Thanks, Alan. We'll need that luck. And lots of it."

Chapter Twenty-Seven

Balboa, Panama City, Panama
August, 2009

It was standing-room only in the auditorium as people jostled, vying for position to get a good view of the stage.

Max cast his gaze across the crowd. He spotted Godfredo, a few feet from the center aisle, and waved. Godfredo beckoned and grinned, pointing to the camera crew that were stationed in the aisle.

"We're gonna be on TV across the whole fucking world!" he said, as Max reached him.

Almost immediately, the vicinity was blasted with artificial light and a production assistant pushed back the crowd. When he was satisfied, he nodded to the camera.

The reporter held up her microphone. When she spoke, she had an American accent.

"I'm live here in the old American High School auditorium in Balboa Street, where we're waiting on the arrival of the President of Panama, who will oversee the official announcement of the winning consortium for the expansion of the Panama Canal. I don't need to tell you this is a huge day for the Panamanian people—indeed, for the world, and hopefully especially for the United States. Of course, the biggest surprise was that China is not competing, which has had everyone speculating over the past two weeks …"

Max looked across the aisle, to where the German engineering team stood together, smiling and waving German flags at the crowd.

"And here comes the official party!"

Camera crews moved like a shoal of fish as black-suited,

wired-up bodyguards wearing sunglasses appeared alongside the Commissioner, José Gonzáles, and Fernando Guardia, Panama's President.

Behind them, came Paco Roco and the heads of the other consortia.

They took their places onstage to a resounding applause.

"The show is about to begin!" Godfredo looked at Max with pure glee. "You ready, *hermano?*"

The Commissioner of the Panama Canal, José Gonzáles, now leaned into the microphone that stood center stage.

The crowd fell silent.

"*Buenas tardes, damas y caballeros* ... Good afternoon ladies and gentlemen ... and a warm welcome to our friends all over the world who are watching this momentous event via our live streaming."

There was an outburst of cheering from the auditorium floor and Max thought, smiling, of Alan's misspelled message, received early that morning: "*Brake a leg young Max.*" He doubted his uncle would be watching the ceremony, but you never know—they had televisions at the local pub, and it would only have been around ten p.m. back in England.

"It is now time to announce the winner of the bidding process for the Panama Canal expansion project!" Gonzáles smiled and nodded to the ongoing applause.

"It has been no small task to assess these submissions, and I thank firstly our team of experts for their willingness to oversee the process, and their dedication and diligence when making their decision." He paused once more.

"I also thank each and every team for their patience, for assisting us with clarifications during the review process, and—today, of course—for accompanying me to retrieve the envelopes from the *Banco Nacional.*"

He stopped speaking as the screen behind him replayed the moment—less than thirty minutes ago—when the official party with armed guards retrieved the plexiglass box from the bank vault.

Max exhaled: had it really been only two weeks since the bids were lodged?

Gonzáles turned to the plexiglass box that now stood on a table in front of the President of Panama.

Inside the locked box, in clear view, lay the envelopes.

"The first-round scores for the technical challenge will now be announced." Gonzáles held up his hand to quieten the crowd. "And shortly afterwards, President Guardia—"

He waited for the cheers to die down.

"President Guardia, the President of Panama, will oversee the opening of each envelope containing the price proposal. A full breakdown and analysis will be available on the Canal Authority website by five p.m. today."

Godfredo slung his left arm over Max's shoulder. "*Buena suerte, hermano!*" He gave Max's bicep a quick punch.

Max grinned. "We've come a long way since the ice hockey team in high school, haven't we?"

"Oh yes, indeed we have."

Gonzáles cleared his throat. "Ladies and gentlemen, in every case, technical bids will receive a score that comprises forty percent of the overall score. Financial bids will receive a score comprising sixty percent of the overall score. Good luck to the bidding teams."

The crowd grew silent.

"In fourth place, with a score of 3,755.5 is the consortium Tobiishi."

The crowd applauded.

"With a score of 3,790.0 is the DBK consortium, with German contractors Löwenhof." He looked up and cast his eyes across the auditorium.

"In second place, with a score of 3,890.5 ..."

Max felt Godfredo's arm tighten around his shoulders.

Gonzáles waited for the noise to die down. "In second place ... the Siegel Group, from the United States of America!"

The crowd roared, and Gonzáles raised his voice.

"With a small margin and the highest score of 3,990.0 … CISCO, the consortium from Great Britain!"

As he spoke the last words, a simple slide appeared on the big screen.

1. CISCO consortium: 3,990.0

2. Siegel consortium: 3,890.5

3. DBK/Löwenhof consortium: 3,790.0

4. Tobiishi consortium: 3,755.5

Max's jaw dropped. He looked at the stage, where Paco, nothing short of ecstatic, had his arms in the air.

As the crowd around them erupted, Godfredo and Tarocco leapt on Max, whooping.

"The highest fucking score on technical merits! Max, you're a fucking *genius!*"

There were flashes all over the room, and Max could hear the American reporter behind him.

"And here's the clincher: if the Americans don't have the lowest price by a respectable margin, they're out! It's all over. They have only one chance, and it's in one of those cream envelopes, up there …"

Godfredo took Max's hand, raising it above their heads, and Max forced himself to breathe as flashlights blinded him.

"Hold your horses, Fredo," Max said, laughing. "It's still anyone's game, if their price is lower than ours."

"And now …" Gonzáles's voice broke through, booming.

The crowd grew silent once more.

"And now … the critical part, accounting for sixty percent of the overall score." He leaned into the microphone. "The envelopes containing the price proposals will be opened."

The dominant sound was the scritch-scratching of Gonzáles's clothing as he walked across the stage, the microphone in his hand brushing against his suit.

When he reached the plexiglass box, he put his hand in to pull out four envelopes.

"In no particular order ..." he began.

He looked at the name on the front of the envelope. "DBK Löwenhof," he announced.

He passed the envelope to the President, who inspected the seal, nodded his approval and handed it back.

"The first envelope has been inspected, and I am free to announce ... in US dollars ... Six billion, eight hundred and seventy-two million, five thousand and eighty ..."

He looked up nervously, stumbling on the huge figure. "Apologies, that's five *hundred* and eighty-seven thousand."

He looked at the big screen.

The crowd was silent.

A string of digits appeared, and the crowd started to chatter and clap.

> DBK/Löwenhof: US $5,400,000,000.00
> Points Awarded: 4,110

"That's it! They're out!" Godfredo hollered. "Two to go!"

Both of them turned to the German team, who were waving their small flags in somber defeat.

The President was inspecting the second envelope. He nodded and handed it back to Gonzáles.

"Siegel," Gonzáles announced. "In US dollars ... Four billion, six hundred thousand."

"*Four billion?*" Max turned to Godfredo, aghast. "That number is so low! It's ridiculous!" He shook his head. He was more than a little disappointed. "We're out. Fredo. We're out."

> Siegel: US $4,000,600,000.000
> Points Awarded: 5,194

With a sinking heart, he pulled his phone out of his pocket and looked at the screen. It was Alex. She'd called four times.

"CISCO Consortium …" Gonzáles's voice ricocheted around the auditorium.

Max slid the phone in his pocket again as Gonzáles opened the envelope.

"In US dollars … Three billion, six hundred—"

Something's wrong.

The crowd's roar became deafening.

Max looked around him. He grabbed Godfredo's arm.

Godfredo's eyes were fixed on the large screen.

Max, too, turned to the screen. "What?!"

CISCO Consortium: US $3,600,500,000.00
Points Awarded: 5,330

Max stared, uncomprehending. *Three billion?*

He turned to Godfredo once more. "What happened? Fredo! What *happened?*"

But Godfredo was still staring at the screen, his hand clamped over his mouth.

"Fredo! Talk to me!" Max shouted.

It didn't matter now what the Tobiishi team achieved. Even with a full score they couldn't win. CISCO were the clear winners.

"*Doctor Burns!* Doctor Burns, tell us how you're feeling right now!" Each camera flash struck like lightning.

Is it possible Godfredo or Paco made an error?

He was dimly aware of Gonzáles's voice under the sea of noise, as the big screen flashed up a final scoreboard.

Base price proposal (in US dollars)
1st place CISCO
US $3,600,500,000.00
POINTS: 5,330

2nd place Siegel
>   US $4,000,600,000.00
>   POINTS: 5,194
3rd place DBK/Löwenhof
>   US $5,400,000,000.00
>   POINTS: 4,110
4th place Tobiishi
>   US $6,100,000,000.00
>   POINTS: 3,900

Then Paco was there.

He grabbed Godfredo, and pulled him roughly toward him. Above the din, with a ventriloquist's smile, he roared: "The cameras are on you, Godfredo!"

Too stunned to do anything but smile, Max stood between the Rocos, illuminated by blinding, staccato flashes. Slowly, it sank in: he—Max Burns—was the chief engineer of the winning team.

Chapter Twenty-Eight

Balboa, Panama City, Panama

The door slammed behind him, and Max fell heavily against it.

Backstage, the long corridor was quiet. The air was mercifully cool.

Ripping off his jacket, Max wiped his brow with his sleeve. It had been like an oven under the lights and the media sun-guns in the main auditorium. And yet he knew this was only the beginning: the media would be waiting for him outside the building.

He pulled out his phone and looked at the screen. Eleven missed calls from Alex. But she'd have to wait until he had some concrete answers.

He dialed Godfredo.

Come on, Fredo, pick up!

The two of them had been separated as the crowd surged, and then he'd had no chance of finding either his friend or Paco.

That is, until he'd seen them—on the far side of the media scrum—leaving the auditorium via a side door.

When he'd tried to push through, to follow them, the media had blocked his way. *"Max! Dr. Burns! This is an incredible financial proposal ... How did you do it?"*

Max now ended the call and loosened his tie, walking slowly along the corridor toward the room his team had been allocated.

He stopped outside the door. He knew he should join Tarocco and the rest of them, but he couldn't go in. Not until he had something to say.

He dialed again.

A group of people were walking toward him and he turned his back, phone to his ear, hoping they wouldn't recognize him.

Once more, he waited as Godfredo's phone rang.

As they passed, Max could hear the people chatting.

"Did you see the look on Siegel's face? I kinda feel sorry for him."

"I know. God, it's gonna be a killer party, though."

Max turned to look: they were Americans. And if they hadn't accosted him by now, it was unlikely they were reporters.

One of the women turned to look at him. She flashed a shy smile.

Without thinking, Max lowered his phone. She had beautiful blue eyes.

She turned away.

They all wore outdoorsy clothes, and the one who'd looked over her shoulder wore khaki cargo shorts and carried a hi-tech rucksack. A part of him wished she would turn back. She'd had a cute smile, and long, dark and wavy hair.

Sighing, he reached for the door handle. He must be out of his mind to be thinking about a stranger's smile at a time like this.

Or maybe it was the perfect time. Because everything felt like a theatre of the absurd.

As if on cue, his phone pinged, and he glanced down to see a message from Alan.

"Bloody hell you done a good job Max. By the way the Liverpool to Leeds canal was half a ruddy lifetime to build so u better make sure u come bac fer a visit before I need a walking frame. I heard it cost em a trucklode more than they thought but don't worry about that bit."

Another message came in.

"The canal I mean not the walking frame. Cost a lot."

131

Max waited, in case there was more to come.

There was.

"*This is Alan.*"

Max gave in to a smile and slipped his phone into his pocket.

He braced himself to face his team.

Chapter Twenty-Nine

Obarrio, Panama City, Panama

The car came to a standstill out front of the Marriott Hotel, and the driver, Fuentes, stepped out.

Godfredo ignored the buzzing of the phone in his pocket, knowing it would be Max. He swiveled in his seat to look at his father. Paco was on the phone to the Italian steel company.

Sensing his son's attention, perhaps, Paco turned. He lifted his free hand and mouthed, "What the fuck are you looking at?"

Godfredo turned away and reached for the door handle.

Paco's hand landed on his arm like a vice.

Godfredo sat back in the seat, and Paco's grip loosened.

"*Ciao, Ciao*, Antonio." Paco ended the call and threw his phone onto the seat between himself and Godfredo. "They're still in," he announced. "They don't like the price one little bit, but they'll do it."

"Nobody likes the price," Godfredo said. "Because it's going to be *fucking impossible* to do this job for less than five billion." He shook his head. "How could you do that?!"

Fuentes opened Paco's door, but Paco reached for the handle and pulled it abruptly. It closed with a slam.

"Why can't anybody ever fucking wait until I've finished talking?!"

Fuentes moved away from the car.

Godfredo leaned forward. "Dad, why the hell did you mess with the price?! And what about our deal?" He was almost shouting by the time he finished speaking.

Without hesitating, Paco brought up his hand and whacked Godfredo hard on the back of the head. "Grow up! It's just a number! You'll get a good slice of whatever we walk away with. And it will be a lot."

"God almighty! Don't *do* that!" Godfredo winced, touching his ear. "You know you're wearing a metal ring, right?"

When Paco didn't respond, he said, "You told me you wouldn't use that number. Because you didn't believe Sofia could have gotten it right. Because 'she's a dumb lapdog.' That's what you said."

Paco turned to him. "Yeah. I said that. And I meant it."

"So why the hell did you change your mind without telling me?"

"Because, after that, the number was confirmed to me."

"What do you mean, 'confirmed'? By who?"

"By José Gonzáles."

Godfredo baulked. "You mean *Commissioner* Gonzáles?"

"Yes. And even then, we weren't absolutely sure that was gonna be the Americans' final figure. So we decided to go lower."

"Jesus. So Gonzáles is the one cutting deals with you?"

"Not with me, Godfredo. With *us*."

"But how could he have known their final numbers?"

"He had an informant. I don't know who it was. He wouldn't tell me. And I believe it's better for us not to know."

Godfredo exhaled and looked out the window, trying to let it all sink in. The traffic alongside them in the street was moving slowly, in fits and starts. Fuentes was now standing patiently by the front bumper of the car.

After a moment, Godfredo turned to his father. "I hope you know what you're doing, Dad, because if you go on springing surprises like this, Max will jump ship. If he hasn't already."

"Max is your department. I just need him to do the work."

"But that's what I'm saying! After this, he might turn

around and tell us to go screw ourselves. And I wouldn't blame him."

Paco leaned forward, his eyes boring into Godfredo. "You listen to me," he said. "I'll make this thing work, like I always do. But you better step up and show me you can take care of your team, and get them ready to shovel some dirt. Can you do that? Or do I need to find someone who can?" He paused. "This game is a shark tank, and right now I can't even tell if you can swim."

Godfredo shook his head. "You should have told me." He reached for the door handle once more.

He heard Paco's door slam; Paco was already striding toward the hotel lobby. Godfredo walked slowly around the rear of the car.

Thanks for waiting, you fat fuck.

"Are you okay, Señor Godfredo?" Fuentes approached him.

Godfredo felt a surge of embarrassment.

"Of course," he barked. "Be here to pick us up at six-thirty."

"Yes, Señor Godfredo."

As Fuentes went back toward the vehicle, Godfredo felt his phone vibrate once again. He stood motionless until it stopped.

He couldn't talk to Max now. Not now.

As Fuentes drove away, Godfredo crossed the street, away from the hotel, toward the tavern. He took a seat in the quiet courtyard, beneath the grapevine canopy, and ordered three bourbons.

"*Tres, Señor?*"

Godfredo let loose a string of expletives, and the waitress scuttled off.

Chapter Thirty

Smithsonian Tropical Institute, Panama

"Wow, these winning designs are actually pretty good." Dalisha was seated on the end of the bed, cross-legged, staring at a laptop screen. She was wearing only her underwear.

"The canal expansion designs?"

"Yeah, they just came online."

Karis laughed. "See? I told you." She tossed a pair of socks into the suitcase that sat on the armchair by the door. "You were getting all worked up over nothing."

She scooped up a pile of clothes and dumped them on top of the socks.

"In fact …"—Dalisha now adopted a secretarial tone— "… I'm pleasantly surprised. Must be because that British geomatics guy is so hot."

Karis laughed. "Yes, I'm sure they took the head engineers' looks into consideration when they were assessing the bids."

She thought again of Max Burns, whom she'd seen in the flesh that afternoon, albeit briefly. Uncharacteristically, she'd been taken by surprise: he'd been far more attractive in real life than onscreen.

She turned to look at Dalisha, and started laughing anew. "And you've decided to wear *that* to the signing ceremony tonight? At the Presidential Palace?"

Dalisha looked down at her underpants. "What's wrong with this?"

Karis pulled out her phone and pretended to take a picture.

"Put it away, Deen." Dalisha laughed and snapped the lid of the laptop shut. She jumped to her feet. "So far the Canal Administration's report on the winning submission looks pretty solid, but I won't be convinced until I've had time to read all their ecological reports in detail."

"Well, if I meet any of the British guys tonight, I'll make sure I send them your way for approval," Karis teased.

Dalisha reached for her purple dress. She slipped it over her head. "I still can't believe the Chinese didn't submit a bid at all. The blogosphere is going crazy about it."

She wriggled, pulling the fabric down over her torso.

"You'd think they'd be first in line to want to build the expansion, wouldn't you?" she continued. "Plus, they have so much freaking money."

"I guess." Karis said. "But you never know what goes on behind closed doors, especially in politics."

"How do I look?" Dalisha put her hands on her hips.

Karis smiled. "Fit for a king."

"Or a hot engineer?"

"Sure. Or a hot engineer. Although ..." Karis paused, a hand to her chin as she considered her colleague. "You might want to consider an armpit makeover?" She raised an eyebrow.

"Ha!" Dalisha snorted. She reached onto her bed and grabbed a small black bag. "Like I have time to give a shit about shaving."

Karis grinned. "I'm teasing. You know I'd never try to tell you what to do. I'd be way too scared."

She slipped on a pair of simple, evening sandals and fastened the ankle straps.

"I'm gonna miss you, Deen," Dalisha said, suddenly.

"Thanks, Dalisha." Karis smiled, looking up. "I'm gonna miss you too."

"You want me to come to the airport with you in the morning?"

Karis shook her head. "No need."

"Do you think you'll be able to come back?"

"Depends how it goes with my family."

Dalisha sighed. "Good luck with that …"

Karis smiled and closed her suitcase. She picked up a small, sequined purse. "I'd kill for a beer," she said.

"Then let's go!"

As she locked the door behind them, Dalisha gave a rumbling laugh and looked at Karis, her expression cheeky. "I have absolutely no intention of behaving lawfully tonight."

"You go, girl," Karis laughed. "I hope you're carrying protection."

Chapter Thirty-One

US Embassy, Clayton, Panama

Larry Roebuck was seated at his desk in full black-tie attire.

He waited, his phone on speaker, while he was patched through to the Secretary of State, Rebecca Eisenhower.

He was unsure what her reaction to the American team's loss would be, but he wasn't in a hurry. He had learned that doing things properly took time, and there was nothing to be gained by submitting to impatience.

He looked out at the Embassy complex and its neat, palm-lined streets, and felt a glimmer of satisfaction as he watched the local workers sweeping up after the rain.

"Roebuck. What in God's name happened?" The speaker came to life.

"Madame Secretary."

"You assured me the Siegel Group was on track to win the expansion project." 'Irate' wasn't an adequate description of her tone.

"Ma'am, I'm as shocked as you are."

"I don't need to tell you what a media circus my staff have on their hands. The President wants answers, and I don't have them."

"Believe me, if I had any insight—"

"What does Siegel have to say about all this?"

"He's baffled. And furious, of course."

"Rightly so. Look, our concern is that the price is so low— dangerously low. Do you think Siegel's numbers might have been leaked? The British offer doesn't make any sense if they don't have a safety net."

"I agree. Has the State Department got any ideas?"

"*None. Our guy in London has told me the UK government is in no way involved or subsidizing, and we have no reason to doubt that intelligence.*" She paused. "*Is there no other information about who might be backing the British consortium? I find it very hard to believe they can complete a project of this size for less than four billion.*"

"Yes. And the cost for Panama to ameliorate a disaster if they don't succeed ..." Roebuck sighed. "It could cripple their entire economy. It could literally bankrupt the canal—and the country."

"*Larry, we need to cover all angles. The canal's expansion is too important to us to have it in the hands of amateurs. I suggest at a minimum John Siegel leave a skeleton team in Panama. Or we send someone who can keep abreast of the project and report on its progress. It's a long shot, but it might be advisable.*"

Hastily, Roebuck said, "No, no, leave it with me. I'll talk to Siegel."

Best not to get more people unnecessarily involved. With a project of this magnitude, the less complications the better.

He was reminded of the original canal and its *fin de siècle* journey, which had been one of disaster after disaster, with monsoons and flooding, collapsing banks of rock, thousands upon thousands of deaths, and massive, expensive machinery lost to bottomless swamps. After four leadership changes in as many years, and a sheer lack of a cohesive strategy, its chief engineer Goethels had been driven mad. The project quite simply broke his spirit.

Roebuck wanted none of that.

Eisenhower cut through his thoughts: "*Keep me posted.*"

The line went dead.

Roebuck exhaled.

When he looked up, his assistant, Summers was standing in the center of the room.

"Heavens to Betsy! You're like a cat burglar, boy!"

"Sorry, Sir." Summers was clutching something in his hand. "A new lapel pin," he said. "I had it made for tonight. For the Presidential Palace." He seemed excited as he handed Roebuck a small American flag pin.

Roebuck wondered briefly if he should have included the lad in the President's typically generous guest list quota for tonight's ceremony. No doubt there would be swathes of young Smithsonian scientists of all descriptions, as well as local dignitaries and ambassadorial entourages.

"Your wife is waiting in the car." Summers said. "Have a wonderful time, Sir."

As Summers left the room, Roebuck opened the door to his en suite, and stood in front of the mirror.

Not bad for his age.

He looked good.

Musing now at his reflection, he considered that, yes, perhaps Summers deserved a night out. He could watch and learn. See how it's done at state events.

With a sudden surge of beneficence, he hollered, "Summers!"

Carefully—proudly—he affixed the ambassadorial pin to his lapel.

Chapter Thirty-Two

Casco Viejo, Panama City, Panama

"What the actual bloody hell is going on?"

Max had just tied his second shoelace, and was seated, wearing full black tie, on the end of his bed in the hotel room.

He was glad he couldn't see Alexandra Wong's face right now.

"Alex, I'm sorry, I don't have answers for you—"

"Well, that makes two of us. Three-point-six billion? Three, Max?"

"It's nearly four—" Max didn't even know why he was bothering to defend the figures. He rubbed his forehead.

"What planet have you been living on? I warned you, didn't I? About your so-called 'friend' Godfredo?"

"We won, Alex. Our design *won*, by a hundred points. Aren't you even a little bit pleased about that?"

"Just ... stop it! Stop it! You know what I mean. The risk here is enormous. What if you can't finish the project because you run out of funds?"

"Alex, stop worrying. Seriously. We're the engineers, here. I know it seems like an overly optimistic budget, but I have no doubts that Paco knows his way around the industry. He has done this his whole life—"

"Have you talked to him? What does he have to say for himself? And what about Godfredo?"

"I haven't been able to reach Godfredo, nor Paco—"

"Well, that's convenient—"

"... but I'll be seeing them shortly, and I promise I'll get you a detailed breakdown."

"*No.*" Alex's voice was firm. "*I'm sorry. You'll have to find someone else if you stay in Panama. I don't want my name associated with this.*"

"Alex, come on! We've come this far …"

All of a sudden, Max felt a wave of exhaustion roll over him. "Can we do this later, Alex? My ride's about to arrive. I need to get to the signing ceremony."

There was no response.

"I'm sorry you feel that way," he said. "We put in a fantastic submission. You should be here to celebrate with us."

He ended the call, and looked out the window, across the hotel courtyard. The pool sat deserted, its green-and-white striped umbrellas rocking in the sea breeze.

He made his way to the door.

Outside, the sun was nowhere to be seen due to the heavy canopy of clouds. The air was suffocatingly hot and humid, the ground still wet from the afternoon's torrential rain.

Max regretted putting on his jacket. It was like being in a sauna.

Again, he tried to put together cohesive thoughts so he would have something to say to Godfredo and Paco. But the experience of the last couple of hours had left him feeling nothing short of schizophrenic.

The reality was, he had no idea what he'd say. Especially to Godfredo, who'd simply disappeared shortly after the announcement, leaving him alone to deal with the press.

A black limousine pulled up alongside him, and the rear window slowly slid down.

"Get in, son." Paco's face appeared, and he waved Max toward the vehicle.

Max climbed in.

"Where's Godfredo?" he asked tightly.

Paco let out an exasperated, "Pfft!"

Max felt his hackles rising. "What does that mean?"

"He's got a headache."

It must be a helluva headache. Instinctively, he reached for his phone.

"I wouldn't bother. He's not answering."

Regardless, Max dialed.

He waited as the phone rang. And rang. And rang out.

"Don't worry about Godfredo. He's a big boy. He'll be on his feet again soon. He's a Roco through and through."

So it would appear.

They drove the short distance to the Presidential Palace in silence and, as they approached the gate, the driver lowered his window. He spoke with the armed guard, who waved them through.

Max wasn't even sure where to start, but he knew that if he didn't ask now, the two of them would be swept into the signing ceremony, and he'd have no chance of getting answers.

The car came to rest behind another limousine, next to the stone steps that led to the majestic whitewashed palace. Three men jumped out of the car ahead of them and posed, all smiles, for a photo opportunity.

"Paco, what happened with the numbers?" Max cut to the chase.

Paco looked surprised. "What do you mean?"

"You know exactly what I'm asking."

"That budget was based on your calculations," he said.

"No, it wasn't."

A doorman reached for Paco's door. Paco slammed on the lock and looked at Max.

"Actually, it was. Your figures are solid. But I've been in this business for a long time, and I know it's dog-eat-dog. In this case, I took your calculations into consideration and I put together a winning budget."

Several horns were now honking behind them. The doorman wrestled with Paco's door, and gave up.

The limousine inched forward to meet the red-carpeted steps.

Max looked directly at Paco. "I know how much work is required for a project of this size, and I'm prepared to step up, to do my part. I only hope you know what you're doing with the allocation of funds. Because from where I'm sitting, it looks unrealistic."

"Max," Paco said. His tone was fatherly. "I understand you know the theory. And you are extremely clever. But—despite what you say—I also know that neither you nor Godfredo have real-world experience on this scale. You need to trust that I've been in this arena for decades. And I wouldn't do anything to jeopardize this project's success. If anything, I see this as the chance to show the world what CISCO Construction was born to do." He paused. "You probably always wondered why I am so tough on Godfredo."

Max waited silently.

"It's because I want him to succeed. Did you know CISCO once belonged to Godfredo's mother and her family? And after doing a spectacular job of running the company into the ground, she and her brothers left me with the responsibility of cleaning up the mess. Which I did, quite successfully, as you can see." Paco's fist was on the seat between them. "And as she seemed to have no interest in us any more, it was up to me to bring up Godfredo."

Slowly, Max nodded.

"Max," Paco said, "you and Alex did one hell of a job on the plans. I know your parents would be proud to see what you've achieved."

He reached out and placed a hand on Max's shoulder.

"Anyhow," Paco continued, "this budget wasn't Godfredo's call in the end. It was mine. Me: Paco Roco. And I take full responsibility for that."

"Okay, then." Max exhaled. "But if you lie to me again, Paco, I can promise you, I'll be on the next flight back to London."

"Of course." Paco nodded. He unlocked his door, and the valet finally had success.

Relief, along with a wave of tropical heat, rolled into the car.

Godfredo had nothing to do with it.

Max stepped out of the car and, alongside Paco, made his way up the marble steps.

Chapter Thirty-Three

Casco Viejo, Panama City, Panama

The bourbon had worked its magic.

Godfredo felt nothing.

He stepped back unsteadily, the full weight of his body now resting on the wall.

Tentatively, he closed the door.

"How do you like it, *Señor?*"

Trying to focus, Godfredo turned to the figure who stood in the center of the room.

He narrowed his eyes. "I don't."

"I'm sorry, *Señor*, you don't … what?"

Fumbling, Godfredo undid his belt. "I want someone *else* …"

He struggled with the buckle; he struggled with his words.

"I want *you* …" He hiccupped. "I want *you* to feel what it's like."

There was silence.

"I want you to be a steaming pile of shit, I want to tell you to do things you don't want to do. All … the *fucking* … *time*." The belt came loose in his hand.

"Okay. You like it rough." The figure—a young man—ripped off his shirt to reveal a surprisingly buff set of muscles. Standing there with a vacuous grin, he looked like a cartoon superhero with acne.

"No, you dipshit," Godfredo roared. "I don't want to screw you! I'm not gay!"

"Then …?"

"Get on your knees, like a fucking dog."

The man got onto all fours on the bed. "Like this?" He flexed like a Chippendale.

Godfredo raised his arm, the belt in his fist. "I'm gonna …"

The man looked at him, expectantly. "*Sí?*"

A wave of nausea hit him, and Godfredo fell to his knees. He felt water on the back of his hands before he realized he must have been crying.

"I can't do it," he sobbed. "I'm not like him. I can't do it."

The young man turned and sat on the edge of the bed. "Whoa. You okay?" He leaned forward and put out a hand.

"Get out! Get the *fuck* out!"

Chapter Thirty-Four

Palacio de las Garzas, *Casco Viejo*, Panama City

Slowly, Max looked up.

Several columns, encrusted with mother-of-pearl, reached from the marble floor of the patio courtyard toward the titanium-white plasterwork of a cloistered balcony. Up there, behind lush, green fern fronds, a string quartet was seated. Light, classical music could be heard above the gentle play of a water fountain.

Behind him, security guards stood discreetly to both the left and the right of massive iron doors.

A man approached, with clipboard in hand.

"Dr. Burns and Francisco Roco from the CISCO Consortium," Paco announced. He sounded proud.

The man checked their names off the list.

A pair of white herons stood in the clear water at the base of the central marble fountain—the long-legged birds were unflustered, eyeing off curious guests.

"They live here since the 1920s," the staffer said, with a broad smile. "Not the same birds, of course. But that's why the Presidential Palace is called the *Palacio de las Garzas.*" He held out a hand to indicate that they could move into the residence. "Please make your way upstairs."

Max followed Paco up the marble staircase, drawing nods and congratulatory smiles from the slow stream of other immaculately dressed guests: men in black tie, and women wearing all shades of rustling, exotic fabrics.

They reached the Andaluz courtyard, where a line of staff stood politely, hands behind their backs. All guests were ushered across the mosaic floor to the elaborate wooden doors of the *Salón Amarillo*.

As they drew closer, Max could see, in the room beyond, massive gilt-framed mirrors and velvet drapes and pelmets. Chairs that looked eighteenth century and French lined the periphery. Chandeliers and gilded wall appliqués shed a warm, glowing light.

A treasure trove of pure gold.

Suddenly, Max faltered: this was a world that was all too familiar. A world of stately homes and opulence and glamor. A world that disappeared abruptly after his parents went down in the helicopter.

Uneasy now, he cast his eye around the room. He was looking for someone; a single familiar face.

There were none. No Alex, no Godfredo, no Alan …

He turned to Paco, standing alongside him.

Paco nodded and smiled as Gonzáles took his hand.

"President Guardia, may I introduce Max Burns?"

Max was thrust forwards.

"This is indeed a wonderful day! Congratulations!" The President shook Max's hand. His English was immaculate: almost Ivy League. He clasped Max's upper arm with his free hand. "I know you will work your absolute hardest for Panama."

Within seconds, the guests had erupted into spontaneous, full applause, and Max was swept into the center of the room.

A handsome man with graying hair and an American flag pinned to his lapel approached Max with a wide smile. He was tall and tanned.

"Dr. Burns. I'm Larry Roebuck. I'm the US Ambassador here in Panama."

Max took his hand: Roebuck's grip was strong and lightly pressing, so that his hand remained on top.

Not someone to be messed with. Max smiled. "Max Burns, sir. Very pleased to meet—"

"So you're the man who beat our Siegel team fair and square." It wasn't a question.

"Guilty as charged," Max said, with a smile. "Of course, it wasn't just me: I have a great team alongside me."

"Well, it's an honor to meet you."

Roebuck moved on to introduce himself to other guests.

A woman's voice broke through. "Oh, there you are!"

Max turned to see a young woman at his side. Her sleek, wavy hair was pushed back over bare shoulders, and she wore a midnight-blue gown that fell in loose, satiny folds to the floor.

And there they were again: those beautiful blue eyes. It was the cute American who'd been carrying the rucksack at the auditorium.

She smiled, and her nose crinkled slightly. "I saw you looking at me this morning."

"You did?"

"Sure. It's what we humans do. It's part of the mating ritual."

He stifled a smile. "Seriously?"

Her laugh was self-effacing. "People expect scientists to say shit like that. It usually works."

"And you're a scientist …?" Max, smiling, held out his hand. "Max Burns."

"Karis Deen—postgrad biologist with the Smithsonian Tropical Research Institute, Department of Paleontology." Her hand was warm.

"Anything else?"

"No." She laughed again. "But it's nice to meet you, Max." She paused. "And … why are you here, then? Did you do something important?"

A smile hovered on her lips, and Max realized she was teasing him.

She leaned in. "You can let go of my hand now."

"Oh, God." He released her. "I'm so sorry."

She was so beautiful.

For a moment, he'd forgotten where he was.

"I'm sorry to interrupt."

Startled, Max turned. The voice came from an older man: Asian, with a broad smile.

"But perhaps you weren't expecting to be treated like such a rock star tonight?"

Karis returned the man's smile. "Hello," she said. "I'm Karis Deen. Smithsonian Institute."

She put out her hand. The man was about Max's own height, wearing rimless glasses. His eyes expressed warmth, the skin around them crinkled at the corners.

"Steven Zhang," he said, bowing neatly. "Pleased to meet you, Ms. Deen. And you …" he turned to Max, "are Dr. Max Burns."

"And I … am going to find some food! Please excuse me." Casting a smile over her shoulder, Karis walked away.

Max tore his eyes away from her, and could only hope the television crews would be allowed in to record the President's address that night, because he had a suspicion he wasn't going to remember a single word of it.

"I do apologize," he said to Zhang. "Yes, of course: I'm Max Burns."

Zhang smiled. "I'm very impressed with what you've achieved. I merely wanted to wish you well as you embark on this immense undertaking."

"Thank you, Mr. Zhang." Max tried to place Zhang's accent. He sounded highly educated. Cambrian, even. "Have you been in Panama long?"

"Actually, no," Zhang said. "I arrived last year." He smiled. "Although I'd been planning to visit for many years. I dabbled in modern languages at Oxford, and often thought Panama would be one of the more interesting Spanish-speaking regions to explore." He paused. "Do you speak Spanish?"

"No," Max said, ruefully. "I can't say I've had a great deal of spare time to learn another language over the past six months. But I expect my schedule will look a bit different from now on."

Zhang's face brightened. "Do you, per chance, play golf?"

"Many years ago. My father taught me. But I haven't had a chance to play in a long time."

Zhang pulled a pen from his pocket. "May I?" He pointed at Max's napkin.

Max handed it to him and, under Panama's Presidential Seal, wrote down a number. "That's my direct line." He folded it neatly and gave it back to Max. "If you happen to have a free weekend, I would be honored to have you as my guest at the Panama City Golf Club."

The thought of playing a round of golf suddenly sounded very appealing.

Far more than facing yet another yacht or island-hopping trip with Godfredo and Sofia and their entourage of partygoers.

"It's extremely generous of you," Max said. "Thank you, I'd enjoy that very much."

"Not at all." Zhang nodded. "Although I should warn you: here in Panama, you'll need to learn to adjust your swing to accommodate the wind. It can be a bit disturbing." He looked at Max evenly. "But I suspect you're smart enough to overcome that particular dynamic."

Max laughed. "We'll see. It's been quite some time. My driving skills will be a little rusty."

"One finds, in life, that one doesn't unlearn skills such as how to swing a golf club. It's simply a matter of adapting to new circumstances." Zhang paused, and bowed. "I look forward to hearing from you, Dr. Burns."

Chapter Thirty-Five

Palacio de las Garzas, Casco Viejo, Panama City

As the President's speech wound up and the official papers were signed, the mood in the room soared. Champagne corks popped and people began once more to mingle. Rounds of cocktails were brought out on silver trays.

Max watched Paco work groups of people into fits of laughter, and rued the fact once more that Alex and Godfredo hadn't attended.

Drink in hand, he ventured into the central courtyard.

In a huddle of people around his own age—over by the colorful, tiled fountain—he caught a glimpse of the long, midnight-blue dress, and Karis's toned shoulders. She was laughing so hard that she was wiping tears from her cheeks.

Instinctively, he smiled.

He looked away, self-conscious; he didn't want to be that creep who lurked in the shadows, staring.

When he stole another glance at her, she was looking at him.

As he watched, she moved away from the group and walked directly toward him.

"Are you finished with the small talk?" she asked, with a cheeky smile.

"I am."

"So … shall we leave?"

"You want to leave?" Max looked around him: it seemed there were even more guests than there had been for the speeches.

"Yes. I thought you'd finished all the important tasks.

Haven't you?" She was still smiling. "Or do you have to sign another contract with the President?"

"No … Right! Of course. My presence is definitely not required here anymore." He smiled and held out an arm. "Well, then … after you, Ms. Deen."

Chapter Thirty-Six

Casco Viejo, Panama City, Panama

At dawn, Max stood on the balcony of his hotel room.

Beside him, Karis Deen was resting her elbows on the stone balustrade. The sea air was mild, and the two of them were wrapped in only large, white bedsheets.

Beyond, lay a broad stretch of restless, choppy sea.

Looking at the turbulent clouds above, smiling, Karis reached out one arm, the palm of her hand facing upwards. She had the look of someone about to leap; to launch herself off into the morning skies. Max wondered what she was thinking. Where she was going.

"So … you're absolutely sure you have to be on that flight today?" he asked.

Her arm dropped to her side and she turned to look at him. He lifted her hand to his lips, tasting the warm rain.

"I'm sure," she said.

"Will you call me when you arrive?"

She smiled, and kissed him. After a moment, she pulled away and looked directly into his eyes. "I won't promise to be in touch. But if I ever come back to Panama—that is, if I ever, by some miracle, finish writing up my doctorate—then I'll definitely reconsider."

He smiled. "Please do. You'll know where to find me."

"Yeah, partying with your consortium on a yacht!" she said, laughing. In response to his quizzical expression, she said, "With that … whatshisname? … that younger Roco guy you work with?"

"Godfredo?" Max grinned. "How do you know about him?"

Karis pulled him toward her. "Don't you read the gossip blogs?" He could tell she was teasing.

He rolled his eyes and wrapped his arms around her waist. "I try not to. Anyway, you can laugh about Fredo if you like—God knows, I do—but that guy was a lifeline after my parents died. They went down in a helicopter accident when I was sixteen."

"Your parents were killed?" Karis shook her head slightly. "That's … I'm so sorry, Max."

Max paused, intending to deliver his usual line: *It was a long time ago.*

Instead, he gave a grim smile. "I might be able to understand it, except it was a suicide; he left me a note. And he took my mother with him."

"Jesus. He must have been really unhappy." Karis's tone was soft.

"It took me a long time to accept that he took her and left me behind. I'm still not sure I understand it." He paused. "I doubt I ever will …" He looked out at the bay and ran a hand through his hair. "Yes," he conceded, finally. "He must have been very unhappy. But you wouldn't have known it. He was such a great dad, you know? Always encouraging me. Challenging me to do better. And he loved my mum. You only had to see them together. They were like Bonnie and Clyde."

Karis held him tightly.

"Alan thinks that was the problem," Max continued.

"Alan?"

"My uncle. Mum's brother. And I think he might be right."

"How so?"

"Dad would have done anything for her," Max said. "I guess I didn't realize it back then—I was just a kid, and I was in boarding school most of the time—but she was pretty wild. She loved entertaining. There were always people at our house, but not regular people; all kinds of colorful characters." He paused. "She was the one who introduced my dad to Rupert Garcia: he was one of her good friends from way back."

"And what happened?"

"He's been locked up since then, thank God, but Rupert persuaded my dad and some of his friends to invest huge sums of money in a scheme that was really just designed to pay off a string of his personal debts. My dad lost everything he and his father *and* his grandfather had worked for." He smiled wryly. "The entire Burns family fortune, and then some."

Karis sighed. "Wow. That's rough."

"The odd thing is, I don't think he cared at all about money and houses, or yachts and ski holidays," Max said. "Even though we had all that."

"Really?!" Karis's eyes sparkled mischievously. "Did you have maids and butlers and people to help you put on your pajamas?"

Max fought back a smile. "We had home help, yes. In London. And on the Sussex estate." He grinned, and brushed a hair from Karis's cheek. "Because it's what my mother wanted. My dad ... He just allowed himself to be sucked into someone else's idea of a good life."

"Your mum's."

Max nodded. "And when it all came crashing down, he ... packed it in and took her with him." He stopped and looked at her. "I'm sorry, Karis. I don't mean to load all this onto you."

"Max ..." Karis started. Her eyes searched his. "Don't worry. I understand." She paused, as though searching for words. "And I think most people do their best with what they have, in here ..."—she placed her hand on his chest—"... and out here in the world." She pointed in the direction of the ocean, and Max turned to look. Dawn light had cast the ocean silver and, for a split second, he felt the press of London traffic and chill, dark nights come rushing back, only to subside with the breeze that now played with Karis's long hair.

He considered her face for a moment. "How'd you get so wise, Karis Deen?"

She gave a dismissive laugh. "I'm not wise. I simply have the view from the shore." She flashed the same beautiful, shy smile that had captured his attention ... was it really only yesterday?

Max felt his blood stirring again.

"So tell me, Ms. Deen ..." he teased. "You've told me you're from Iowa. Where, exactly?"

"A small town," she said, brightly. "I'm ninety-nine-point-seven percent sure you wouldn't know it."

"Try me." He pulled her closer once more and kissed her deeply. He felt her body respond to his touch.

Suddenly, she pulled back.

"Shit!"

"What?!"

"My flight! It leaves in ..." She peered into the room behind them, toward the clock by the bed. "*Shit!* Less than two hours!"

In a matter of seconds, she had dropped the bedsheet and was sliding the midnight-blue dress over her head.

Quickly, Max pulled on his clothes, and the two of them ran barefoot through the hotel and out into the street.

"*Goodbye, Mrs. Señor Max!*" came the ever-cheerful voice of the bellboy, as the door closed behind them.

Max, laughing, pulled opened the door of the first of the taxis in the rank.

He turned and reached for Karis's hand.

"I enjoyed being with you," he said, as he leaned in to kiss her cheek.

She squeezed his fingers. "Me too. I guess I wasn't expect-ing ..." She stopped. "Well," she said, with a wry smile, "I've never been much good at timing. Take care, Max Burns."

And, without a backwards glance, Karis Deen was gone.

Chapter Thirty-Seven

CLASSIFIED BY: Roebuck, Ambassador; REASON:
1.4(B), D)
August 9, 2009

1. (C) During an August 8, 2009 conversation
with the Ambassador at the signing party
in the Presidential Palace in Panama, John
Siegel, Jr. (Siegel's chief engineer) expressed
again serious concerns about the British
Consortium's bid, saying, "There is no way
an expansion can be completed with CISCO's
winning base price. We see a real possibility
they might fail."

2. (C) A subsequent email exchange with Siegel
outlined a proposal that the Siegel Group
keep a skeleton team in Panama, with a view
to keeping a close eye on the progress of the
British Consortium.

Chapter Thirty-Eight

Dulles Airport, Washington, DC, USA

Karis Deen stepped through the sliding doors and scanned the line of faces.

She hadn't really expected to recognize anyone standing so close to the arrivals gate, but she looked at each face, regardless. Force of habit.

Once she was satisfied nobody familiar was immediately there, she moved her attentions further afield.

A man stood against the wall on the far side of the terminal, right under the International Arrivals sign. He wore civilian clothes: a Yankees baseball cap, and a faded denim, collared shirt.

Exactly as he'd been described.

"Agent Deen?" he asked.

She nodded briefly, and together they started moving toward the pickup bay out front of the terminal.

A black SUV pulled up alongside them.

Karis took the front seat.

With only a brief glance at the rear vision mirror, the driver took off.

Chapter Thirty-Nine

Panama City, Panama

It was precisely nine a.m.

An Asian man hopped out of the front passenger seat, and stepped quickly through the spotting rain with an umbrella.

"Doctor Burns?" The man bowed his head slightly, extending his right arm to indicate the car. "Please." He held the umbrella above Max's head and moved to open the rear door.

Taking his cue, Max hopped in.

He scanned the rooftops as the car took off, stopping himself only when he realized the English boy in him was looking for a clock.

He smiled. Not a single clock on a single building in the Old Town of Panama City worked. They were armless, or rusted beyond recognition, or simply stuck on a random time.

The land that time forgot.

A few minutes later, he saw the street that led along the foreshore of the Old Town: *Calle 2 Oeste*. It was the same stretch of seafront where he'd sat with Karis, on the wooden bench, less than a week before, right before they'd gone back to his hotel room.

As the car made its way slowly along the street, it dawned on him: this street was a dead-end. A cul-de-sac with a popular tourist bar and restaurant, and several foreign embassies.

He had the feeling Steven Zhang was not a restauranteur.

As the car pulled into a battle-axe driveway, the assistant

slid the window down long enough for a uniformed guard carrying a rifle and white bayonet to see him and deliver a crisp salute.

The iron gate slid open.

At the end of the driveway stood an elegant, white Spanish colonial home.

At the top of a flagpole flew an unmistakable flag—red with yellow stars.

Max Burns entered the Embassy grounds of the People's Republic of China.

Part Four

Chapter Forty

Undisclosed location, Virginia, USA
September, 2010

From inside the Bell Huey, Karis Deen couldn't see much.

It was only when the helicopter landed and the door slid open that she saw a cluster of austere, sandstone buildings and long, minimalist glass façades overlooking spacious lawns.

Following her colleagues, she ran, hunched over, away from the heli, as she'd done many times over the past months. All of them keeping pace; all of them wearing marine pattern camouflage.

And yet this was no forest gap or river trail.

"This way!" came the instruction from the front of the pack.

The group was led toward the front entrance of the largest building. Its glass door was acknowledged only by a pair of silk trees.

Once inside, Karis stopped. The foyer was spacious, carpeted and strangely quiet. Its surfaces and joinery were without blemish or fault, bar a long, raw sandstone wall that stretched the length of the building—a cloister of sorts—with views onto a modern courtyard.

A Brancusi-esque white, stone figure stood amid sparse, long grasses.

"Okay, now I'm confused."

Karis turned to the man who was standing alongside her.

"Me too," she said, her voice hushed. "But don't you dare pinch me." She grinned. "If this has anything to do with today's task, I seriously don't want to wake up."

The two of them moved across the foyer to catch up with the group.

Jay Stevenson was, by now, a friend. He had been through the entire year with her, the two of them forging a solid camaraderie as the training became increasingly challenging and the numbers of fellow recruits were whittled back from the original hundreds to—now—less than fifteen.

As they entered the intimately lit auditorium, Karis was surprised to see about forty unfamiliar people—also wearing uniform—already seated in low backed chairs.

They made their way toward a couple of spare seats at the back of the room. From the fresh smell of leather, Karis suspected they were the first people to sit on the upholstery.

"Good morning." A woman's voice—modular and commanding—broke through the general chatter. "Welcome to the Abbey!"

The room grew silent, and Karis turned to see a petite woman walk toward the lectern at the front of the room. She had stylishly cropped blond hair, and she stood at ease, hands behind her back.

"I see you're all ready for the day's training." The woman smiled and looked around the group. "Today …" She paused. "Today, your task will be to find your apartments and get to know the place. This is your new home."

There was a stunned silence.

Karis cast a look at Jay.

"I'm Agent Erika Fisher," the woman continued. "I'm the Director at our new facility." She smiled again. "As of this moment, nobody knows you're here. And you are the only ones who know of the place's existence."

Fisher now looked around the room, her attention resting on individual agents from time to time.

"Over your past many years of service to the United States, you have proven yourselves by going above and beyond expectations. Moreover, in the past year—since you signed up for special training—you have consistently delivered excellent performance, and you've shown us that you take the survival of your respective units seriously. Out of the more than three thousand personnel who applied from the various different agencies and military divisions across the country, you are the ones who have earned the right to sit on these chairs." She paused. "Congratulations."

The people around Karis began to loosen up—they turned to each other with nods or smiles.

Karis realized she'd been holding her breath.

"So, where are we?" Fisher began with a rhetorical question. "You may be aware, there were a number of Congressional Committee Hearings a couple of decades ago as part of an effort to get a Defense Clandestine Service off the ground. Are any of you familiar with this?"

"Monarch Eagle." A man in front of Karis spoke up. "It was to be under the Defense Intelligence Agency."

"Correct." Fisher nodded. "It was designed to streamline the broader Department of Defense intelligence, which was deemed to be increasingly inefficient. The various units were starting to overlap in their efforts."

She paused.

"Two years ago, in 2008, under the direct wish of President Nash, the Defense Clandestine Service—the DCS—was put back on the table, to be independent from FBI and CIA, to report directly to the Pentagon, thus directly to the President of the United States himself."

She paused to look around the group.

"You are our first intake of personnel."

Karis turned to Jay. He had a look of pure glee on his face.

"But let's take a step back." Fisher herself now moved away from the lectern and became more animated. "As you all know, the locus of global power has shifted a great deal over the past years. In the eyes of the world, the United States is no longer indisputably number one. This is—in part—due to the way former administrations have dealt with challenges in the past. However, we are living in a very different time than that of the men and women who served before us. We face very different threats, very different infrastructures and flows of information. If the United States is to regain its standing and its control on the global stage once more, we recognize that we need to take new roads—do things differently. Find new ways to run our economy, our government, and also our intelligence."

She raised a sculpted eyebrow. "Which of course doesn't mean we go ahead and eliminate everything we've created. The CIA and other agencies will continue to do their great work. But we ..."—she looked around the room—"... we are different. The DCS will be able to achieve things that the older, less agile agencies have failed to achieve over the past twenty years."

She stopped for a moment, perhaps to let this sink in.

"Our approach will be iterative and it will be fast. We will regularly revisit and analyze the geopolitical landscape, and we will target issues of strategic interest. Some of the powers in that landscape are China and Russia, as well as those smaller countries and organizations that are striving to become nuclear powers. Any questions so far?"

Jay raised his hand.

Fisher turned to him and nodded. The auditorium became still.

"Ma'am? This 'Abbey', as you call it ... I mean, sure, it looks like a monastery, but does that mean we have to live like monks?"

Fisher smiled. "I can see it may look like that ... Agent Stevenson, is it?"

Jay nodded.

"The reality is: this is a training facility, but it is also our home. And a home must be a safe haven: a place that allows you to step into the world fully prepared to face whatever may come. So, in the same way you would leave your apartment in New York to go to work and come home at night, you will be sent into the field periodically, and you will come home at the end of your assignment, to evaluate, feed back to the team, assess and recharge your batteries. And you *will* need time to recharge, because your job—our job—can, and will, be dangerous and very demanding." She paused. "Let's not make the mistake of thinking we are—or can ever be—part of the everyday world. We aren't. And we can't be. We made the choice, some of us less recently than others, to serve our country in ways that others are simply incapable of." She looked around the room once more. "As I said, your training will be central to this. So that when you show up in that arena out there, you'll be able to infiltrate the highest levels of business, government and society, be that at the wedding of a real estate tycoon's daughter's in Hong Kong or betting and having tea at the horse races in Ascot. And to do this, you and everyone in this room will be taught skills and given knowledge you would not expect to learn at an old-school governmental or military facility."

She paused.

"The eagle is indeed the call sign of the President of the United States. But on a golf course in Dubai?" She smiled archly. "It's one stroke less than a birdie."

There was a round of laughter, and Jay grinned.

Fisher continued: "You're laughing now, but these are exactly the nuances you'll need to be aware of if you are to operate successfully, with your cover intact."

She paused briefly. "From a personal point of view, I look forward to getting to know each and every one of you. I have long believed in, and worked toward, establishing this facility, and you can be sure I'll do whatever it takes to help you achieve the excellence and lifelong surety that you've earned."

She smiled now, and returned to the lectern.

"Meanwhile, all your personal belongings from your previous stations have already been stored away. We trust that you'll find everything you need in your apartments here at the Abbey. And if you need anything in particular, please mention it to reception and we'll take care of it."

Karis turned once more to Jay, whose face exhibited a mix of disbelief and joy.

"That's all for now." Fisher had raised her voice over the rustle of movement as people turned to each other. "There will be a briefing here tomorrow at zero-seven-hundred."

Chapter Forty-One

The Abbey, Virginia, USA

Karis heard the soft click of a lock disengaging as she touched the door handle of her new apartment.

Hastily, she removed her hand.

The door locked itself again.

"*Dios mio!*" The words came from a man who was standing in front of the door of the neighboring apartment, across the broad hallway. "This place is so cool!"

"Definitely better than a field tent and mosquito net," she said, laughing. The guy was darkly tanned and well groomed, and his otherwise symmetrical face bore subtle signs of an old injury—perhaps from combat. Karis liked him immediately.

"Okay, I'm going in!" He pushed open the door. As an afterthought, he said, "Agent Tucker Santiago Avila. Remember that name!"

She laughed again. "*Encantada*. Karis Deen."

"*Oh, tu hablas Español?*" He broke into a joyful smile, revealing a set of straight, white teeth.

"*Si, bastante.*"

"Even better!" He gave her a sailor salute, Broadway-style, and disappeared into his apartment.

Smiling, Karis touched her door handle again, and—this time—pushed open the door.

She stepped across the threshold.

Immediately, roll-blinds on all windows opened and began to ascend, allowing her to see the almost fully open plan apartment with its views across the forest and the grounds. A modern, white stone-and-glass kitchen ran the length of one wall. Leather sofas and an understated floor rug delineated the spacious living area.

Instinctively removing her shoes, she walked across warm ash floorboards toward the kitchen. Downlights and appliance interfaces came to life as she approached.

She opened the refrigerator briefly: it was stocked with fresh vegetables and a selection of gourmet-style, jarred condiments. No ketchup, she noticed.

Another, smaller, glass fronted refrigerator was stocked with beer and bottles of wine and champagne. She pulled out a bottle of white wine and looked at the label. For all she knew, it could have been a good one, or it could have been a five-dollar job. She had no way of knowing.

She placed the bottle on the bench top and made her way toward the bedroom, where a large bed was made up with white linen, and a blond wood bookshelf carried volumes, floor to ceiling: classic novels alongside philosophers and military strategists, scientific works, religious texts and poetry.

She ventured into the walk-in wardrobe.

At the far side, a long mirror reflected a young woman in camouflage uniform. Her long, dark hair was pulled back, and she carried herself with the carriage of a dancer.

Karis turned away.

A row of freshly ironed shirts and several long evening gowns hung below a shelf of jeans in various shades of designer-style denim. Bra-and-panty sets sat alongside brand-name tanks, and wool and cashmere sweaters.

She ran her hand along the row of fabrics: it was one thing to have the sum of your life packed into a trunk without your knowledge, but it was something else altogether to walk onto a stage where your presence is a foregone conclusion.

Her fingers rested on the satin of a black evening gown that resembled her own midnight blue one. Except this one was without a doubt ten times the quality, its fabric heavy and soft.

For a moment, she was accosted by the memory of suffocating heat, salty fish and ocean breezes of Panama.

And the night with the English engineer.

She withdrew her fingers quickly.

The woman in the mirror shed her uniform, and pulled one of the designer t-shirts over her head. She stepped into a pair of jeans.

Karis now wondered if she'd wake up shortly to find herself back in her CIA digs at Langley or—worse—somewhere in the godawful Midwest wasteland where she'd grown up.

"*Clean up your goddamn mess!*" Her grandmother's voice rang in her head, and Karis had the sudden urge to laugh. Her response, back in the eighth grade, had been the same every time: "*I'm organized in my head, and that counts for more.*"

In fact, her grandmother hadn't disagreed. But—then again—the old woman had been a drunk.

Karis now turned as there was a gentle chime that she could only assume was the doorbell.

As she approached the front door she saw a screen had come to life, and she had a full view of the hallway, where Jay looked to be engaged in animated conversation with her new neighbor, Avila.

She opened the door, smiling.

"Karis!" Jay said. He was sporting new jeans and a black t-shirt. "I just came to …" He peered into her apartment.

"Confirm that it's all for real?" She laughed. "Looks like it is."

He exhaled. "I've obviously died and gone to heaven."

"Tell me about it." She laughed.

Jay now stepped back a little. "Me and Avila just decided we're gonna go take a look around. Wanna join?"

Avila flashed a broad smile. "I heard they have an underground swimming pool and shooting range!"

Within minutes, the three of them were walking back through the foyer of the building and across the lawns.

It wasn't yet lunchtime.

Chapter Forty-Two

The White House, Washington, D.C., USA
January, 2011

As Secretary of Defense, Bill McKenzie was a regular attendee at meetings of the National Security Council at the White House.

Today, he was running late.

The first person he saw as he entered the Situation Room was Rebecca Eisenhower: the Secretary of State. She nodded as he entered.

He looked around the room, his gaze resting on the chair of the council, the President of the United States—Richard Nash—who sat at the head of the table.

"Apologies, Mr. President," McKenzie said, and took his allocated seat, across from Eisenhower.

Nash smiled in his usually breezy, midwestern manner and looked at the agenda on the table in front of him. "Good morning, Bill." He looked up at McKenzie with a smile. "So we're all ready to start. First topic of the day: Nicaragua."

McKenzie removed his glasses. "We've just learned the government of Nicaragua is in secret talks with a Chinese businessman, with a view to building a canal cutting across *Lago Nicaragua* in the south of the country."

"Are they crazy?" Rebecca Eisenhower laughed, shaking her head. "Nicaragua is ... well, 'complicated' would be an understatement."

There was a murmur of concurrence around the room: she'd clearly been referring to the 'Iran-Contra' affair of the 1980s, in which covert funding—not approved by US congress nor, allegedly, by the then President, Ronald

Reagan—enabled US weapons to be sent to Iran via Israel for the supposed safe exchange of hostages in Lebanon. Except once the hostages had been released, those weapons had been sold off and the money—and more weapons—rerouted to aggressively right-wing contras in Nicaragua, effectively overthrowing Nicaragua's socialist Sandinistas.

The Soviets had not been happy.

"Complicated: yes." McKenzie nodded grimly. "But not impossible. A new canal in Nicaragua would certainly explain why China didn't bother entering a bid to compete for the expansion of the canal in Panama: they probably want to have their own."

"So what's behind it? Is it just a show of muscle?"

McKenzie pursed his lips. "Could be. But if the Chinese succeed in building their own canal, it will definitely increase their foothold in the region."

Eisenhower looked at the President. "Admittedly, sir, this is the first I've heard of it, but I can't help thinking that it would be very much in China's interests to see the Panama Canal somehow weakened. You remember that report we received two years ago from Ambassador Roebuck in Panama? About the British consortium winning the bid for the expansion?" She looked around the room. "The number they came up with for their bid was unrealistically low, and we still don't know if they'll be able to finish the expansion successfully."

"Go on."

"We made inquiries at the time, and London reported that the UK government was in no way involved or subsidizing the British consortium. And it's doubtful they'd interfere in any way. So we still don't know if the British consortium are running alone, or if there are some other forces behind them that we're not aware of yet."

Nash nodded slowly. "So humor me," he said. "If the ongoing Panama Canal expansion were to fail, who would benefit?"

"At a minimum, it would buy public approval for the Nicaragua canal, wouldn't it?" The suggestion came from the Vice President.

Nash looked over to McKenzie. "Bill, what intelligence do we have coming in? You think the Chinese could have a hand in the expansion project in Panama?"

"To further their own interests?" McKenzie held up a hand. "I'm not ready to make that call. For the moment, I suggest we watch and we continue to gather intelligence about the British consortium and the progress of their work."

"Sir?" The White House Chief of Staff leaned in to the President and spoke to him in a low voice.

President Nash stood. "You'll have to excuse me for a few minutes," he said to the group.

There was a moment of general discussion, while the Vice President had a word to Nash on his way out.

McKenzie took this opportunity to sit back in his chair and stretch. It had been a long week.

From her seat on the opposite side of the table, Rebecca Eisenhower leaned toward him.

"Say, Bill, how's the new Clandestine Service shaping up?" Her voice was lowered. "What did you call it? The Abbey?" She smiled.

McKenzie nodded. "Erika Fisher has it well in hand."

"Are they operational already?"

"I'm told they'll shortly be a force to be reckoned with."

Eisenhower gave a curt nod. "Let's hope so."

Chapter Forty-Three

The Abbey, Virginia, USA
February, 2011

"If you'd told me a couple months ago I'd be able to code in C++ and Python, I'd've thought you were completely mad." Tucker Avila turned to look at Karis and Jay.

The three of them had been jogging in the forest for about half an hour, and it was cold. A low mist hung in the hollows on the forest floor.

The only one who didn't seem to notice the cold that day was Avila, who wore the same form-fitting, three-quarter leggings he'd worn since they'd very first arrived at the Abbey; he claimed they suited his physique.

"Turns out, I'm quite good at analyzing patterns," Avila continued. "On a large scale."

"So you think you could already hack into China's State Council mainframe?" Karis teased him.

"One step at a time. Let's just say I aced the function parameters and arguments test."

Jay snorted, good-humoredly. "Yeah, you know all about arguments—"

"Hey, is that Fisher?" Avila slowed his pace.

A figure in dark sweats with a hood was running toward them.

"I think so."

As they drew closer, Karis saw the short blond hair that escaped from under one of the DCS issue hoodies, and recognized it as that of her boss.

"Good morning!" Fisher pushed back her hood. She slowed to a walk.

Karis came to a standstill alongside her colleagues, her breath now clouding in front of her in the stillness of the forest.

"Agent Deen, do you have time for another round?" Fisher asked. She smiled. Straight to the point.

Karis nodded. "Sure. I don't have class till this afternoon."

Waving at Jay and Avila, she fell into step alongside Fisher. They were well matched, with a similar stride.

"How are things for you, Agent Deen?"

Karis nodded. "Great, thank you, Ma'am. I still feel the need to pinch myself daily. Or every time there's a new delivery of wearable technology." She laughed, and pointed at the hi-tech running shoes she was trialing.

Karis appreciated her boss's attempt at communication. She appreciated even more the fact that Fisher hadn't resorted to first names. Too many women in positions of power did that, like there was some tacit camaraderie, or a secret club based purely on the basis of their physiology. In reality, she had less in common with most women than she did with agents in general.

"So, Agent Deen, what can you tell me about yourself?"

"Other than what's in the files, you mean?" Karis grinned. "Not much!"

"Indulge me," Fisher said congenially. "I like to get to know my reports. And you, Agent Deen, are one of the more challenging ones."

Karis laughed. "I don't mean to be. I guess I've never been a pack animal." Her whole life, she'd seen and heard her peers—girls, and then women—chit-chat about themselves, explore their feelings about their tastes, their dreams, their friends, their families. Swapping clothes and whispers. It was like another language. "Well, I wasn't, until I joined up."

"I can relate to that," Fisher said with a smile. She paused for a moment. "You grew up with your grandmother, is that correct?"

"Yes. Until she died. I was fourteen. Then I lived by myself, and then I signed up for the marines." She wondered if she should beef up the combat and patriotism talk if she wanted to impress Fisher. But the fact was, Fisher didn't come across like most of the personnel she'd worked with, who came from long strings of folks lining up to receive the triangle-folded flag for their fathers' coffins. Fisher's patriotism seemed to come from somewhere else.

"We don't have information about your father or your mother." Fisher interrupted her thoughts. Her tone was curious.

"I don't have any, either. I only know what other people like my grandmother have told me."

"And what did she tell you?"

"That my mother was a junkie and she OD'd. That she didn't know who the father was." In the stillness of the forest, the story died almost the instant it passed her lips. Karis gave a short laugh. "My grandmother used to say all kinds of whacko stuff."

"Like?"

"Like, 'You're a mistake. You shouldn't be here.'" Karis paused. "When I was a little kid, I didn't understand that at all—that a real, live person could be a mistake, when they haven't even had time to do anything in their life yet." She gave a wry smile. "She also told me that when my mother was pregnant with me, she tried to kill me by stabbing herself in the belly with knitting needles."

Fisher inhaled sharply. "She told you that?"

"Yeah. I don't know if it's true. Maybe it was. But after she said that, I decided everything that came out of her mouth was pretty much bullshit. Excuse my language."

Fisher shook her head. "Did you ever see your mother again?"

"I only saw her twice, and both times she seemed surprised that I was still alive."

"That must have been rough."

"Honestly, it's so long ago it feels like someone else's life now. Or a movie." Karis picked up the pace a little, to keep the chill at bay.

She looked at Fisher. The older woman had a thin film of sweat across her brow. She wondered if her story had somehow triggered something. But Fisher now turned to her with a gentle smile.

"I can see why you excel at your job," she said. "It takes exceptional strength to have achieved what you've achieved. Especially to have made it as far as the Abbey."

"Thank you, Ma'am." Karis wasn't sure what to say. She hadn't spoken about her grandmother's stories to anyone before, and she wasn't sure how she felt. Vulnerable, perhaps. It wasn't a bad feeling.

After a moment, she said, "Ma'am? Have you ever had doubts about your job?"

Fisher started laughing. "Of course. My whole life!" She turned to Karis. "Are you having doubts?"

Karis shook her head. "No. I just ... I guess you've been in service a long time."

Once again, Fisher laughed. "You could say that. It's been over thirty years." She smiled at Karis. "And of course I've had many doubts over the years. But I've never been particularly good with personal relationships. I've always looked for a group, rather than a mate. And probably that's why I've been so successful. Lucky, even." She glanced at Karis. "Love never obscured my view."

She slowed the pace slightly. Karis fell into step.

"I was brought up by my father," Fisher continued. "He was a very devoted man. He gave every spare minute of his time to the church. To drop-in centers, halfway houses. To people who had never quite managed to find their way. I admired him for that. And, at a certain point, I knew I had a choice: I could do as he did—devote my life to God's work—or I could find something else."

"Although religions are organized," Karis said. "Their processes are tried and true."

"Yes, they are. But underneath the attempts at organization—the politics and the ceremonies and the work—the church is fundamentally only trying to find a worldly way to live with gray areas. With God and love and fear, and suchlike. And I'm sure I don't need to explain to you that there *is* no common language there. Which makes finding ways of achieving real, lasting impact very difficult. And very time-consuming."

Karis waited for her to continue.

"Protecting the United States is tangible," Fisher said. "And it's a much-needed reality. So, when you ask me if I've ever doubted my job, I'd say of course I have. Every time I'm handed a new mission, or there's a change in global or local power." She looked at Karis briefly. "But the net effect is always that I am more determined than ever to have our country grow in strength. And my way of doing that has always been to train the best of the best so they, in turn, can teach others." She flashed a smile. "I have a meeting shortly," she said, now slowing to a standstill. "I look forward to an opportunity to do this again some time."

"Thank you, Ma'am. I'd like that."

Fisher nodded, and took a couple of steps back. "And, by the way, I'm very impressed with your skills on the shooting range." She turned away.

Karis watched as Fisher started backtracking along the path on the forest's perimeter.

Smiling—with a sense of contentment—Karis continued, picking up the pace again. Her breathing, and the occasional snap of old bracken underfoot, were the only sounds in the forest.

Chapter Forty-Four

The Abbey, Virginia, USA

As she jogged away from the younger agent, Erika Fisher's face was grim.

Of all her reports, Karis Deen was the most resilient, and she was the most interesting. She was also the one that most reminded her of herself as a younger woman.

She stopped jogging, to catch her breath.

Christ. She couldn't really be breathless in under twenty minutes, could she?

She grit her teeth and began again, picking up the pace this time. Determined to make the full circuit without raising a sweat.

She thought once more of Karis. The conversation with the young agent had left her with an uneasy feeling. In some ways it was understandable, of course; she herself had been young once, and subject to the worries and concerns of a woman who was still young enough to find love. To have a family.

It was no use: she stopped and bent forwards, resting her palms on her knees.

She looked at her watch and stood straight once more, emitting a furious, "Shit!"

There was no way around it: she'd need to find a doctor. And preferably before she had to undergo her annual physical.

Breathing heavily, she continued walking at a pace.

Chapter Forty-Five

US Embassy, Clayton, Panama
May, 2011

US Ambassador Larry Roebuck hovered behind Summers, reading over his assistant's shoulder.

The afternoon was wretchedly hot, and the air-conditioning in his office seemed to be on the blink. Summers's office was cool, though, so he'd made himself at home there, in order to go through the official communications.

"Okay, read what you've got so far." Roebuck stepped back from the desk. He folded his arms across his chest and closed his eyes as Summers started reading.

"One: In his February 3, 2011 status report, John Siegel, Jr (Siegel chief engineer) wrote [quote]: 'Regarding our calculations, we predict the CISCO consortium are in deep financial trouble and must run out of money soon.' [See attached full report.]

"The Embassy hasn't been able to gain certified information about CISCO's bookkeeping to verify their level of liquidity."

Summers paused, and looked up at Roebuck. "Is that right?"

"Yes. Good job. Next paragraph?"

Summers read the screen. *"Two: Local intelligence have reported seeing the British Consortium engineer, Max Burns, playing golf almost weekly with the Chinese Ambassador, Steven Zhang, and meeting with him afterwards at the Chinese Embassy."*

Roebuck sighed. "Where did you get that from? That sounds like gossip."

"I took it from the internal intelligence brief that came in yesterday."

"Take it out. We can't put gossip into formal reports to the Secretary of State."

"Okay, sir."

Roebuck left Summers's office and returned to his own.

Air-conditioning or not, he'd had enough of the office altogether that day.

He flung himself in his chair.

Puffing air into his cheeks, he arced up his desktop computer and pulled up a browser.

"*Sir!*" The hollering came from the hallway, a few minutes later.

Roebuck closed his eyes.

What now?

"Mr. Ambassador! It's the Secretary of State on line one!"

Summers now appeared, breathless and flustered, in his doorway. "I'm so sorry, sir. I'm so sorry! I made a terrible mistake!"

"What are you talking about?" Roebuck looked at his phone: the light was blinking.

"Sir, I sent the entire Siegel report to Washington ... including the bit about the Chinese."

"Sweet Jesus!" Roebuck sprang to his feet. "Out!" Furious, he pointed to the door.

Summers, obsequious, backed out.

Roebuck sat, took a deep breath, and picked up the receiver.

"*Larry, what's this about the English engineer and the Chinese Ambassador?*"

"Good afternoon, Ma'am." Roebuck paused, but there was silence. "Right, well, yes, I wasn't even sure if I should send it through, it could be just some local gossip—"

"*It could very well be much more than that.*"

"What do you mean?"

"*A Chinese investor is looking to build a canal in southern Nicaragua.*"

Roebuck almost sprang from his chair once more. "What?"

"*We believe that's why the Chinese didn't compete in Panama's expansion. It may be they are trying to sabotage the Panama Canal in order to get some leverage for their Nicaragua project.*"

"In order to get leverage …?" Roebuck echoed her, fumbling for words.

"*Yes. Your intelligence about the British engineer is the first concrete connection between China and the Panama Canal.*"

"Oh. I see," he said. "Of course."

"*Thanks, Larry. And let me know if you get any more information from your end.*" The line went dead.

Slowly, Roebuck hung up the receiver.

He pulled a handkerchief from his pocket.

What the hell just happened?

He pressed the handkerchief to his brow and stood up.

A Nicaragua Canal? To be built by the Chinese? Sabotaging the Panama Canal?

His heart was racing.

What the hell is that Max Burns up to?

Chapter Forty-Six

Washington, D.C., USA
July, 2011

Erika Fisher ran down the wooden staircase in the old building and flung open the main door.

Outside, the spring air was jaw-numbingly cold.

She barely felt it.

People jostled to get past, and she stepped back, away from the push. She pressed her shoulders to the concrete wall.

Numb, she thought of the black-and-white x-rays she'd seen last week, clipped to the lightbox. The milky definition of the bones in her chest cavity. And the doctor's furrowed brow.

She'd been expecting a 'flu. Or—at the worst—pneumonia, but her appointment this morning had changed all that.

"It's not good news, I'm afraid, Mrs. Andrews. You have advanced lung cancer. The blood work has confirmed it."

The doctor's words echoed in Fisher's head.

"We'll need to do another CBC test—"

"A what?"

"A cancer cell count—we'll need to do another test in two weeks, to see how fast it's advancing."

"How ..." Fisher fumbled for words. "How much time do I have?"

The doctor shook her head slowly. "I can't say."

"That's not an answer!"

"Is there someone you'd like me to call?"

Fisher looked away and breathed, holding unwelcome emotions in check.

"A family member, perhaps?"

Fisher stared at the doctor, unable to process her words. "A family member?" she repeated. "Right. The family."

Who? Who the hell would you call?!

She felt anger rising.

The doctor glanced down at the paper in front of her. "I see you live in the city … Is the right, Mrs. Andrews?"

"That's what I wrote," Fisher responded.

"Great. My receptionist will book you an appointment at the hospital today. You'll get all the help you need there." She stretched out her arm to reach for some brochures. "Here." She slid them across the desk, then looked down to write a prescription. The skin on her finger bulged out, either side of a gold engagement ring. The stones looked to be either fake or of bad quality.

"Does it show up in a regular blood test?" Fisher asked.

The doctor looked up. "I'm sorry?"

"Cancer. Does it show up in a regular physical exam?"

"No," the doctor said. "Not in a basic blood test." She looked quizzically at Fisher for a moment. "Perhaps that's how it was missed." She signed the prescription. "This should help with the pain. My receptionist will walk you through the next steps."

Fisher took the paper and walked directly toward the door. She needed air.

"Mrs. Andrews?"

It took Fisher a moment to realize the Doctor was calling her. She paused in the doorway.

"It's not a weakness, you know. Nor is it your fault. We don't have a choice in these things."

For a moment, Fisher stared at the doctor. "You do this job five days a week?" she asked, suddenly.

The doctor nodded, with a smile. "Sometimes six."

"And you … what? You sit there—on that chair—all day, every day?" She didn't bother to hide the sneer in her tone.

The doctor didn't respond.

"You see ... I'm fit," Fisher said. "I'm *extremely* fit. I don't indulge, and I don't allow sloppy, weak behavior into my life. And yet, somehow—" Her voice broke off. "Somehow, *I'm* the sick one."

She turned on her heel and left.

Now, as she scanned the seemingly unceasing flow of unfamiliar faces on the downtown sidewalk, she set her jaw.

When the light turned, she pushed through the press of pedestrians—sheep at a crossing—and walked briskly toward the drugstore on the corner.

Chapter Forty-Seven

The White House, Washington, D.C., USA
December, 2011

The Secretary of Defense, Bill McKenzie, took his seat in the Situation Room at the White House.

This time, he was early.

President Richard Nash greeted the other members of the National Security Council and took his seat at the head of the table. Without further niceties, he turned to McKenzie.

"Nicaragua," he announced. "Get us up to speed, Bill."

McKenzie nodded and spoke to the room. "The Nicaragua's National Assembly has just approved a bill to grant a Chinese private investment company a fifty-year concession to build and manage a new canal through their country."

There was a general murmur of disquiet.

McKenzie continued: "Our team in Nicaragua has sent us leaked plans for their proposed canal." He looked around the room. "These plans say the canal is due to be thirty meters deep. That's nearly a hundred feet."

"A *hundred* feet?" The Secretary of State, Rebecca Eisenhower interjected. "That seems a bit excessive."

"Precisely. The original canal in Panama is operating at a depth of forty feet, and the new channel will be operating with a depth of sixty feet, in order to accommodate the post-Panamax vessels. And that's what's got us worried. There'd be no need for such a great depth if the Nicaragua canal was only being built for commercial use."

"So what are they up to?"

"We ran an analysis, and the lake itself—*Lago Nicaragua*—is around forty-five miles by ninety-five miles. That's about as big as the state of Connecticut." McKenzie smiled grimly. "With a depth of a hundred feet plus those parameters, we've now established that the Chinese could be planning to build a full submarine base in the middle of Central America."

There was silence.

"Completely undetectable by us or anyone else," he added.

President Nash started tapping his pen on the table: a sign that he was thinking. After a moment, he said, "Bill, how far is Managua from Washington?"

McKenzie knew what Nash was thinking. "Only two thousand nautical miles," he responded. And his meaning was implicit: intermediate range ballistic missiles have a range of up to three-and-a-half thousand nautical miles.

Nash looked at McKenzie. "A full underwater military base ... masquerading as a shipping channel ..." He shook his head. It was at times like this that Nash's slow, midwestern pace and wry humor showed itself most strongly. "Well, that sure is one for the books!"

"So what are we *doing* about it?" Rebecca Eisenhower emphasized her words with a fist on the table in front of her. "For a canal in Nicaragua to be seen as a legitimate business proposal they'll need to attract other countries toward their shipping route," she said. "But the Panama Canal is already well established. Even after we gave it back to the Panamanians in 2000, it's still really well administered. Big shipping companies would have no reason whatsoever to change their trade routes unless the canal was sabotaged or running into disaster."

There was a long pause as President Nash looked around the room.

Eventually, he looked at McKenzie. "As this is an issue of national security, Bill, you're in charge." He got to his feet. "I'll be damned if I'll stand by while China builds an arsenal of nukes on our doorstep. What did Sun Tzu say in

The Art of War …?" His tone was rhetorical, and he rested his fingertips on the table. "'*In battle, there are not more than two methods of attack: the direct and the indirect. Yet these two in combination give rise to an endless series of maneuvers.*'" He paused. "We may not have any control, nor do we fully understand what exactly is going on in Nicaragua, but we will definitely not allow the Chinese to make a fool of us in Panama. Not on my watch."

Chapter Forty-Eight

The Abbey, Virginia, USA

The floor of Jay's apartment was much warmer than the floor of the gym, on account of the in-slab heating.

Karis settled herself, prone, on the white woolen rug by the gas fireplace, with a cushion under her head. They'd spent the previous two hours taking turns spotting and belaying each other on the climbing wall overhang, and she was looking forward to a large meal.

"Here," Jay said, as he handed her a glass of red wine. "See if you can guess the year."

"Ooh, aren't you all fancy now?" Karis teased. She sat up and took the glass he offered. "You couldn't just give me a good, old-fashioned beer?"

Jay laughed. "Nope. You have to earn it."

As they'd been shown, only a few weeks previously, she swilled the wine in the glass and sniffed it.

"I'll never be able to tell you the year," she said, with a groan. "But I can tell you it's Italian, it's most likely savory …" She took a sip and washed the liquid around in her mouth as they'd been shown. "The olive comes forward. It's off dry … and …" She shrugged. "Something else?"

Jay's laugh exploded as he popped a bag of potato chips. "Not bad, Agent Deen! Now, if your climbing was as good as your wine knowledge—"

Karis threw the cushion she'd been resting on at him. He dodged it expertly.

"You know, climbing is good and all," she said, "but I'm not looking to bulk up. I totally get it that if I'm in the field, I'm supposed to have ninja agent powers. But at the same time, I wanna look—you know—*normal*. Not like a massive beefcake."

Jay threw his head back and laughed. "How do you know you don't already look like a beefcake?"

"Oh, ha ha," she said, drily. She took another sip of her wine. "So tell me … what did you miss most when you were in Sudan?"

"Sex."

"No, really."

"Really. I was there for three years."

"Three years?" Karis exhaled. "You never told me that. You only said you were in Darfur with the UN Peacekeepers." She took a sip of wine. "There are a lot of UN there, right?" She didn't know details, but she knew enough: Darfur was a hotbed of fighting, despite a recent peace treaty.

Karis took another sip of her wine and assessed Jay for a moment. "Sudan wouldn't be on my list of preferred destinations," she said.

"Me neither. To wade into a shitstorm that intense you either gotta believe you were born to change the world, or you gotta have a death wish. And if you think you were born to change the world, you're probably either colossally unhinged or a sociopath."

"Hmm. Death wish or psycho …" Karis smiled grimly. "Not really a win–win situation, is it?"

"No, but war never is." He looked at her. "You're a marine, right?"

Karis nodded.

"Why didn't you start with Defense Intelligence instead of going back to civilian: to the CIA?"

She cast her mind back for a moment. "A bunch of us were on leave in Colombia and I got hooked into the network out there," she said. "It's just the way the wind blew. I wanted a change, so I made a few enquiries, and I liked the CIA set-up back home. So that's where I started."

Jay grinned. "'Just the way the wind blew.' I like that about you, Deen. You're a free spirit." He gave her a sideways look. "I don't suppose you'd wanna …?"

"Have sex?" Karis laughed again. "Sure, why not? It's been a while—" She stopped herself. "Actually … It's nothing personal, Jay. I probably would have, back at Langley, if you'd asked." She gave a half smile. "But here at the Abbey?" She looked around his beautiful apartment. "I feel like I'd be jinxing myself or something. You know what I mean? It's all so … perfect."

Jay's face showed good-natured frustration. "Fair enough," he said. "I personally don't feel that way whatsoever."

"Of course you don't," she said, with a laugh.

A low chime interrupted them, and a screen above the fireplace came to life with a message from the Abbey's Hub.

> *From: Agent Fisher*
> *To: Jay Stevenson; Karis Deen; Tucker Avila*
> *Briefing*
> *Conference Room A*
> *20.30 Hours*

Jay looked at Karis. Without hesitation, he said, "That's in five minutes. You need to get anything from your apartment?"

Karis put her glass on the kitchen counter. "Thanks for the wine, Jay. I'll see you in a bit."

Chapter Forty-Nine

The Abbey, Virginia, USA

"Thanks for your promptness."

Fisher strode across to the lectern. She took a sip of water from her bottle and turned to the group.

Karis was with Avila and Jay in the first row of seating.

"I'm briefing you this evening on Operation Sea Bass."

Karis felt her pulse go up a notch.

Fisher touched the screen of her tablet and the beamer came alive, bearing a map of Central America, on which a long, red line ran, zig-zagging through the wetlands in the southern part of Nicaragua.

Fisher turned back to the group.

"This is the proposed site for the new Nicaragua Canal," she said. "To be built by a Chinese investor in collaboration with the Nicaraguan government." She paused. "We—like the rest of the world—can reasonably assume that behind every big Chinese investor is the government of the People's Republic of China. I won't go into all the details now, but we have reason to believe that this proposed canal is a front for China's real plan: a submarine base in Lake Nicaragua."

Jay and Avila both shifted in their seats, and Karis felt a small thrill run through her body: were they about to be sent to Nicaragua?

Fisher placed her hands on the lectern. "The Pentagon is pursuing all leads in Nicaragua. It's our job to find out what's going on in Panama."

Panama?

Karis stiffened, as her heart rate quickened.

"The two of you …"—Fisher pointed at Karis and then Avila—"… are to be deployed a little earlier than we'd anticipated. Agent Stevenson, you will be their contact here at the Abbey."

She looked at the three of them in turn.

"We're sending in two separate units. I've already briefed the first unit. They'll be collecting intelligence from other leads we have on the ground, specifically on the Panamanian side, among the canal workers. You won't have any direct contact with them. As this is a classified, high-level operation, the information flow will be strictly on a need-to-know basis."

Fisher now stepped away from the lectern to address the three of them directly.

"From the Chinese point of view, right now would be an ideal moment for the expansion of the Panama Canal to run into insurmountable difficulties," she said. "And if that came to pass, the implications for United States interests in the region—and the world—could be irreversibly catastrophic."

She cleared her throat and took another sip of water.

She turned to Karis. "Excavation on the expansion site has just uncovered what looks to be an ancient feeding ground—megalodon teeth and shell fossils and the like. You'll need to read up on it, because it's a very big deal with regard to geodating. It also gives you a very convenient shoe-in to return to your post at the Smithsonian Tropical Institute in Panama."

She pulled up another image, this time of an Asian man. "This is Steven Zhang, China's Ambassador in Panama."

"I think I've met him!" Karis said.

Fisher turned to her quickly. "You did?"

"Yes. At the signing party for the expansion of the Panama Canal, at the Presidential Palace."

"Yes. That was probably him. Zhang's family has a long history of interest in the canal. His predecessors worked on the construction at the turn of last century, returning to China after the canal was built. Zhang himself grew up in China, studied in England, and his father is an important figure in the political landscape." Fisher paused. "Zhang was given the Ambassador post in Panama only three years ago, and we had believed the reason was the canal expansion project. But, as it turned out, the Chinese didn't even enter a bid to compete, so we now believe his assignment may have been for another reason. And this is what we need to find out."

As the next image came up, Karis baulked.

"Max Burns." Fisher turned to the group. "Burns is the geomatic engineer and brains behind the designs that won the bid for the expansion of the Panama Canal, against our American team." She turned to Karis. "Did you see him at the signing ceremony, as well?"

"Yes, I did." Karis wondered if she ought to say something about their night together.

"Good," Fisher continued. "You'll need to find a way to get close to him. He meets with the Chinese Ambassador almost every week, on Wednesdays. We need to know why."

Karis nodded. She decided now was not the moment to give full detail about her encounter with Burns.

Fisher glanced back at the screen. "His construction company is owned by a guy called Paco Roco and his son, Godfredo Roco. At this stage, we don't know much about them, or how much they're aware of Burns's contact with the Chinese." She paused. "If you get even a whiff that he might be helping the Chinese or anybody else to sabotage his own project, I want to know about it."

"Understood." Karis nodded curtly.

Fisher looked at the three of them in turn. "This is a container mission: you won't have any support from the local embassy, as they won't be told of your presence in the area. Reason being: we don't want any noise around this until we have proof of China's activities in Panama. We don't want to run any political risk."

"And if we need back-up?" Avila asked.

"The second team will be there to assist you in case you run into trouble. Besides, this operation will be under my direct supervision here at the Abbey."

The door opened, and a young man with a buzz cut and a three-day growth walked in, carrying a cardboard box.

"This is Agent Marc Hussain," Fisher said. "He's going to explain your new communication devices for this mission." She stepped to one side as the man placed the box on the table.

"Hi, I'm Marc," he said, with a smile. He looked at the group. "Yes, you could call me M. But please don't."

He grinned at Fisher, who handed black cellphones to Avila and Jay. Marc passed one to Karis.

"So what do we have here?" Marc started. "These are our Abbey communication devices." He pulled his own phone from his pocket. "They are of course hooked into the agency's database, ClassNET, so we can communicate with the broader organization and community. But what's really cool is this screen …"—he brandished his phone in the air. "It's what most people will see if they pick up or touch your device. It looks like a regular phone." He paused. "Now look at your own device."

Karis looked down at the screen in her hand and, immediately, the app icons all slid to one side. An interface with the word *DROP* opened up.

"Wow, that's cool!" Avila said. "Fingerprint recognition?"

Marc smiled. "No. Face recognition. And it even works if you have a hangover, or if you're unshaven."

Fisher smiled archly and looked at Karis. "That's good to know."

"What does DROP stand for?" Avila asked.

Marc turned to him, impassive. "Nothing. I always drop my phone, so I called it that."

Avila's laugh exploded, and even Fisher started laughing.

"The device has several sensors built in and transmits data

like your vital signs, as well as information about your location and environment, which gives us, back at the Abbey, the ability to analyze situations you're in." He smiled, clearly pleased with himself. "So if, for example, you're unable to communicate because you're unconscious, your body will tell us. And we'll be able to send back-up."

"Even if we're not holding the device?" Karis asked.

"We only need a range of ten feet."

After a short pause, he said, "DROP also gives you access to an international concierge service at any time, to help you book your flights, restaurants or even tee times at golf clubs and so on." He looked at Fisher.

"Thank you, Marc."

Marc nodded, and left the room.

Fisher waited until the door had closed behind him.

She turned to the group.

"Everything else you need to know you will find in the files we have already sent to your mobile devices. Good luck. Your transport leaves at zero-five-thirty tomorrow."

As Fisher left the room, Karis stood and looked at her colleagues.

Avila grinned and got to his feet. "*Ciudad de Panamá! Aquí vamos!*"

Panama City, here we come.

Jay gave Avila a hug. "Good luck, bro." He put his hand on Karis's shoulder. "Go get 'em, Deen."

"So much for the designer ballgowns and golf clubs," Avila said, laughing, as the three of them left the room.

Karis shook her head. "I can't believe I'm going back to Panama." She laughed. "Oh well. I'd better go find my nerdy scientist outfit again!"

Part Five

Chapter Fifty

The Panama Canal, Panama

The day promised to be fine; it was already hot and humid.

Karis Deen stepped a path in her sandals across bare basalt. She carried her brushes and trowels in a small bag, and—in one hand—Dalisha's large, round shaker screen for sifting dirt.

As she reached the topmost point of the incline, she turned back and waved Dalisha on. "Hurry up!"

"Hold your horses!" Dalisha carried a rucksack crammed with full water bottles. "I may be slow, but you don't want to cross me. I carry the life source!" She stopped, out of breath, at Karis's side. "You'll thank me later, when you're calling for mercy from the sun god."

Laughing, the two of them walked over the rise.

The canal expansion site lay below them. The steel towers of the Centennial Bridge could be seen in the distance, its white suspension cables just visible through the morning haze.

Karis shielded her eyes.

She had prepared herself to view the dig site, and she knew it was going to be big; it was the Panama Canal, after all. Yet, now—seeing the broad, gaping canyon stretching alongside the existing canal, north to south, with no end in sight—there was nothing to do but stop and stare, simply in order to process the pure size of it.

"They've dug so much out already!" she murmured.

"Well, what'd you expect?" Dalisha grinned. "Technology is advancing. We're not living in the industrial age anymore."

The two of them started toward the dig site and, for a moment, Karis thought of the thousands who'd lost lives—perhaps some of them on the very path they walked now—when the original canal was being built, more than a century ago. Years and years of hard labor spent attempting to impose order on the steamy, willful environment.

The Las Cumbres area, where they were working that day, was on the western bank of the waterway, and it had once mostly been dense tropical forest. Now, it was dusty and bare; quarries and rock faces for miles upon miles.

The archaeological dig zone itself looked much like any others Karis had seen over the years: demarcated with a white string grid like an empty chessboard hovering just above the ground. The thing that differentiated this site from any other, though, was its scale: it was massive. Bigger than any Karis had seen. It marked out a huge area on the incline of what looked like mainly basalt.

They approached the small, enclosed wooden caravan that housed their equipment. It sat alongside a worn, white tent: their field headquarters.

"So how's your brother doing?" Dalisha's words interrupted Karis's thoughts. "Have you sorted everything out with your family?"

Dalisha dropped the rucksack to the ground. It landed with a thud.

"He's fine," Karis nodded. "He just needed hand-holding to deal with the accounts."

Dalisha unlocked the door of the caravan. She handed Karis a couple of the large plastic soda bottles and swung the rucksack inside, out of the sun. Karis could see the caravan's rudimentary shelving was already loaded up with plaster-and-burlap jacketed specimens, all labelled with black marker in Dalisha's neat handwriting.

"And your supervisor at the university?" Dalisha asked. "Was she okay with you coming back? How'd you swing that?"

"She wasn't thrilled about it, but I still have some of the funding left from the first round, so I cut a deal. Plus, this kind of discovery doesn't happen every day."

"You got that right!" Dalisha laughed. "The Director had a freaking *conniption* when they first discovered the teeth in the quarry. You should'a seen him. He was all over the expansion construction team like a rash."

"Really?" Karis laughed.

"Yeah. But he got them to stop digging!"

"How'd he do that?"

"He negotiated with the consortium, and they gave him until New Year. So I guess we'll be working over Christmas!" She chuckled. "Like we've got anything better to do …" She paused. "Come on. Let's get to it, before it turns into hell's own oven out here."

As the two of them made their way across the already baking dig site, Karis was well aware there was no way around it: she had to put in her hours on the job in order to play the part. Still, she knew the more she immersed herself in her cover identity—the more she embraced it—the easier it would become. She could almost say she was looking forward to the work, crouched over sections of rock, poring over the minutiae with paintbrush or hammer and chisel. There was something compelling about being on a dig. Like panning for gold.

"Want one?" Dalisha had pulled a pack of jelly snakes from her pocket. "Me and a few of the other guys are going to this new fish restaurant in the Old Town tonight," she said. A red snake hung from the corner of her mouth, and she pulled it till it snapped. She started chewing. "The guy who runs it thinks he's the Iron Chef. You wanna join us?"

"Thanks," Karis said, taking a snake. "Another time. I'm actually … I was planning on dropping in on a friend tonight."

"A guy?" Dalisha cast a curious look at her. "You never told me you met someone! Is this the way you treat your loyal roommate?"

"It was nothing serious," she said, with a grin. "I just met him briefly the night before we left."

"You met him at the signing party?! Awesome! I had no idea! Way to leave the country with a bang! Will I meet him?"

Karis laughed. "Probably not. I'm not even sure if he'll remember me. It's been almost two years."

"Course he'll remember you!" Dalisha scoffed. "Anyway, if he doesn't, I'm sure you can find a way to remind him."

Karis laughed. "I'm sure I'll find a way."

Chapter Fifty-One

Panama City, Panama

Karis stood in the long, swing drive out front of the Smithsonian Institute for Tropical Research. Alongside her, a plastic fir tree, complete with fake snow and blinking Christmas lights, sat dwarfed by a huge, vine-swathed corotú tree.

A rundown, yellow cab pulled up.

She held the skirt of her simple, floral sundress bunched up in her hand and slid into the back seat. She could feel the sunburn on her arms and her nose from the long day at the dig site.

"*Buenas tardes*," she said. "And, may I say, you're looking pretty suave today, Señor Driver."

Agent Tucker Avila turned to her with a look of pure joy.

"Hot isn't even in the *ballpark!*" he said. "I'm on fire! You like my shirt? I'm going for a kind of '70s *Hawaii Five-O* meets *CSI Miami*."

Karis laughed. "Well, normally I'd say it's a good way to get noticed … except I gotta tell you, my fairy-footed friend, you're not the only one around here who likes pineapples and Elvis sunglasses. And I'm sorry to say, less than three of the guys I've encountered are likely to be gay."

Avila's expression was one of mock horror. "Less than three? How many have you encountered?"

"Four." She broke into peals of laughter.

"Very funny." His tone was haughty. "I should warn you, Agent Deen: you're treading on dangerous ground, making gross generalizations. And assumptions about my preferences."

She grinned and rifled through her purse. "Trust me. I can always tell which way someone swings. Sometimes before they even know it themselves." She looked up and blew him an air kiss. "So I have the same Smithsonian cellphone I had last time. Same number and all." She handed him a card with the number on it.

"You want me to lodge the details with the Abbey?"

She nodded. "Thanks."

Avila swung the taxi out of the drive and onto the main thoroughfare, and proceeded to follow the winding road downhill.

"I do like this place," Avila said emphatically. "Not at all what I expected, but I *like* it."

"I told you." Karis beamed. "So you know where we're going?"

He nodded, and Karis didn't doubt him: Avila had a photographic memory.

Within a few minutes, they'd reached the top of the hill, and the staff entrance on the east side of the Panama Canal Administration building.

Karis hopped out.

Without looking back, she said, "I'll check in later."

Avila drove off.

Pausing to take in her surroundings, Karis made her way toward the main entrance.

For the first time in her career, she was really nervous. And it had nothing to do with the armed guards that were stationed in the foyer of the building. All the usual preparations had been done before she left DC in case she encountered secondary screening: her cover story was watertight, and she had the Smithsonian paper trail to back her up. Fisher had even equipped her with a newly acquired, shabby, secondhand suitcase to ensure there would be no trace of explosives.

Usually, when she headed into the field, she had never met her target. In this case, though, there was Max Burns.

Not for the first time, Karis admonished herself that she'd let her guard down just that one time. She realized, now, it had been a mistake: exactly the kind of situation they'd been warned about in training.

"A non-natural disaster is never an isolated event. It is the result of a long story: a series of bad decisions leading up to that point. Each and every decision matters. Each and every moment."

Inside the building, a guard took her passport.

"I'd like to see Dr. Burns," she said. "I don't have an appointment, but maybe you could tell him I'm here?"

The guard nodded. He was enormous, but—like many of the local guys she'd encountered—not at all intimidating. "Dr. Burns doesn't work in this building."

"I believe he's here for meetings."

The guard nodded. "Of course. I'll let him know. You can wait in the foyer." He pointed her through.

Karis wasn't worried that Max might not be there: technically, his office was situated opposite the Administration Building, but the intelligence Fisher had garnered already told her that he was reliably in the grand old hallways for meetings every afternoon.

She passed under a maritime clock and between two substantial white-and-black marble pillars, into the heart of the quiet space under the dome. At its highest point, a tiny ring of oculars allowed light to diffuse, giving more visibility of the high gallery and a detailed panorama painting that depicted the epic story of the canal's origins.

She continued to the far side of the dome, where a French door looked out onto a huge flagpole and patio balcony. At the foot of the marble steps, a stone obelisk stood at the center of a large cul-de-sac. Palm trees lined the boulevard that stretched away from the building.

Idly, Karis walked the periphery of the rotunda, where marble busts commemorated great men.

President Franklin D. Roosevelt's words were there, cast in bronze.

"It is not the critic who counts; not the man who points out how the strong man stumbles ... The credit belongs to the man who is actually in the arena, whose face is marred by dust and sweat and blood; who strives valiantly; who errs, who comes short again and again, because there is no effort without error and shortcoming ... who at the worst, if he fails, at least fails while daring greatly ..."

"Are you looking for the great women? Because you won't find them. They were in a different arena."

Karis turned. Her heart was racing.

"No," she said, smiling, attempting to keep her voice even. "I was thinking it's very ... I don't know ... *dramatic* to strive, isn't it? People seem to like to say they're striving valiantly."

Max stopped walking, and she couldn't read his expression. She wondered if she'd said the wrong thing, right out of the gate. She pressed her lips together, fighting the flush that was rising in her cheeks.

Then Max started laughing. "I once met a great woman who said something very similar," he said.

"You did?" She felt the doubt lift: this was the Max Burns she knew.

"Sure," he said, with a grin. "She said, 'Most of us are doing the best we can.'"

"Wow, she sounds very wise. Would you mind introducing me to her sometime?"

He nodded. "Of course! Except ..." his eyes glinted with mischief. "She has this strange habit of disappearing. Just when you think you've discovered something amazing ..."

Karis felt the laughter rise up inside her, and she stepped toward him, the memory of his arms wrapped around her more vivid, more visceral, than she'd anticipated.

"It's good to see you, Max." She was about to embrace him before she came to her senses.

Turning her head, she allowed him to kiss one cheek, and then she stepped back.

Immediately, she saw the confusion in his eyes, and she regretted not trusting their bond, however tenuous. But she knew the risks: it was one thing to be making love, thinking you were about to leave the country for good, and another thing entirely to be standing in the heart of the Panama Canal Administration Building in the middle of the working week, face to face with the target of your new assignment.

She wondered if he had even the slightest idea of what he'd gotten himself into.

"Don't worry, I'm not here to hold you hostage to the past, Max Burns," she said, smiling. "I only wanted to pick your brain."

"I've heard that before," he said, with a wry expression. He tipped his head to one side, rubbing his shoulder with his free hand. "It's been a long day." He sighed. But then he broke into a broad smile. "Well, I have to say, it's a nice surprise to see you back here, Karis Deen. Where are you staying? Would you like to join me for a drink?"

Karis laughed. "I thought you'd never ask."

Chapter Fifty-Two

Panama City, Panama

Max glanced across to the passenger seat, to where Karis Deen was sitting quietly.

He knew he shouldn't have expectations: he barely knew her, and it had been a very long time since their one, solitary night together.

And here she was, sitting in his Land Rover.

He hoped she didn't regret anything.

"Max, I feel like I should apologize to you."

He shook his head. "No, no, you don't need to—"

She interrupted him with a short laugh. "Just wait and listen, Dr. Burns!"

"I'm sorry … what do you mean?" He steered the car across the intersection.

She smiled. "Max, I'm not apologizing about our night together, or about the fact that I haven't been in touch." She seemed amused by his confusion. "I'm apologizing because I want to talk about work, and I realize it's after hours for you."

"Ah. I see." Max kept his eyes firmly on the road as the reality sank in: she was more interested in Max-the-engineer than in Max-the-person.

But that had been his experience generally over the past year or so: everyone seemed to want to talk to him because he was the one the media had blithely labelled 'the expansion's brainchild'—the expert engineer that everyone called on for comment. He'd almost become the CISCO spokesperson.

Wearily, he switched back into work mode.

"So let me guess: you're back because of the prehistoric feeding grounds. You're not the boss, but you figure you're on a first-name basis with the chief engineer, so you want to find out how much we can massage the schedule to allow you to excavate at the site as long as possible. Am I close?" He glanced at her.

Karis nodded. "Good guess. You're not just a pretty face."

Suddenly, he felt irritated. It had been a long few weeks where he'd been at loggerheads with Paco over the timeline for the concrete pouring and, frankly, he didn't think he had it in him to try and decode whether the woman was flirting or not. Mixed messages were tedious at the best of times.

"I've negotiated four weeks already," he said drily, as he came to a stop for a red light. "I can't give you longer. There are too many stakeholders that can't be put off at this stage."

Karis nodded. "I thought you might say that. Oh, well, it was worth a try."

He pulled up in a vacant parking spot alongside a café that was nestled between two blocks of bay side terrace houses. The café—along with many other establishments—had sprung up over the past year. That happened a lot in the *Casco Viejo*, what with the money being poured into the expansion, and the thousands of employees who were now working on site at the canal.

There was a free table overlooking the waterfront, and Max directed Karis towards it.

As they sat, she started laughing.

He looked at her quizzically.

She pointed to the plastic holly and mistletoe wreath that garnished their table.

"It's so crazy," she said. "It was snowing when I left the US."

"You know there's an ice rink down on the causeway?"

"Really?"

"Yes, inside a huge tent. Can you imagine? Ice-skating in the tropics—"

"Max!"

Max turned at the sound of his name.

"I thought you must've died of overwork!"

"Godfredo! What the hell happened to you?!" Max jumped to his feet: Godfredo's face had stitches down one side, and he wore a large sticking plaster above one eye.

The two embraced warmly.

"God, you smell like a brewery!" Max said, laughing. "Had a long lunch, did we?"

"Small accident with the jet-ski. I guess I jumped a bit too far this time."

"Far out, Fredo, you're going to get yourself killed one day." Max shook his head, and placed his hand on Godfredo's arm. "Can I introduce you to Karis? Karis, this is Godfredo."

Godfredo's face froze in an affectation of a star-struck feint as his eyes alighted on Karis.

"*The* Karis?" He took her hand and kissed it.

"Don't mind him," Max said mildly. "It's all show."

"You told him about me?" Karis turned to Max and smiled; that shy smile that made his knees go weak.

"Don't move a *muscle*, Karis!" Godfredo said. "Sit here." He pulled out a chair. "Max will get us some drinks."

"You can get your own drinks, you lazy sod," Max said, laughing. Nevertheless, he waved over a waiter, and ordered beers for all of them.

"How is it I haven't met you before?" Godfredo now leaned his elbows on the table and looked at Karis intently. "Usually pretty girls like you don't take long to find me … in this tropical paradise …"

Max rolled his eyes to the heavens. "Give it a rest, Fredo, you great big egomaniac." He turned to Karis. "I apologize in advance for any uncouth behavior or inappropriate language. I'm afraid I have no control."

"But Max!" Godfredo opened his arms wide. "*Hermano!* You know people are more likely to trust you if you swear! It's a scientific fact!"

Karis immediately started laughing, and Max allowed himself to relax: she could hold her own, no question.

"Well, since you ask," Karis said, "I haven't had time to 'find' you yet, as I've been back in the US. I'm with the Smithsonian Institute. I'm doing a postdoctorate." She paused. "And you're one of Max's work colleagues?"

Godfredo nodded. "CISCO is my dad's company. We're part of the British consortium; we've been contracted to build the new locks for the canal."

Karis's eyebrows shot up. "So you're Godfredo Roco!" She seemed impressed. "You look different than in the local gossip magazines!" She grinned. "So ... technically ..."— she slid a glance at Max—"... he's your boss?"

Max laughed. "Well, I'm sure he'd like to think so, though it's not quite as simple as that."

"It never is." She flashed him a smile. "So when is the expansion going to be finished?"

Godfredo leaned in. "You ask a lot of questions for a Smithsonian girl."

"I'm a scientist," she said. "What'd you expect?"

"Well, you should come out and see the construction site with us one time. It's really something," Godfredo said.

She smiled. "I know. I was out there today."

"She's one of the paleontologist crew," Max said. "She likes bones and teeth."

"She does?" Godfredo looked at her with more than a little innuendo.

"Yeah. But only the ones that are millions of years old," Max countered.

Karis nodded. "True. We're trying to beat the clock before the concrete kings move in."

"Aha! So you're the one to blame for our delays!"

"Yep," she said, cheerfully. "We've just discovered a huge

deposit of shells and teeth, and we think it might be a prehistoric feeding ground. Much older than we thought. Like, about *twelve million* years older than we thought. Very exciting!"

Max couldn't help but smile at her enthusiasm.

He turned to Godfredo. "So tell us how your face remodeling happened."

Godfredo launched into the tale, and Max watched as his friend relived the boating collision with animated hand gestures.

Not for the first time, he mused that Godfredo was a bit of a mystery. After Paco's interference in the figures for the bid, Godfredo had simply dropped off the radar for several weeks, leaving Max and Paco to put together the teams that would move forward with the project.

Not that it was a bad thing, in the end, as Max had finally had the opportunity to work with, and observe, his friend's father closely; to see the way he operated. And, unexpectedly, his mind had been put at ease. He'd been impressed with the speed at which Paco got things done. His ability to rally suppliers and contractors for steel and materials as well as dredging and excavation equipment was hardly trivial, but it was his hard-nosed bargaining and dogged pursuit—and, ultimately, engagement—of the big players that had made the most impression. Max often wished he'd been a fly on the wall at some of the meetings from which Paco had emerged triumphant.

It made him think of all those years he and Godfredo had been at school together, when he'd had no real picture of Paco's capacity for—and momentum with—his work. And how easy it had been, as a teenager, to jump to conclusions about Godfredo's home life.

Whatever the dynamic between the two Rocos was, Max knew it was not something he could ever understand. Because Paco was, after all, Godfredo's father. And perhaps it was better to have an unpredictably explosive father than none at all.

In any case—after they'd won the contract, when Godfredo finally showed up after being off the radar for three weeks—he'd acted as though nothing had happened: he jumped back into his role as Paco's right-hand man without any explanation. Every attempt Max made to discuss the goings on had been met with stonewalling or dodging, and Max had all but given up on finding out where he'd been. He'd even considered contacting Sofia, but eventually opted to assume Godfredo's behavior wasn't out of the ordinary. The fact was, he hadn't seen his old friend or lived in close proximity to him for going on twenty years, and he had no real way of knowing what was usual and what was extraordinary in Godfredo's world these days. The two of them were so different—and always had been—that it wasn't worth taking to heart.

Max now looked across the table at Karis, who was doing an admirable job of listening to Godfredo's story about yet another nautical incident from several years ago, this one involving a catamaran and a speed boat.

"You hungry?" Max spoke to her in the lull between words, as Godfredo had mercifully stopped talking to take a swig of his beer.

She shook her head. "I should go, and at least unpack." She slid her half empty glass to one side, retrieved her bag and pushed back her chair. "Take it easy, Godfredo." She smiled warmly.

Max followed her out onto the street, resisting the urge to pull her toward him.

"So would you like a lift—?"

"Are you around tomorrow night—?"

They'd spoken at the same time, their words a jumble, and she giggled.

For a moment, he wasn't sure what to say: he certainly hadn't been expecting her to ask to see him again.

"Tomorrow would be lovely," he said, tentatively. He pulled a card from his wallet and handed it to her. "These are my contact numbers."

She held it in her hand. "Okay, great. Thanks."

"Wait, tomorrow is Wednesday, right?" he asked. "I can't meet tomorrow. I have a standing arrangement with a friend."

"Oh. Okay." She seemed disappointed.

"But maybe you can join us? It's my friend, Steven. You'll like him. He's the Chinese Ambassador. Maybe you met him last time, at the signing ceremony?"

"Maybe." She frowned. "I don't remember. But is it a formal thing? I don't know if I'd have the right clothes."

Max smiled. "No, it's not formal. He's always off duty when he's with me. We usually just play a game of cards or go out to eat. You'll like him."

She nodded slowly. "Okay. As long as I'm not interrupting."

"Not at all. Steven will be excited to see you again." He wanted to reach out and brush a stray hair from her cheek, but he knew he had absolutely no idea what was going through her head.

"'Bye," she said.

"Yes. Right." Puzzled, he watched her walk away. "See you tomorrow."

The beautiful Karis Deen.

Pushing all thoughts of her from his mind, he started back toward the café; he had more than one man's share of work on his plate already, without having Karis Deen mess with his head.

Chapter Fifty-Three

Hippodrome, Panama City, Panama

Paco Roco waited in the shade offered by one of the large horse trailers. It was late afternoon, and the stable hands weren't in evidence, most likely taking siestas, having been up at five or earlier to start the day's training.

Paco peered into the trailer. Like most of the vehicles in the compound, it was empty, except for the swathes and bales of hay that were piled against one end. It looked big enough to hold a Los Bravos revival band, plus twenty or thirty screaming fans.

"Francisco. Thanks for meeting me."

Paco turned to see José Gonzáles approaching him along the broad avenue-like stretch of dirt road that formed the backbone of the stable complex at the Hippodrome.

Paco held out his arms. "Good to see you."

Gonzáles embraced him. "I'm sorry. I've had a lot on my mind. Unfortunately, things aren't going quite as planned. Walk with me."

Gonzáles put a hand on Paco's back, and the two men walked.

"Do you know anything about your kid having any contact with the Chinese Ambassador?"

Paco shook his head. "Godfredo, you mean?"

"Anyone. Godfredo. The English engineer …"

"Yeah, Burns sometimes plays golf with a Chinese guy called Steven."

"That's the one. Steven Zhang. Do they meet often?"

Paco frowned. "What's bothering you?"

"My contact … He thinks there's something more going on."

Paco turned to look at his friend. "What do you mean?"

"He says there are powerful people—and I think he means the Chinese—who might try to sabotage the whole project, so we need to get moving."

Paco roared with laughter. "Sabotage the project? Jesus. And I thought I had that dubious honor!"

"You're being hired to do the job, you moron, not sabotage it." Gonzáles clearly wasn't in the mood.

"Christ. Someone got out of bed on the wrong side today." Paco sighed and patted his friend's arm. "It will get done. As we discussed. No need to lose the rest of your hair."

Gonzáles looked at him, but his stare was empty: he was clearly thinking about something else. He shook his head. "The sooner this is over, the better, I tell you. I can get Rosa to the Caymans …"

Paco nodded, his hand still on Gonzáles's arm. "Yes, yes, my friend. And it won't be long. We just released the last payments to you."

"And you?"

"Taken care of."

"Okay," Gonzáles nodded, exhaling. "And you're sure there will be no paper trail?"

"I'm sure. I'll be putting out a press release within the month, and then your guys can go ahead with the audit." Paco started laughing. "They sure as hell won't find much. In every sense."

Gonzáles cracked a smile. "Good. Very good." He ran a hand through his thinning hair. "Jesus. I'm getting too old for this kind of pressure."

Paco forced a laugh, though privately he thought Gonzáles might be losing his edge.

"Well, make sure you don't leak anything to the press," he said. "Not yet."

"No, no, of course not," Gonzáles said. He clasped Paco's

arm, then broke away, walking toward the timber construction at the end of one of the small side roads.

Paco watched his friend for a moment, then began walking to keep pace.

Something was going on, but he wasn't sure what.

He followed Gonzáles to the stable hands' hut. Inside stood a simple arrangement of equipment: a hose, a couple of stools, an icon of Jesus on the wall.

Nobody was around, so Paco felt it was safe to speak. Still, he kept his voice low.

"José, you need to tell me if you're involved in something bigger than our plan. Something you can't handle."

Gonzáles paced. He still seemed nervous. But he shook his head. "It's okay. As long as you haven't seen any of those Chinese sniffing around."

"Come on, José. They're all working in the Mini-Marts, selling vegetables."

"Hey!" Gonzáles stopped pacing and pointed at Paco. "Quit being a smartass. You know what I mean. You need to be careful, in case there are some bigger fish involved here. We need to watch our backs."

Immediately, Paco took Gonzáles by the lapel of his jacket. "No you listen to me, José. You need to tell me who this 'contact' of yours is, or you'll have no insurance. I won't be able to help you if things go wrong."

He released Gonzáles, and straightened his friend's jacket for him.

Gonzáles shook him away. "I can't tell you. You know that. It's for your own safety, Francisco. There are powers involved here that neither you nor I can handle." He paused. "You do your bit, and I'll do mine." He wiped dust from his sleeve. "Let me know when you're ready to move ahead, and I'll meet you one more time to go over the final details. But after that, I don't want any more contact. You hear me?"

Paco held up his hands in a gesture of acquiescence. "Of course, old friend."

Gonzáles shifted uncomfortably in his jacket. "How are the yearlings?"

"Fine. The trainer is a prick, but he's doing good work."

"Okay." Gonzáles nodded slowly. "Okay."

He nodded once more and walked away.

Chapter Fifty-Four

The Abbey, Virginia, USA

Agent Jay Stevenson was standing at a large, waist-height console. Commercial-display-sized screens were mounted in front of him, and there were ten other consoles with operators at standing desks stretching along the length of the theatre-like room.

He turned to Fisher. "Agent Avila is online."

"Put him up."

Tucker Avila's face appeared in a video conference window in one quadrant of the large, mounted screen. Fisher—head to waist—appeared in the other.

"Agent Avila."

There was a slight delay, but then Avila spoke. "Ma'am, Agent Deen has made contact with Burns and Zhang."

"Already?" She paused and looked at Jay. "Is Agent Deen's DROP device transmitting?"

Jay looked at his screen. "Yes. I'm getting her biometrics." He glanced up at Fisher. "But she didn't activate the transmission function."

"Okay." Fisher turned to Avila. "Tucker, would you please make sure both of you always activate the transmission function when you engage with a target?"

"Of course, Ma'am. I will make sure of that."

"So please go on."

"Agent Deen has reported nothing suspicious so far. She thinks it's a dead lead."

Fisher frowned. She could believe Deen's instincts were good, but were they *that* good?

"How can she know this after one meeting?" she asked.

"I watched the restaurant and they were there for three hours and seven minutes. So it wasn't a brief meeting."

"And afterwards?"

"She was taken in Zhang's car back to the Chinese Embassy."

Fisher baulked. "Sorry, did you just say the Chinese Embassy? In the Ambassador's car?"

"Yes. But they were only there for a short time. Then they left."

Fisher bit back a smile: the girl was good. "And you followed, of course."

"Yeah, that was a bit of a problem. I had to fall back because Agent Deen got out of the car with Burns at his apartment. They talked in the street, and then they went off for a walk."

"In the middle of the night? Why didn't you park and pursue on foot?"

Avila pulled a frustrated face. "Ma'am, the path they took was right through the middle of the old town. There's no way to follow without being seen. It's the middle of the week: the place is deader than a graveyard after midnight, except for a few locals and about seven hundred cats. And the locals all know each other. It's not like the weekend, when it's crazy as a circus." He smiled briefly. "So I made the call to back off."

Fisher nodded. "Okay. You think she'll get a second meeting with Burns?"

Avila nodded. "I'd say so."

"So what was her impression of Zhang?"

Avila shook his head. "She was at bit at a loss, I'd say. She said both Burns and Zhang are quite academic, and they talked about stuff like posh food and golf."

"Posh food and golf," Fisher repeated slowly, with more than a little sarcasm.

"That's what she said, more or less."

"We're not in the more-or-less game, Agent Avila. When I want your opinion, I'll ask for it. Shall we start over?"

"Yes Ma'am." Avila cleared his throat, and announced, "Agent Deen reported that she laughed a lot, because of their attention to detail when it came to quails' eggs and *amuse-bouches*. Specifically, celery sorbet. She said Zhang is very well travelled, and he understands a great deal about the culinary arts."

"And golf?"

"Zhang likes golf, but Agent Deen got the impression that over the past year Ambassador Zhang has been overtaken by Max's skill in the game. Zhang expressed what she termed ..." He looked at his notes for a moment. "She called it 'good natured frustration.'"

"Zhang was frustrated?"

"Ma'am, I think the point was that he is good-natured."

Fisher folded her arms across her chest. "Avila, what's your take on Deen's approach to this? Would you say she was overstepping?"

"I wouldn't rule it out. She may be playing it a bit close to the line—with Burns, I mean. It got a bit hot out there, after they were dropped off by Zhang."

"Meaning?"

Avila shrugged. "I think she'll do whatever it takes." When there was no response, he added, "Ma'am."

"Thank you, Agent Avila." Fisher nodded, and indicated to Jay to end the call.

"Agent Stevenson," she said, "before Agent Deen left, did you get the feeling she was nervous?"

"Nope." Jay shook his head. "She trained as a marine. I doubt she'd know the meaning of the word."

Fisher looked at him silently. "Do you think she's spent time with Burns before? On her previous assignment in Panama?"

"She only mentioned that she'd met him at the signing party, and he seemed like a nice guy."

"Thank you Agent Stevenson."

Fisher left the room.

Chapter Fifty-Five

Panama City Golf Club, Panama City

Cursing to himself, Paco Roco walked the long stretch on the green. His shirt was wet, his forehead dripping. And, as if it wasn't enough that he was getting rained on, he could even feel rivers of sweat sliding down the back of his legs.

"I'll be playing a round alone. Meet me at the fifteenth hole."

"Why not the club house like normal people?"

"Too many ears."

Gonzáles hadn't been as spooked as he was the last time they spoke, at the racetrack, but he had reminded him that—after this—there was to be no more contact.

Paco squinted through the drizzle, knowing it was only a matter of time before the sky unleashed torrents.

Gonzáles was probably that speck out there on the fifteenth hole.

The horn blared again: the one that told everyone to vacate the golf course on account of the weather. The sky was dark. Thunder could be heard from afar, and the wind was picking up.

Like anyone would need a horn to know we're about to be hit by a fucking lightning storm.

Golf was a game Paco had never understood. All that standing around and shunting a ball from A to Z, using the time in between to talk strategy or have meaningful heart-to-hearts in small groups of soft-assed fairies. There was no point. The roar of the entire fucking crowd was right there with you at the racetrack, and when your horse came in … Well, there was no feeling like it in the entire world.

"You got it wrong, Paco, it's about the mind," Gonzáles had reprimanded, when Paco once questioned his time spent on the course. *"It's about having the staying power and the balls to stick with your game. It's just you out there. You against the opponent … and yourself. Trusting your abilities. And besides, all the deals I ever made that were worth anything were deals I made on a golf course."*

Well, at least he now had an explanation for how Gonzáles had climbed from a nobody Argentinian contractor working for CISCO to high-ranking government official in Panama since they parted ways twenty years ago.

He trudged on in the suffocating humidity, heading for cover: that thick swathe of trees that cut alongside the fairway.

Or the midway or the causeway or whatever the fuck you call it.

Once under the canopy, away from the direct rain, his mood improved slightly. Puffing as he walked, he conceded that perhaps he'd been a bit harsh. Gonzáles was, after all, looking after his—Paco Roco's—interests.

But as for China … Paco snorted with laughter as he thought about it. Really, what was there to sabotage any further? He, Paco, held all the cards himself. Didn't he?

As he strode across the green, he wondered who else would benefit from a delayed end date. Perhaps some trade would be lost, but the canal itself wasn't under threat. Their plan was straightforward: make sure they win with a very low offer, cry bankruptcy, and ask for more money from the Canal Authority in order to be able to finish the expansion project. And now? Now they were so far into the game, they wouldn't dare replace the existing team—the time it would take for a new team to step in would increase their costs even further.

Yes, Gonzáles's plan was definitely well thought out.

Paco's lips twitched into a smile.

He was keen to see how the next step was going to pan

out. The Burns kid didn't have any idea that they had already shifted all their profits to an offshore bank account in the Bahamas, nor that there were no funds available to finish the expansion project.

He was still a few hundred yards away—approaching from behind—when he saw Gonzáles.

He wasn't alone after all.

Paco stopped walking.

There was another man. They were both looking away from Paco—out towards the next hole, perhaps—and it wasn't one of those yes-sir caddies that follow you around with golf clubs.

Maybe that's why Gonzáles wanted to meet; maybe he changed his mind, and this was the 'informant.'

Yes, that was it. Clever Gonzáles! He was claiming his insurance, in case the whole thing went belly up.

Paco started walking faster toward his friend, a smile on his face.

Gonzáles swung his club.

As he watched the ball arc away from the two men—a tiny white dot shooting into a dark mass of black cloud—Paco saw the other man's club come down hard on Gonzáles's head.

Gonzáles crumpled, his knees buckling.

Paco froze, unable to turn away.

Without breathing, he watched as the man pulled out a gun.

Immediately, Paco threw himself to the ground. The knoll would barely hide his bulk, despite the shrubs.

The warning horn blew. And then again, as the rain began to fall.

Cautiously, Paco raised his head: Gonzáles lay on the ground, unmoving. The other man was walking away. Toward the clubhouse.

Inch by inch, Paco pushed himself back, away from the scene. Down the incline.

There, he lay inert, breathing fast, rain coming down onto his face, his entire body.

Instinct told him to get out of there. Fear told him to freeze.

He clambered to his feet and, as fast as he could, Paco Roco ran for the trees.

Chapter Fifty-Six

Obarrio, Panama City, Panama

"Get your flabby ass over here."

Godfredo looked at the phone as it went dead. This was a new level of charm, even for Paco.

He grabbed his work tablet and, within sixty seconds, was at his father's suite.

"Yup, whaddaya want?" he called out.

Paco was nowhere to be seen. Rain whipped the massive floor-to-ceiling window panes as the storm outside continued its fierce tirade.

"Dad?"

"Don't fucking 'yup' me!" His father's voice came from the bedroom. *"Get in here and shut the door!"*

Godfredo made his way to the bedroom.

Paco was frantically scooping belongings together, throwing them into a large suitcase that sat on the bed. He was drenched.

"What's going on?" Godfredo stood in the doorway. "What are you doing?"

Thunder shook the apartment.

"Dad?"

Paco now stopped and faced him square on. He was short of breath. "Gonzáles is gonna be reported as missing. And I don't know when they're going to find him. But I do know it'll be after this fucking storm stops, and I do know they won't find him alive."

Godfredo's mouth hung open. "How …? What?"

Paco went to the en suite and swiped bottles of cologne and toothpaste and hair products into a plastic bag.

"Dad? What the fuck did you do?"

"I didn't fucking kill him," Paco bellowed. He came back to the bedroom. "But I *saw* it." His face was contorted. "I was supposed to be meeting him at the golf course."

"Shit. Really? Did anyone see you?"

"I don't think so," Paco pushed back his wet hair with both hands. "Just one man, it was. Some other golfer. I don't know. Maybe there was another guy lurking around."

"And you know for sure he's *dead*?"

"He's dead, okay! Shot in the head!" Paco started a frenzied round of pulling clothes from cupboards and drawers.

"Okay, so they didn't see you. That's a start."

"No, you idiot! That's the fucking *end*! Don't you see? Gonzáles was our surety that the Panamanian government would get behind us when we run out of cash!" Paco dumped collared shirts onto the pile.

"Wait … When we run out of cash? What are you talking about?"

"Our profit has been syphoned off and allocated, that's the way we were playing it. But Gonzáles was our goddamn insurance that we'd be able to get more to finish the project!" The rain from his hair was still dripping down his forehead. Outside, forks of lightning speared the sky.

"But who would want him dead? There wasn't *anyone* else who was in on this arrangement?"

"No!" Paco started wrestling with his sodden jacket, in an attempt to remove it. "It was between Gonzáles and me. All I know is he had an informant, the one who got the figures we needed from the American team for the bidding."

"And who is it?"

"I don't fucking know! Gonzáles wouldn't tell me." He wrenched the jacket off his body and threw it to the floor.

"Great. So now what?"

"I'm going to make an announcement to the press today that the money's mysteriously gone, and that I believe Max Burns is responsible."

Godfredo's jaw dropped. "Are you insane?"

"No, I'm trying to survive."

"This is just …" Godfredo held up his palms, at a loss. "I don't even know why I'm arguing about the logic of this. We can't do this to Max … *I* can't do it."

"No! You listen to me, you little shit!" Paco pointed a finger at Godfredo. "I already have a history with Gonzáles. He used to work in our Buenos Aires office. It was a long time ago, and most of the records are buried, but I need to act fast, in case the authorities link our names before I have a chance to get on a plane. We need to divert their attention and Max is our only option."

"Dad, this has nothing to do with Max!"

Paco exploded. "I will *not* go to jail in this country. You hear me? We don't have any other way out."

"And then what? Run away to the Bahamas?" Godfredo looked at him, shaking his head. "You're such an asshole."

Slowly, Paco turned to Godfredo. His expression was bilious. "You don't speak to me like that."

His fist connected with Godfredo's cheek.

Godfredo reeled, stumbling.

Paco pointed to him once more, as—outside—the storm made its presence known and thunder shook the windows.

"Don't you disrespect me. We talked about this right from the beginning. And I warned you." Paco slammed the lid of his suitcase. "I'm making this call, and I'm also doing it for you. If you had half a brain, you'd start acting like a Roco."

Chapter Fifty-Seven

Casco Viejo, Panama City, Panama

At the same time as the driver, Max Burns jumped out of the black sedan. He ran to the other side of the vehicle to greet Karis, and opened the car door.

The driver, apparently unmoved, returned to his seat.

The streets were wet and steaming. Torrents of water gushed down the street's broad drains, and the sky was spitting its last reminder that this was, indeed, the tropics.

Karis was wearing sandals, and that same, simple, midnight blue dress she'd been wearing at the President's Palace, two years ago.

"I hope it's not too much," she said looking up at him, a fold of the long, satin-like fabric scrunched nervously in one hand. "I was having a major wardrobe crisis because I wasn't sure how informal it was."

Max laughed. "You look perfect."

He closed her door and ran back to the other side of the car. He could barely take his eyes off her: her long hair was swept up at the nape of her neck into a loose chignon. She twisted stray locks of hair, pushing them behind her ear, attempting to tuck them in. She seemed nervous, but he'd noticed she was often far more relaxed when they were alone together than when they were in public.

"You don't have to keep opening doors and pulling chairs out for me," she whispered, as he slid into the seat beside her.

He smiled and pulled her hand toward him. "I know. But it's how I grew up. My father did it—for everyone, not just women." Max paused, and looked at her face. "Well, it doesn't matter," he said with a smile. Then he did what he'd been longing to do all week: he kissed her. He almost wished they weren't expected at the dinner so he could have her all to himself.

Karis pulled away and gave a shy smile. "So did you whip his ass this morning?"

"You mean Steven's?" Max had to take a moment, to switch gears. "No. He got held up with some meeting or other, so I started the round without him."

"That sounds like fun," she said brightly, but Max knew she was teasing.

"All good practice," he said, with a grin. "I had to finish my round early anyway, because of the thunderstorm. It was bedlam. I met Steven for drinks at the clubhouse afterwards."

Karis was gazing out the window. "Can you not keep on playing after the rain?"

"Normally, yes. But that storm was huge. It'll be like a marshmallow out there. I don't think anyone will be on the course until tomorrow."

The phone in his pocket started buzzing, and he pulled it out in time to see a missed call from Alan's home number.

He switched the phone off: a night with Steven Zhang was bound to be interesting, and Alan always appreciated a good story. He resolved to call him in the morning.

Before long, they were on the waterfront in the Old Town. Several yellow taxi cabs were lined up along the foreshore by the low, stone wall, and people were milling around the mouth of the cul-de-sac, already in weekend party mode.

The sedan wheeled slowly toward the guards at the gates of the Embassy of the People's Republic of China.

The driver's window slid down, and there was a brief exchange. The guard peered into the rear of the car. He nodded to the driver and waved them in.

Out the front of the embassy building, the car came to

a standstill. Max smiled at Karis, and they waited as two valets opened their doors.

As they entered the foyer, a member of staff led them through to a comfortable sitting room that Max hadn't seen before. It had exquisite silk furnishings, tapestried in one of the ancient Chinese traditions. Modern, black, teak furniture was arranged around an antique red, upholstered lounge chair that formed the room's centerpiece.

Steven Zhang entered, his arms held wide.

"Max! How glad I am that you are able to join me!" He took Max's hand and turned to Karis. "Ms. Deen. So very good to see you again. I know you're going to find tonight's menu captivating."

Zhang bowed, excusing himself, as more guests entered the room, one after the other. They were clothed in designer shirts and shoes: flamboyant waistcoats, asymmetrical jackets, and a voluminous tartan dress that—thanks to having spent so many years with Sarah—Max knew could only be a Vivienne Westwood.

Karis was staring at the intricately painted ceiling. She turned to Max, her expression unreadable.

He took her hand.

"Apéritif," a waiter announced.

Tearing his eyes away from her, Max looked down to see small, clay cups clustered on a bamboo tray.

He released her hand and took two cups.

"Thank you."

He handed one to Karis as the waiter moved away.

"I'm going to bet it's spring water," he whispered. "Or filtered celery juice."

She started to laugh. "Really?"

"Steven's a big fan of hydration." He smiled.

Simultaneously, they lifted their cups and drank.

"Yep," she whispered. "Celery juice."

"Welcome, everyone!"

Breaking through the excited chatter now, Zhang

introduced guests that hailed from Beijing, Toronto, Cape Town and New York. It wasn't difficult to tell from their introductions that they were in the rare company of foodies: bloggers, reviewers, food chasers.

"Please come this way!"

The dozen of them were ushered into the Embassy's substantial, industrial-sized kitchens, where two long trestle tables with six chairs apiece were positioned in front of the largest of the kitchen's stainless-steel benches. It was more science lab than kitchen.

Silently, Zhang moved to help people find their seats. Max and Karis were seated on the far side, in the second row.

Each table was decorated with three small but elaborate floral displays set equidistant from pairs of table settings. A low, black bowl sat in front of each place; white, liquid nitrogen seeped over each rim, its fingers of cold creeping along the tablecloth.

"You smell it?" Karis murmured.

Max nodded. There was a scent of sage—the barest whisper. A strange first course that couldn't be eaten.

A short Asian man wearing thick, black-rimmed glasses now stood to one side of the front bench. He wore a chef's black-and-white-checked pants and plum jacket. A streak of blue hair was pushed behind his ear, under a chef's hat. Two sous chefs stood behind him, alongside several tall canisters with metal lids and rubber tubes with dials attached.

Zhang now spoke. "It is my absolute privilege to introduce esteemed molecular gastronomy expert, Chef Michael Wu."

Chef Wu bowed. "I am honored to be able to give this experience to you."

One of the sous chefs lowered the lights on the guests' side of the kitchen, leaving the main bench floodlit.

Karis rested her hand lightly on Max's arm.

The Chef worked quickly with a knife and small boxes

of ingredients. Smoke began to emanate from a glass bulb above a Bunsen burner, and one of the sous chefs was working with a crème foam.

After some minutes, a small cube was placed on a piece of black slate, alongside a black ramekin, inside which was the crème foam.

"To begin: spring vegetable soup with crouton."

Chef Wu bowed, and the plated delicacies were distributed.

As Max put the first spoonful of foam into his mouth, he noticed a wheat-y, toast-like flavor. Within moments, the foam had crystallized into crisp breadcrumbs.

All around the room, guests were uttering exclamations of surprise.

Karis, beside him, was laughing in delight. "Try the crouton!" she said. "It's incredible!"

Max lifted the crouton to his lips with a pair of black chopsticks. As it touched his tongue, it dissolved into a delicately flavored warm soup.

A spontaneous round of applause broke out and, looking at Max with pure glee, Karis gripped his arm. "I've never …" Her voice trailed off as she glanced over his shoulder, distracted.

Max turned.

Zhang's assistant was now at Zhang's side. He leaned down and spoke.

Zhang immediately stood, and moved silently out of the room.

The assistant straightened his jacket, and looked directly at Max.

He held his gaze as he approached.

"Dr. Burns, the Ambassador would like to see you in his study."

Max looked at Karis, then back at the assistant.

"Er, of course." He stood, placing his napkin on the table. "I'll be right back," he said softly to Karis. "Excuse me."

Ambassador Zhang was waiting in the corridor, not far from the kitchen.

He was holding a large envelope.

"Steven?"

Zhang started walking. "Please come. We don't have much time."

Through a back exit, past dumpsters of dirty linen and a hive of activity in the bowels of the building, Max was led to an underground parking lot.

"What's going on?" Max asked. "Is it some kind of emergency? Karis is back there—"

Zhang spoke quickly in Mandarin, and his assistant handed him a set of keys. The Ambassador walked directly to a small, white Honda sedan. One of the doors had a long score along it, and the license plate was hanging at an odd angle. Its darkened windows were dirty and scratched.

"Steven, is everything okay?" Max asked.

Zhang looked at him and nodded. "Get in, please. We need to go."

Chapter Fifty-Eight

The Abbey, Virginia, USA

Erika Fisher sat in her leather office chair. A small vial and a glass of water sat on the desk in front of her. She reached out and tipped a white capsule into her hand. She put it in her mouth, took the glass of water to her lips and swallowed.

There was a knock at the door.

Fisher slid the glass to the side and the vial into her drawer. She picked up a dossier.

"Enter."

"Ma'am, I've just received priority intelligence from Panama."

Agent Jay Stevenson was standing in the doorway.

"Go ahead." Fisher put down the dossier and indicated the free chair.

"The Panama Canal's Commissioner, José Gonzáles, has been killed. His body was found on the course at the Panama City Golf Club."

Fisher narrowed her eyes. "Accidental?"

"Doesn't look that way. He was shot in the head."

"Has the news broken?"

"No, it's not in the media yet. The body was found less than an hour ago. Sea Bass Two also reported Commissioner Gonzáles had called the American Embassy several times. We don't know who he was calling. However, he also received a call on his cellphone this morning."

"He *received* one?" Fisher sat up straighter. "Who was it?"

"Ambassador Roebuck."

"Do you have the transcript of their call?"

"Yes. It was very short. He told Gonzáles to meet him. Guess where?"

"At the Panama City Golf Club?"

"Exactly."

Immediately, Fisher stood. "I want no contact with our Embassy in Panama—at any level—until I can get to the bottom of this."

"You're going to Panama yourself?"

She nodded. "There's more going on there than we originally thought. Walk with me."

She left the room with Jay in tow.

"Get Marc Hussain to my office within the hour for a full briefing." Fisher spoke to her secretary.

She turned to Jay. "No need to inform the other teams that I'm going in." She paused. "It won't look good for the country if an American Ambassador is involved, so I want absolute discretion until I know what we're dealing with."

"Yes, Ma'am." Jay Stevenson took his leave, and Fisher made her way toward her living quarters.

As she crossed the lawns, she was aware of pain in her chest. Her mouth was dry, and it wasn't from fear or adrenaline. The doc had warned these pills would have side effects.

As she walked, she thought of Richard Nash, the President of the United States himself.

"He's a Godly man," her father had once said. *"He cares about our country."*

Even today, there was a quietly powerful body of senators and other politicians who believed it was worth putting every resource into retaining the United States's ever more tenuous foothold in Central America and, indeed, the world. Consciously or not. Building the Panama Canal was one of those pivotal projects that had seeped into American identity. The incredible undertaking had literally catapulted the United States onto the world stage—as visionaries, as leaders at the forefront of the industrial age. It was the stuff of legends.

And nobody wants to see a legend fall to its knees.

Once in her apartment, Fisher opened the refrigerator door and reached for cold water.

As she made her way to the bedroom, she was, for the first time, glad of the seemingly endless supply of fancy mineral water that appeared daily in her refrigerator.

She drank thirstily for several seconds, her eyes closed, before realizing her grip on the glass bottle was tight.

She looked at it. It was an idiotic, blue designer variety, the water doubtless from some random European mountain spring.

Small luxuries.

Which are entirely unnecessary, unless you yourself are somehow deficient.

She hurled the bottle at the bed with an intensity of rage she'd not felt in decades.

She was damned if she was going to let her hard work go to dust, no matter the cost.

End up on some flowchart or infographic at the next Congressional Hearing?

Not in her lifetime.

Fisher reached for her duffel bag and pulled fresh clothes from the closet.

Chapter Fifty-Nine

Embassy of the People's Republic of China, *Casco Viejo*, Panama City, Panama

Four exits, if you count the high windows.

Karis surveyed the room.

What did Zhang want with Max? Why did they leave the room so unexpectedly? Something must be wrong.

The other guests seemed barely to notice Zhang's departure, so enraptured were they with the food.

Does Zhang know who I am?

She pressed her lips together, thinking fast; this was an eventuality she hadn't fully prepared for. Everything about Max's life—his simple apartment, his orderly filing systems, even his lean contacts directory in his email and on his phone—everything was transparent. None of the usual clutter that enabled questionable behaviors to coexist. Even their background files and research showed that he'd had little or no time to do anything beyond his teaching load. Not to mention that demanding girlfriend.

Karis smiled politely at the man in a Tom Ford shirt, who had turned to look at her.

I couldn't have got Max wrong, could I?

But there was no time to analyze it now.

Avila … He should be right outside the embassy by now, or at least within a few minutes' reach.

But could she get off the grounds?

She felt an urge to speak aloud: to say something that might be picked up by the DROP app, but the phone was in her bag, on the seat behind her, and she couldn't risk calling attention to herself.

"Ms. Deen?" The voice was soft in her ear.

Karis turned to see the Ambassador's assistant.

"Would you kindly step outside for a moment? And please bring your belongings."

"Of course," she stood immediately. "Is something wrong? Where's Max?"

She didn't expect a reply. She spoke only to sound like a real girlfriend.

In the foyer of the embassy, the Ambassador's assistant stopped and turned to her.

"Dr. Burns sends his apologies. He will contact you later. I must ask you to leave the premises." Out of earshot of the other guests, his voice was not as polite as it had been. He was unsmiling.

Karis frowned. "Are you sure? He didn't say anything about—"

"I must respectfully ask you to leave the premises." He gripped her arm and directed her toward the door.

"Of course." Karis walked down the steps. She made the short walk to the guardhouse, then out onto the street.

She felt her heart rate go up. There was no chance her cover was still intact: not any more. That guard's manner had told her everything she needed to know.

Swiftly, she crossed the street, pushing her way through the Friday night partygoers.

She started running.

Through the mêlée, Karis could see the yellow cab outside the bar at the far end of the street. Avila himself looked to be embroiled in a heated discussion with a guy in a traffic warden's waistcoat.

Damn. Get rid of him, Tucker!

As she drew closer, she could see it wasn't a traffic warden, but one of the *bien cuidados*: the guys who dressed themselves like government employees, claiming custodianship of the scarce street parking in the Old Town.

He was facing off with Avila.

"*Fuera de mi area!*" *Get out of my zone.*

Avila wasn't having any of it, it seemed, until he saw Karis coming. Hastily, he handed the guy a dollar bill. "*Aquí tienes un dolar. Ahora tranquilízate!*"

The guy nodded forcefully—like he'd just kicked a winning goal—and stood with his arms folded, waiting for Avila to leave.

Karis wrenched the door open and flung herself in the front seat.

Without a moment's pause, Avila took the driver's seat, and pulled out into the busy street. He leaned on the horn to clear a path.

"Talk to me!" Karis demanded, scanning the street behind them. She punched the car radio into silence. "What the hell is going on? The Chinese have got Max!"

"What? Who has him?"

"Zhang took him somewhere! I don't even know if he's still on the embassy grounds. What do you know?"

"Did you check your messages? Did you see the news? About the Commissioner?"

Karis shook her head. "No. How could I? I've been off the grid, eating freaking pulverized prawn eyeballs—"

"Aw, shit." Deftly, he swerved the cab to avoid any contact with the tightly parked cars on the curb. "The Canal Administration Commissioner is dead: murdered!"

Karis's mouth dropped open. "What?! Gonzáles was murdered? When?"

"During the thunderstorm this morning, on the golf course. They just found the body."

"Oh my God." Karis's hands went cold. "Which golf course?"

Avila looked at her briefly. "The Panama City Golf Club. Why?"

"That's the club Max and Zhang play at."

Avila cast her a look. "They were there this morning?"

"Yes. And now they've both disappeared."

"Shit …" He pumped the horn at a guy on a moped. *"Muevete, imbécil!"*

"Tuck, did you see any vehicles come out of the Chinese embassy while you were watching?"

"A white laundry truck, and a beat-up Honda. Also white. There were two people in the Honda, but only one that I could see in the laundry truck—"

"Look out!" Karis said, as they narrowly missed the curb. "Pull over, Tuck, before you get us killed." She pulled out her phone and dialed Max's cellphone number.

Avila swung the cab into a dead-end side street and stopped the engine.

"Damn. His phone's switched off." She looked at Avila. "I need to get to Max's apartment in case he shows up. That's the only way I can get in contact with him. It could be the Chinese have taken him off the embassy grounds in one of those vehicles, but—in case not—you should go back and watch the embassy. When you get any news, let me know immediately." She got out of the car and slammed the door. She leaned into the open window frame. "I don't think Max is involved and I'm worried he might be in danger. And I don't know why."

"Karis, do you think you're in a position to make a fair judgement?"

"This is my job, Tuck. I know how to separate my feelings from my assignments."

There was a pause. "Okay, Karis. I trust you." Avila reached for the passenger side glove compartment. He pulled out something wrapped in a faded, blue bandana. He handed it to her. "Take this. You might need it."

She took it. It felt like a Glock.

Karis ran the few blocks to Max's apartment.

The street was busy, being a Friday night, so she made a few passes of his building, checking side streets—watching for watchers. Just a precaution. She couldn't see either of the cars Avila had described as leaving the Chinese embassy earlier that night. Not that she expected to, but perhaps she hoped to.

She looked up at Max's front window. The apartment lights were off.

Laughing to herself, she realized she wouldn't need her superior lock-picking skills: Max had entrusted her with a key.

She pulled it from her purse.

The foyer was lit with an old deco-style chandelier, so she didn't loiter but made her way up the main staircase to his apartment. There, she didn't bother turning on the hall light, but moved directly to Max's door.

Instinctively, she reached for her bag, for silicone gloves, but of course there were none: the bag was a satin number— beaded, with only her cellphone and a lipstick. And the gun. In any case, her prints would already be all over the place, so she unlocked the door and stepped inside.

Chapter Sixty

Casco Viejo, Panama City, Panama

The interior of the car wasn't in any better condition than the car's chassis. Vinyl seats were splitting at seams, and there was damage to the ceiling.

Steven Zhang seemed unfazed, his eyes on the flow of traffic ahead of them as he expertly navigated the small car away from the city's Old Town.

"Max, I do apologize for the circumstances," he said. "I have just learned that something of significance has occurred, and it is in my country's best interests that I distance myself from you at this time."

Zhang now pointed to the large envelope that sat above the dash.

Max looked at it. "Is this a joke?"

Zhang nodded at the envelope, his hands both on the steering wheel. "Unfortunately, history tells me it is likely that, under the circumstances, the Americans will point fingers at China."

"What for? What circumstances?" Max slid his finger under the seal. The envelope opened easily.

"As you know, my government did not deny reports that there will be a new passage through the continents with the Nicaragua canal." Zhang paused. "We believe that's why they have an agent on you."

"An agent? Come on!" Max laughed at the absurdity.

Zhang pulled out a sheaf of digital images.

Slowly, Max turned to look. "Steven, this isn't funny …"

In his hand was a picture of Karis Deen.

Zhang said nothing as he navigated the traffic.

Max looked again at the images in his hand, uncomprehending.

Karis Deen in the street.

Karis Deen entering the Presidential Palace with the Smithsonian scientists last year.

Karis Deen ... in a CIA bulletproof vest.

Max put a hand to his jaw in a fruitless attempt to erase the tension. He leafed through more images.

Can pictures like this be fabricated?

And yet there was one image of Karis that was irrefutable: Karis Deen with Max Burns—just last week. There she was: sitting next to him, leaning her head on his shoulder, on that wall by the waterfront.

"She can't be CIA," he murmured, looking at the bulletproof vest she wore in one image. "That's an old picture, from years ago. Look at the date ..."

Still Zhang said nothing.

Max let the images fall to his lap. He turned to the window of the cab.

He registered only dimly that they were now on the main esplanade, heading east of the city, along the bay.

"You've been watching me," he said, his voice hoarse. "You've been watching ... everyone."

There was a pause. "You understand—"

"No, Steven, *stop!*" Max snapped. "I understand you've had people watching me when I believed us to be friends." He felt the anger surging through him. "Let me out of the car—*now*."

Zhang immediately indicated, and veered the car toward the road's shoulder. Traffic swerved and sped past them, horns honking, as they slowed to a stop.

As Max put his hand on the door handle, Zhang reached out and grabbed his arm.

"Max—"

But Max shook him off. "You know, after what you just

told me—with all your intelligence and covert spying and bullshitting to your so-called friends—how do you expect me to believe a word you say?"

"I have absolutely no expectations."

"Of course you don't," Max said. His tone was bitter. Shaking his head slowly, he looked at the face he'd grown to trust. "Is China involved in something to do with the expansion?" he asked quietly. "Are you setting me up so you can build your canal in Nicaragua?"

He waited, but no response came.

Zhang looked away, and Max's fingers gripped the car's door handle tighter.

When Zhang spoke, he didn't meet Max's eyes. "I will always be available for my friends, but I am first and foremost the Ambassador for the People's Republic of China. I am not in a position to discuss details with you." His voice was even. "Max, I don't know exactly what happened at the golf course today before we met, but I have to ask you to get out of the car now."

"At the golf course? What are you talking about?"

Zhang didn't respond.

Max looked at him, incredulous. He had no words.

Stunned, he opened the car door and stepped out, alongside frantic, Friday night traffic.

The door slammed behind him.

The car took off.

Chapter Sixty-One

Costa Del Este, Panama

Max turned, his head reeling, as the white Honda disappeared into the night.

Karis.

Mind numb, he started walking in the same direction the car had travelled. Horns honked, and Friday night partygoers whooped out car windows as they passed in gusts and whooshes, causing his jacket to flap like a scarecrow in the wind. The smell of remains from the city's fish markets hit him in gusts of sea breeze, the salty trace of offcuts more prominent, perhaps, now that the sun had gone, and the day's hubbub had died down.

What the hell had just happened?

It must be big, if the Chinese Ambassador was willing to risk his own reputation to get him off the embassy premises.

And what had happened at the golf course?

Max pulled out his phone and switched it on.

He searched: *Breaking news Panama.*

He inhaled sharply.

"*Canal Commissioner Gonzáles murdered.*"

And there it was: Gonzáles was dead, on the course at the Panama City Golf Club.

Max squeezed the phone. It was almost surreal.

And yet … Steven was the one who had been late to their meeting that day.

"Shit!" He ran a hand through his hair and cast a look up the street.

He looked at his phone and saw, now, a message from Sarah.

Hesitating, he touched the screen. Sarah had long ago told him she'd wanted no more contact. And he knew she wouldn't be contact him unless …

"Alan in hospital. He had a stroke. Please call me as soon as you can."

"No!"

With shaking fingers, he punched in her number.

Suddenly, he stopped. What if Steven had been sent to set him up? What if the CIA was tracking his cellphone?

Fumbling now, he cancelled the call.

He switched off the phone.

For a long, awful moment, he looked around him.

Across the avenue, lit up by the city's streetlights, the leaves of tall palm trees shifted gently in the warm breeze. Pedestrians walked in packs along the sidewalks, traffic honked, open-topped buses were jammed in between taxis and luxury cars and beat up little family cars like the one he'd been in not minutes before.

Lifting his head, he watched the blinking lights of planes coming in to land, of other aircraft passing overhead.

How did it come to this?

Slowly, Max made his way up the strip and toward the flow of traffic heading east. He put out an arm. He didn't hold out much hope of hailing a taxi on the freeway, but he had no choice.

It was less than a minute before a yellow cab pulled up alongside him.

"New Horizons," he said, as he stepped in. "Do you know it? *Lo conoces?*"

"*Sí, Señor.*"

The cab took off, a breeze from the Bay of Panama coming in the open windows. The driver—an older, snaggle toothed man—was singing a Latin pop song at the top of his lungs.

Max looked at the phone in his hand. In one swift move, he threw it out the window.

"*Usted está solo?*" The driver's words interrupted his thoughts. He seemed not to have noticed the phone as it smashed on the roadside. "You go solo tonight?" The driver winked at him in the rear vision. "At New Horizons?"

Max nodded. He was tired beyond belief.

"Please," he said. "Just drive."

Chapter Sixty-Two

Casco Viejo, Panama City, Panama

Karis Deen pulled the Glock from her purse, and felt its familiar weight in her hand.

Slowly, methodically, she scanned Max's apartment.

A light was on in the bathroom, but otherwise it was dark and appeared to be uninhabited.

She went into the living room.

The voicemail light was blinking on the phone's handset.

She moved across and picked up the receiver.

An automated recording: "*You have ... three ... missed calls and ... one ... new message.*"

Then a female voice: English. Tense. "*Max? It's me. Sarah. Where are you? I've tried your mobile. Call me back as soon as you can.*"

Karis placed the handset on the table. Briefly, she wondered what Max's life had been like in London.

"Come on, Max," she murmured. "Where are you?"

Silently, she looked around the living room.

Everything appeared to be in order. Even the papers on the dining table were in neat piles.

The last time she'd been in the apartment was under entirely different circumstances—mere days before—and for a moment she felt a real, sharp pang of loss: loss of that intoxicating levity she felt when she was with him.

Of course—levity aside—she'd managed to work her way through every single possible drawer and storage nook while he showered a few nights ago.

And, even thinking back on it now, dissecting everything

she'd seen, she was still unsure: Max Burns either had nothing whatsoever to hide, or he was an extremely good actor.

Unfortunately, at this point, she knew it could go either way.

Chapter Sixty-Three

Obarrio, Panama City, Panama

"Mr. Roco! Mr. Roco! We've just learned that after the terrible thunderstorm, Commissioner Gonzáles was found murdered on the golf course. Do you have anything to say?"

Jesus Christ.

Godfredo, alarmed now, jumped out of the car and pushed through the media scrum until he was standing at his father's side.

Paco's face showed deep sorrow. "I'm at a loss," he said, his voice gruff. "It's a terrible, terrible thing to happen, and our hearts go out to Commissioner Gonzáles's wife and their family."

"Señor Paco, we just learned that you're currently undergoing an extensive auditing process with the Canal Administration. What does that mean? Is the British Consortium in financial difficulty?"

Godfredo felt his pulse shoot up: to his knowledge, Paco hadn't released any details to the press about the audit yet, nor his relationship to Gonzáles. Moreover, he didn't look overly surprised to see journalists waiting on the hotel doorstep.

"This has been a trying period for us, I won't deny it," Paco said.

Nervously, Godfredo scanned the hungry faces with microphones and sun guns. He raised a hand, shielding himself and his father from the cameras.

"That's all, everyone," he said. He pulled Paco by the arm, and broke free of the scrum.

"Señor Paco! We're also trying to get in contact with the consortium's chief engineer, Max Burns, but he's not responding. Do you know of his whereabouts?"

Paco stopped walking.

Don't stop walking, you idiot!

Godfredo turned back and tried to pull his father away.

"I do not," Paco said, looking at the journalist earnestly. "Unfortunately, we haven't heard from our chief engineer in a couple of days. And it's terrible timing, given the auditor's findings."

That set them off.

"Is the British consortium in trouble? ... What kind of findings?"

"You mean Max Burns has *disappeared*?"

"I'm sure there's a good explanation," Paco continued, obviously playing dumb. "He's very experienced with budgeting on this scale. And I should add that he's an extremely reliable and trustworthy man, despite his tragic family history—"

Godfredo's mouth fell open.

Oh, for fuck's sake.

Never mind the bald-faced lie about Max's involvement in the budget ... Did Paco really just bring Max's family into the equation?

"That's all! That's all! No more!" Godfredo bellowed, dragging Paco away from the clamor.

"Señor Roco, are you confirming that CISCO is in financial trouble? What do you mean by 'family history'?"

Paco paused for a moment, then turned back to the media. They fell silent.

"Please, don't ask me to do your job for you. I have nothing more to say on the matter."

Godfredo strode across the hotel lobby ahead of his father. It was all he could do to try and keep from hitting his father's face with his fist.

As they stepped into the elevator, he turned to Paco, shaking.

"I don't know what you think you're doing, but this is the *last* time I will speak with you. You're on your own now!"

Paco pressed the elevator buttons repeatedly, as though the action would somehow speed up the process. "You're in this just as much as I am, Godfredo," he said, as the elevator started moving. "You knew the numbers were forged, and guess what? You're a Roco, just like me. So, like it or not, we go forward together."

"No, fuck you, Dad!"

"Grow up, Godfredo. I needed to deflect attention, and now I've said my bit."

The elevator pinged, and the doors opened.

"And now, if you'll excuse me, I'm picking up my bags, and I'm going to the airport."

Paco went directly to his room, and the door slammed behind him.

Chapter Sixty-Four

Casco Viejo, Panama City, Panama

Erika Fisher was seated in the front passenger seat of the black sedan. Outside the car, the streets were teeming with people.

She was en route to the American Trade Hotel, at the heart of Panama's Old Town.

Fisher ran her tongue over her teeth and swallowed.

Her mouth was so dry.

"*Ma'am?*"

She cocked her head to one side, listening to her earpiece.

"*The Ambassador looks like he might be about to leave the hotel. Orders?*"

"Stay put. I'll be on site in less than a minute." She issued a further set of instructions to her driver. "You wait outside, I'll direct him off the premises."

With a passing glance in the mirror, she arranged her cropped, gamine hair so that it softened her face slightly. She'd had to apply blush that morning in order to hide the increasing pallor.

Quickly, she turned away from her reflection.

As the car pulled up at the hotel's elegant front façade, she opened the door and stepped out. She was met with a wave of suffocating humidity that caught her off guard for a moment.

There was time to scan the foyer of the hotel before she was approached by a member of staff.

Smiling but disengaged, she bypassed formalities and walked across to the bar.

The eyes of most guests—men and women alike—were on her as she navigated the tables, but she was used to that kind of attention. As a young woman it had bothered her; it had felt as though she hadn't earned it.

Fisher nodded to the barman, who had half an eye on the small television behind the bar.

"I'll have the same." She pointed to Roebuck's glass.

As expected, her words caused the Ambassador to look up.

For a moment, she was startled by the intensity of his eyes; the symmetry of a handsome, older face. She recognized the look of an Alpha who has just sensed his mate. Or his match.

Roebuck opened his mouth to say something, but his eyes flicked away and he turned to the television screen. The sound was low, but audible.

"… *where we have just witnessed a disturbing interview with Francisco—known as 'Paco'—Roco, CEO and President of CISCO, head of the British consortium's contractors …*"

"Turn it up!" Roebuck barked. Fumbling with the remote, the bartender obeyed.

"… *an audit currently being carried out, is expected to confirm Roco's statement, but in the meantime, there are concerns that missing British engineer Max Burns is responsible for the consortium being close to bankruptcy …*"

Roebuck's mouth hung open.

"*This information comes on the back of the news about the brutal killing of the Commissioner for Panama Canal's Administration, José Gonzáles, the man responsible for initiating the audit on the CISCO files …*"

The screen now showed a photo: Max Burns shaking hands with Commissioner Gonzáles at the Presidential Palace.

"Wow," Fisher said, coolly, as a gin and tonic was placed in front of her. "Who would have thought they'd suspect the British engineer of murder?"

"Huh?" Roebuck looked at her. His tone changed to one of concerned urgency. "Terrible news, indeed. I must …" He looked at his phone once more. "Please excuse me."

He stood, and waved to the bartender for the bill, while dialing.

"Mr. Ambassador, I think you should join me."

Roebuck lowered his phone.

"Have we met?" His expression was one of irritation.

Fisher flashed her badge and immediately her agents appeared: two men hovering within meters of them.

"Fisher. Defense Clandestine Service."

Roebuck looked at her incredulously. "Defense Clandestine? I'd have been informed if there was any clandestine activity in Panama."

"For various reasons, this operation was not communicated to the Embassy."

"What is this?" He sounded incensed.

"I'll explain in due course, sir. Right now, I'm asking you to come with me."

Roebuck nodded.

Slowly, he picked up his briefcase and followed her toward the exit. They made their way to the first of the two vehicles.

"Please." Fisher opened the front door on the passenger side of the first sedan. She cast her eyes around the immediate vicinity as he got in, then made her way to the driver's side.

The driver looked up as she opened the door. "Ma'am?"

"Join the other unit, please," Fisher said. "And wait for further instructions."

"Of course." Obediently, he unbuckled, then jogged to the second car.

Fisher got in. It was mercifully cool in the air-conditioning.

Without looking at Roebuck, she buckled herself in and checked the mirrors.

Roebuck looked at her. "Where are we going?"

Ignoring his question, she started the engine.

Chapter Sixty-Five

Costa Del Este, Panama City, Panama

Ignoring the driver's small talk, Max Burns handed over dollar bills.

The cab took off, into the night.

Max walked toward the neon yellow sign at the end of the strip that heralded New Horizons. A fake, concrete boulder with accompanying plastic flamingos stood guard at the gate.

Dull street lights sputtered as he passed, and storm-damaged palm leaves hung limp across the perimeter fence. Many more leaves, sticks and debris had accumulated in mounds along gutters and building foundations.

Once inside the gate, Max saw one orange metal garage roller door after another, all of them closed. Occupied.

As he jogged down one row and turned into the next, he drew some consolation from the thought that nobody who knew him would ever suspect him of hiding out here, among folks who were taking lovers to a pay-by-the-hour motel.

For a brief moment, he thought of his uncle: of the fresh, black-and-white movie calendar that Alan had pinned to his wall, not long before they'd said their farewells.

Distraught, Max stopped jogging.

That calendar was last year's now.

How many terrible beans-on-toast meals had he missed? How many beers in front of the telly?

Walking slowly, now, he could only think that he trusted Alan with his life, and yet—here, in Panama—the only person he felt he could really trust was Sofia: a prostitute who worked as a night manager in a push-button motel.

How a life can change in a moment.

Skirting around to the next row, he spotted a dimly flickering green light above an open roller door. He ducked inside.

He crossed the small garage space toward an illuminated, red button on the left wall that was well within reach of a driver's car window.

He pushed it, and the roller door behind him started to close.

A halogen light went on above a black door to his left.

There were no instructions. No swipe card unit.

He opened the door and went in.

Immediately, he was hit with the smell: chlorine, and cheap cologne.

Long, velvet curtains hung, pulled back, at either side of the room. A table with a pair of gold framed Elvis sunglasses sat immediately to his right, and several diamanté-strewn jumpsuits on hangers hung along one wall. To his far left, an electric guitar was poised on a stand next to a large amplifier. Cables were coiled on the floor like snakes and in front of him stood a microphone stand. To his right: a floor-to-ceiling dancer's pole.

"Okay …" he said, slowly. The smell of chlorine was strong.

He ventured further into the room, which was lit with warmly glowing lava lamps of various shapes and sizes. The far wall was papered with a classic, black-and-white photo-graph of hysterical rock concert fans. In the center of the room, mirrored ceilings reflected a round bed, sheeted with faux-satin leopard skin and adorned with pillows like big, fluffy red lips. An elaborate, ivory-and-gold telephone was positioned on the bedside table, along with a menu of fast foods.

Presuming it wasn't just a prop, he picked up the phone's receiver.

Immediately, he was greeted by a female voice.

"*Buenas tardes, bienvenidos a New Horizons—*"

He recognized her voice.

"Sofia?"

There was a pause.

"*Who is this?*"

"Sofia? Is that you? It's Max."

"*Max! Don't move! I'll be with you in a second.*"

Moments later, Max turned to see Sofia standing in the doorway. Her face—usually so composed—registered pure shock. "What are you doing here?"

"Sofia, I have nowhere else to go."

She started running across the room. She was carrying an open laptop.

"What did you get yourself into?" She showed him the screen of her laptop. "Look! Look!"

Horrified, Max watched as a large image of his own face was superimposed behind the news reader onscreen.

"*… suspect in the Gonzáles murder …*"

"What …?"

"*The Commissioner's body was found earlier this evening …*"

"What is this?" Max turned to Sofia. "I'm a suspect?"

But Sofia held up a manicured fingernail for silence, her attention riveted to the screen.

"*Max Burns hadn't been seen for two days, having not shown up to work this morning …*"

Max looked at Sofia again, incredulous. She was shaking her head in disbelief.

"*… police traced his movements to the Panama City Golf Club, but CISCO's CEO Paco Roco holds grave concerns for the British engineer. With the British consortium now crying bankruptcy—*"

"Bankruptcy?!"

Footage of Paco and Godfredo in front of the press came up on the screen.

Sofia scrolled as she read aloud: *"Burns on the run …
Prime suspect in Panama murder …"* She looked up at him.
"Dios mío, Max, I'm so sorry."

Max sat heavily on the bed beside her.

"Paco sold me out," he said. "Paco and Godfredo … They
set me up." He shook his head, unable to comprehend.

"What can we do?" Sofia asked, her voice urgent. "Shall
I take you to the police?"

Max shook his head.

She closed the laptop. "Would it help if we called the
British Embassy?"

"It's too late for that. You saw the news. They want me for
murder. There's not much the Embassy could do for me."
The words were thick in his mouth.

"Do you want me to call a lawyer? I know a few."

"I … I don't know," Max stammered. "I don't know who
I can trust anymore." He paused, looking at her, her face
oddly unfamiliar without its layers of makeup.

"Is Sofia your real name?"

She was silent.

"I'm sorry. I didn't mean to insult you."

"It's okay. You're right. Sofia's not my real name—"

There was a loud knocking on the door.

Max jumped to his feet. "You didn't tell anyone I was
here, did you?"

She shook her head.

"Sí, quien es?" Sofia called out.

A woman's voice came from behind the door speaking
Spanish.

Sofia looked at Max. "He's here!" she said. She stood up.
"Godfredo's in my office."

Chapter Sixty-Six

Costa Del Este, Panama City, Panama

"Max!" Godfredo Roco stood in the doorway. "Thank fuck!"

"You *asshole!*"

Max threw himself at his friend and punched with all his strength. The two of them struggled like teenagers, locked together.

Once more Max lunged, taking Godfredo by the collar and punching. With a squeal, Sofia grabbed Max's arm, and Godfredo fought back.

Max felt his friend's fist connect with his cheek.

"*Basta!*" Sofia yelled. "Stop it! Stop it, both of you!" She tried to pull them apart, but Godfredo pushed her to one side.

Immediately, she turned and slapped Godfredo's face.

Stunned, Godfredo stopped. He looked at Sofia.

"Did you just … *hit* me?" Blood dripped from his chin.

"I did, you crazy bastard! Look at what you're doing!" She let off a string of fast Spanish and, meekly, Godfredo stepped back, breathing heavily. The front of his shirt was stained crimson, and his cheek was grazed.

He turned to Max. "*Hermano*, I'm so sorry. This all got so fucked up."

Max looked at his friend in shock. "I'm not sure I heard you correctly," he said drily. "Are you *apologizing*? To me?"

"I won't let you down again," Godfredo said. "I promise. I'll fix this. Dad went too far this time—"

"Where is he? Where's Paco?" Max demanded. He touched his cheekbone gingerly.

"He left the country. Right after he spoke to the press."

"Really?" Max rubbed his bruised knuckles. "And you didn't go with him? Why not? Taking the easy way out is more your style, isn't it?"

"Max, please." Godfredo looked at his hands, which were now covered in his own blood. "I'm not going to leave you to fight this one on your own, *hermano*. You must know me better than that." He looked at Max, his face imploring. Max was silent. "I'm the only one who can testify that you had nothing to do with the scam my dad and Gonzáles came up with."

"Wait … Paco and Gonzáles? Wow. This gets better and better." Max's voice oozed sarcasm. But then it hit him: *Did Paco kill Gonzáles?*

He looked at Godfredo.

"No, no! Dad's not a killer!" Godfredo had anticipated his question. "There's somebody else, but I don't know who it is."

"And I'm supposed to believe you?"

"Really, Max, I don't know who it is! Dad never told me. Maybe he didn't know either."

"Think, Fredo!" Sofia urged. "You don't have *any* idea who it could be?"

"No," Godfredo said. "And I don't want to know. Not after today."

Sofia turned to Max. "Someone with a big reputation."

Steven. Of course.

Steven was the only one who knew he'd be at the golf course that morning when they killed Gonzáles.

Max sat heavily on the bed once more, a wave of fatigue rolling over him.

Whatever this thing is, it's much bigger than me.

He looked at Sofia. "Can I borrow your phone?"

She nodded, and quickly handed him her cellphone. It was encased in hot pink, with champagne diamantés.

"Who are you calling?" Godfredo asked.

"Karis. She's the only one who can deal with this. The local cops aren't going to believe me."

Godfredo contemplated this for a moment. "So ... you're suggesting a Smithsonian scientist can help you solve a murder?"

Max sighed. "Fredo, Karis is an undercover agent with the US government."

"Oh. My. God! That makes her even *hotter*!" Godfredo's triumphant expression froze. "Wait, you're not serious." He looked at Sofia. "Is he serious?! Oh my God. How fucking *cool* is that?! Max! You've been screwing a CIA agent—!"

"Shut *up*, Godfredo," Max said, wearily. "Really. For once in your life, *stop talking*."

"Okay," Godfredo said, backing off. His eyes were sparkling. "So ... Let's go!"

Max turned to his friend. "No, Fredo. You've already caused enough trouble for me. You wait with Sofia until I call you. I have to do this on my own."

Chapter Sixty-Seven

Casco Viejo, Panama City, Panama

Dropping the television remote, Karis ran to the window of Max's apartment. Standing to the side, in shadow, she shifted the venetian blind slightly with one finger, and surveyed the street below.

A local police officer stood there, looking up. He was talking into his radio.

Behind her, the television broadcaster's words delivered their sting.

"The Panama Canal expansion project's chief engineer Max Burns is on the run after bankruptcy and embezzlement claims. Speaking at a doorstop a short time ago, Paco Roco, head of the British Consortium's contractors, CISCO, spoke about the company's financial catastrophe ..."

She didn't wait to hear more.

Max must have known about this. He must have.

How could I have misjudged him so badly?

Karis's heart rate increased as the door clicked softly behind her. She ran along the corridor to the fire exit at the far end. She took the stairs two by two, slipped out the emergency exit and found herself in a gated courtyard with old stone walls.

A tree stood in the corner. She knew it would be easy climbing and, indeed, within seconds, she was crouched in the lower branches, assessing her options.

In her hand, the Abbey phone started vibrating silently.

She didn't pick up: to break the silence and talk right now might mean the difference between being spotted or getting away.

She kept her eyes on the street, but she was only half concentrating: she—of all people—couldn't baulk at the idea of Max being a Chinese asset. Coming from her—an undercover agent—that would be ridiculous. But if he was involved in the death of Gonzáles ... that was another matter. That would make Max Burns a cold-blooded killer.

The police officer made his move, entering the building via the main entrance, and Karis prepared to step across to the wall and jump. She landed on the pavement below, startling a pair of cats. They skittered across the street.

As she moved along the sidewalk toward the nearest cross street, her phone started vibrating again. She looked at the screen.

Her hands went cold and she stopped walking.

She accepted the call and waited, silently.

"*Agent Deen?*"

Karis's stomach somersaulted. It was Max's voice.

Softly, she said, "You know, then?"

"*Yes.*" His voice was neutral.

She didn't speak. She didn't know where to start; how to explain.

"*Can we meet?*"

"Max ..." She spoke slowly. "I need you to hear me: if it was you who killed the Commissioner, I won't be able to help you. Do you understand?"

There was silence for a moment.

"*I know who killed Gonzáles. I think you need my help more than I need yours.*" His tone was icy.

"Okay. Where do you want to meet?"

"*Why don't we meet out front of the Smithsonian?*"

"The ... Smithsonian? Come on," she said, defeated. "I was just doing my job."

"*Right. And you're really good at it.*" There was a long pause.

"Okay," she conceded. "Give me ten minutes."

The phoneline went dead.

Karis allowed herself a moment to pull her scattered thoughts together. She took a couple of breaths before starting to run along the street toward Avila's location.

Gripping the phone, she dialed.

"Tuck? Where are you?"

"I'm headed your way. The white Honda came back to the Chinese Embassy, and there was only one occupant."

She peered up the street. "Wait. I see you!" She ended the call and sprinted the last stretch toward the yellow cab as it approached. It came to a stop on the side of the street.

Breathless, she flung the door open and climbed in. "I need to get to the Smithsonian!"

"Why?"

"Drive, Tuck! Max called me."

Avila looked at her, without moving the car. "You trust him?"

"What choice do I have?"

After a moment, he nodded. "Okay."

He swung the wheel and they headed out of the Old Town.

Chapter Sixty-Eight

Balboa, Panama City, Panama

"Dead bodies," Erika Fisher said, under her breath.

She turned the wheel, taking the car off the main road, and drove toward the broad tree-lined avenue that was *Calle Roberto F. Chiari*.

"I'm sorry?"

Fisher looked at Roebuck. "That's what the transoceanic railway was used for." She pointed in the direction of the railway that passed alongside the canal. It was just out of view. "Even before it was completed, it was shifting hundreds and hundreds of dead bodies, to get them out of Panama. To get them home to their loved ones."

She gave a grim smile. Not at the grisly history of deaths at the hands of malaria and abysmal working conditions on the Panama Canal construction site a century ago, but—rather—at her own words. A couple of weeks ago she wouldn't have dwelled upon the missteps of the past, nor on the tribulations of strangers, opting instead to look to the future.

A lot can change in a few weeks.

She could feel Roebuck's calculating gaze on her as she drove.

"What exactly is your directive, Agent Fisher?" he asked. There was an edge of challenge in his voice: he was clearly trying to gain the upper hand.

"I think it's you who killed Commissioner Gonzáles yesterday at the golf course," she said.

Roebuck attempted to protest, but she cut him off. "Don't

get me wrong: it was an interesting plan. And it might have worked out—getting our American engineers back into the Canal project after it was declared bankrupt." She glanced at him. "I can well imagine you: swooping in to offer a helping hand on behalf of the mighty United States of America. And in exchange regaining our stake in the administration of the canal. It's a very neat solution to a very messy situation." She smiled grimly. "You'd have been the hero of the day, Larry! And wouldn't that have given you a huge step up in Washington—?!"

"You have no right to accuse me of anything!"

Fisher was calm. "Sir, that's precisely the problem we face: you feel you're above the law. But we have a record of you speaking with Commissioner José Gonzáles on several occasions—"

"Have you been surveilling my communications?! I'm an Ambassador for the United States!" Roebuck's tone was harsh.

Fisher was impassive. "My team had—for other reasons—been intercepting the calls of Commissioner Gonzáles; not yours. But you made the mistake of calling him on his cellphone." She glanced at Roebuck. "*You* might have been on a secure line, but *he* wasn't. That's how you put yourself on our radar." She sighed. "In any case, it's a moot point. Right now, you can see you've put me—and our country—in a very difficult situation. How do we explain to the world that we have power-hungry Ambassadors running around killing people?"

"You're grossly overestimating my ambition. I'm just a patriot from a small town in Indiana, who wants to serve his country."

Fisher laughed, her tone brittle. "I know." She kept her eyes on the road. "That's the error we all make at one point or other, when we're in this patriot business: we start to believe our own hype."

"You're not making sense."

"Okay, let me make it plain." She fixed her eyes on him for a moment. "As I see it, there are two options. First: I bring you to justice. But you need to be aware that if I turn you in, you will be put on trial in the Panamanian and US courts, and the international media will have a field day—"

"I get it, I get it." He cut her off. "What's the second option?"

"The second option is that you give me your gun."

"What?"

"You heard me."

"What makes you think I'm carrying a gun? Don't you think I'd have thrown it away already, even if I was stupid enough to use it? Which, by the way, I have not admitted."

Fisher slowed the car. She took a turn onto the street that led to the CISCO Construction Group's head office. They were only a few hundred meters from the Panama Canal Administration Building.

"Sir, I don't think you would have thrown the gun away. You of all people know an Ambassador is well protected. You have complete diplomatic immunity. Nobody would ask you—nor suspect you—of carrying a firearm. That's how I know you kept it, and how I know you're carrying the murder weapon with you as we speak." She turned the wheel and accelerated. "And so I'm going to ask you again to hand it over."

There was silence for a long stretch.

Fisher worked to control her facial expression: if the gamble didn't pay off she'd have nothing.

She exhaled slowly—mostly to try to expel the pain that was in her chest.

For a moment, she wondered if she need worry that he might pull the gun on her. But she was sure he'd realized by now that he was in too deep for that.

"I assume you didn't register the gun," she continued mildly.

He kept his silence.

As they reached the parking lot out front of the building, she slowed the car to a standstill. The place was badly lit, bar a couple of lamps that illuminated the main entrance to the building.

"You know what's funny?" Fisher said, as she switched off the engine. "We really thought the Chinese were behind this." She cast a look at Roebuck, curious to see his response. He clutched his briefcase close to his body. "Can you imagine? We already had two clandestine teams on it." As she remembered the look of abject concern on the Secretary of Defense's face, she fought back a smile. "Implicating the Chinese in the failure of the canal expansion would have given your plan a real boost, you understand that, right?"

Slowly, Roebuck nodded.

It was the first indication that her gamble was going to pay off.

"I got spooked," he said. He turned to her and he shook his head. "To get the Chinese involved was never part of my plan."

She nodded, and he held her gaze.

"But when it happened … I needed to pull out," he said. "It was getting out of control. It had to cut any ties that would connect me with Commissioner Gonzáles."

"I understand," she said. She inclined her head toward the sprawling whitewashed building. "This way, sir."

They got out of the car.

Chapter Sixty-Nine

Smithsonian Institute for Tropical Research, Panama City, Panama

From where he stood by Sofia's tiny red Toyota, Max could see the cab's headlights approaching.

He heard the sound of tires crushing fallen leaves and twigs as the car came to a standstill some distance from him. Two figures got out. One of them was Karis Deen.

She approached him alone.

Max's pulse started racing.

Perhaps ten feet from him, she stopped. "Max, what happened to your face?! Are you okay?"

She was so very beautiful.

"Is caring about me also part of your job?"

"Come on, Max." She was unsmiling. "Tell me what you know."

Immediately, Max shut down any feelings he may have had. "It's the Chinese," he said abruptly. "Steven never signed in at the golf club this morning, but he made sure I was there to meet him." He paused. "He *always* signs in. I think the Chinese are trying to frame me for Gonzáles's death."

In the half light, he saw a flicker of confusion on her face. "You think the Chinese also set up CISCO to destabilize the expansion project?"

"I'm not sure what Paco's connection with Gonzáles was, and when it started. Godfredo told me that he and his dad didn't know who was pulling the strings behind Gonzáles. I guess when the Chinese realized that the Americans were increasing their intelligence, they decided to get rid of their main contact, Gonzáles. Or maybe killing him was always part of their plan."

Over her shoulder, Max saw the second figure—a man—was now approaching. "I've got Jay," he announced. He had a cellphone in his fist.

He handed it to Karis. It was on speaker.

"Jay, it's Karis. I'm with Avila and Max Burns. Max believes the Chinese may be the ones behind Gonzáles's death."

"Karis, no. You were right. The Chinese have nothing to do with it. It looks like it was one of our own."

"What do you mean?" She turned her back to Max.

"It's the US Ambassador in Panama: Larry Roebuck. And Karis … Fisher's in Panama."

"Fisher's here? Why?"

"She didn't trust your report about the Chinese. And when she learned about the possible connection with the US Ambassador she decided to go to Panama herself. She instructed us not to inform you. And we believe she's with the Ambassador now."

"You believe …?"

"We don't know for sure, but we just received word from her back-up team that she secured the Ambassador and then stood her team down."

"Why the hell did she do that?"

"I don't know. And a few minutes ago, she deactivated her DROP cellphone."

"No way! So you can't track her?! Where did you last see her?" Karis turned, and Max could see her face was grim.

"Avenue Morgan."

"The Canal Administration Building," Avila murmured.

"Thanks, Jay. We'll call you as soon as we know more." Karis ended the call. She turned to Avila. "We're on our own. So let's go to—"

"I'm coming with you," Max interjected.

Karis turned to him, her expression one of surprise. As though she'd almost forgotten he was there.

She shook her head. "Agent Avila and I will sort this out. I've got your number, I'll contact you when—"

"No way," Max cut her off. "I'm not standing around here while other people try to take everything away from me again. I've been there before, and I'm not going to let it happen. I'm not letting you out of my sight."

Karis tipped her head, observing him for a moment. "Okay. Why would they go to the Administration Building?" she asked. "What could they be looking for?"

"I don't know. Let's find out."

Karis nodded slowly. She turned back to Avila. "Tuck, you go to the American Embassy to see if they show up there. "I'll take Max to the Administration Building. If you get in trouble, call me."

Avila nodded and made his way swiftly toward the cab.

Karis looked at Max. With no trace of emotion in her voice, she said, "We'll take your car. You can drive."

Chapter Seventy

Balboa, Panama City, Panama

With Max at the wheel, they made their way along winding streets. Debris from the storm—leaves and sticks—came into sharp relief under the car's headlights.

As they drew closer to the majestic Panama Canal Administration Building, Max slowed the vehicle and scanned the roadside. He glanced at Karis.

"You want me to park around here somewhere? In the shadows, maybe?"

Karis's lips twitched, and Max could see she was fighting a smile. "It's okay, you can go a bit closer." She turned to look at him. "Wait, *stop!*"

Max hit the brakes.

Karis was pointing to the other side of the street. "Over there! That's Fisher's car."

Max peered through the windshield.

Sure enough, a black sedan was parked in the corner of the otherwise deserted parking lot, out front of the cluster of Spanish-colonial-style buildings that had housed CISCO headquarters for the past eighteen months.

"My office …" Max said. He turned to Karis. "What would they be doing there?"

"They want the CISCO files," she said. "What's in them?"

"I have no idea why they'd want my files." Max shook his head. "But maybe they're not looking to get something," he said slowly. "Maybe they're looking to *leave* something."

"What do you mean?"

"A gun? The murder weapon?"

"That doesn't make sense. I can't see why Fisher would frame you for the murder of Gonzáles." Karis was silent for a moment. Then she pointed toward the parking lot. "Drive that way," she instructed, coolly.

Max turned the wheel, and a sign became visible: *CISCO Construction Group. Employee and Visitor Parking.*

"And you're sure it's Fisher?" he asked. He drove directly into the parking lot.

She nodded. "I worked here for quite some time, Max. I know the kinds of cars we use in Panama."

In the far corner of the lot, Max slowed the car to a standstill.

Hands still on the wheel, he turned to Karis. "How do we know they're not in the car?"

Her eyes were on the entrance to the building. "We don't," she said. She opened her door.

As he pulled on the door lever, Max felt the cold snap of metal against his other wrist.

He tried to pull back.

"What the …? What are you doing?!"

She had handcuffed him to the steering wheel.

Unable to find words, he gaped at her.

"I'm so sorry," she said, softly.

He tried again to wrench his wrist free, but only succeeded in sparking a pain that shot up his arm.

"You can't do this!" he shouted.

"Shhh! Keep your voice down!" She hissed. "I have to do my job, Max. You're not trained to enter this kind of situation. It's not safe for me, or for you."

He reached across with his free hand, trying to catch her arm, but she slipped away and stepped out of the car.

"Karis," he said, his voice urgent. "This is *me* here. I'm not some random civilian. That bastard did this to me! You can't stop me from defending myself! It's not right!"

She placed a hand on the top of the car door and turned to look at him.

"Karis, stop! Remember I told you once about my father?" Max's words were fast; desperate. "And how that con artist Rupert Garcia screwed him over?"

She hesitated.

"You're the one who told me to let it go … That he did the best he could under the circumstances." Max leaned toward her as far as he could. "And you were right. But now you're screwing it up for me! I can't do anything if I'm tied to a goddamn … bloody … steering wheel!" He fought the handcuff. "This is my future, Karis! It's *my fight!*"

He could only watch on, numb, as she closed the car door and started to run toward the main building.

Enraged now, he thumped the steering wheel. He fought the cuffs; he punched the car seat.

Until, close to tears, he conceded defeat.

He leaned back on the headrest, and he watched her run.

If this was the end of the line, then so be it.

Max Burns knew he'd done his best.

But then, suddenly—miraculously—Karis stopped running. Poised, with gun in hand at her side, she turned.

Max sat forward. His heart leapt as she started sprinting back to the car.

Without speaking, she pulled open his door and released him.

"Thank you," he said, rubbing his wrists. He got to his feet. "Thank you."

When he took her hand, she looked up at him and kissed him, and for an impossibly small sliver of time he forgot everything as he breathed her in; wrapped his arms around her.

Then, abruptly, she broke away, and the two of them ran—together—into the darkness.

Chapter Seventy-One

Balboa, Panama City, Panama

Uplights in the foyer cast a gentle, ambient light. Enough that Fisher could see framed photographs of the Expansion signing ceremony along two walls: Paco Roco with the President of Panama; Max Burns on the construction site with a safety helmet on. Various configurations of the new CISCO team as they visited the expansion site.

The signed agreements stood in a glass display case along the back wall, although she noticed Larry Roebuck averted his eyes as they passed.

Her own footsteps, in sync with Roebuck's, were the only sound as the two of them moved toward the corridor that took them to the northern wing of the building.

Within minutes, they had reached the office she was looking for.

Dr. Max Burns
Chief Engineer

The door was large and of a dark, polished wood. She turned the brass handle and wasn't surprised when the door swung open.

"Hmm. No security cameras and the doors aren't locked. Not big on security in the tropics, are they?" she murmured. She turned to Roebuck, ushering him into the room. "But I guess the likelihood that someone would abuse their position is pretty low. Under normal circumstances."

Roebuck appeared to ignore her sarcasm and stood, unmoving, in the center of the large, marble floor. It was an office that suited well the title of Chief Engineer.

Fisher stepped inside, taken aback for a moment by the view. Generous windows and a patio looked straight out over the canal itself, and above a dark canopy of tropical foliage was the faraway glow of illuminated steel that delineated the Bridge of the Americas from the inky, tropical night.

With the aid of a small penlight, Fisher moved across to the desk and switched on the desk lamp.

As the room's contents became visible, illuminated but the glow of the lamp, she grew aware that she was in the office of a man whose focus—not unlike her own—was almost entirely on his job: the place was absolutely tidy, with no photographs of family or loved ones on the desk; no clumsy crayon pictures or unidentifiable, childlike clay creations collecting dust on shelves. Just a couple of golf balls and an orange golf tee in the corner of one of the bookshelves, alongside a neatly folded paper napkin. The napkin bore the seal of the Presidency of Panama.

"What are we doing here?" Roebuck asked, his voice steady.

Fisher opened a few of the filing drawers and removed some of the folders.

"What are you doing?" he persisted.

"Sir, I'd ask you to place the gun in the drawer. Wipe it clean first."

Roebuck didn't move.

"Mr. Ambassador, I know you have it. Please put it in the drawer. Now."

Slowly, Roebuck opened his briefcase.

He pulled out a .45 caliber gun.

He pointed it at Fisher.

"My agents know you're with me," she said, unwavering. "And they know you spoke to Gonzáles on the phone this morning."

"And yet, as of now, you're the only one who knows I killed him—"

There was a noise from the hallway, and both of them turned to look at the door.

Silence.

With renewed urgency, Fisher said, "Please, sir. I'm asking you to put the gun in the drawer so the authorities can find it here."

Roebuck narrowed his eyes. "You'd blame the English engineer to save my hide?"

"It's not about you!" Fisher felt herself snap. "You're … nothing! Less than nothing. What have you ever done in your life? Who have you ever served other than your own sorry, political ego?"

At her words, Roebuck smiled, and Fisher berated herself for losing her cool. For giving him anything of herself.

"What's in it for you, then?" he asked. She heard the mock curiosity in his tone. And suddenly she was tired of the man. Tired of his arrogance and grandstanding.

In one swift move, she took her own weapon from her belt and aimed it at Roebuck's face.

Roebuck's hand remained steady.

"If I hand you over to the authorities and they find you guilty," she said, "the United States will never gain control of the Panama Canal again. We'll never be trusted to step in, in any capacity at all. We'll be the laughing stock of the world. But perhaps you didn't think about that when you started playing your little war games?" Her tone was scathing. "Killing me gets you nothing," she snapped. "In fact, I'm your best insurance. Now put the goddamn gun in the drawer!"

Fisher felt a bead of sweat slide down her temple.

Roebuck's attention flickered across her face, and a trace of a smile crossed his lips.

"They don't know where you are, do they?" he said. His finger tightened on the trigger.

My God. He's going to shoot me, and he's going to sleep like a baby tonight.

Fisher grit her teeth: she could kill him now and it would all be over …

"There are always casualties of war," she said, softly. "And, this time, Max Burns is one of them. It's unfortunate. But he's a likely candidate because he has links to the Chinese." She paused. "The Chinese would not hesitate to take advantage of our weakness. And I don't intend to let that happen."

She waited patiently.

"Let's finish what you started."

Chapter Seventy-Two

Balboa, Panama City, Panama

"There are always casualties of war. And this time, Max Burns is one of them ..."

Fisher's words ricocheted around Max's head.

He stood with his back to the wall outside his office door, his mind reeling.

He—Max Burns—was nothing more than a scapegoat in a massive power struggle being played out right there, within arm's reach.

On the other side of the doorway, Karis Deen was mirroring Max's pose. In the half-light of the corridor, he could see her eyes searching his. She seemed focused and calm.

In the room beyond, Roebuck's voice broke the silence.

"So ... you'll let me go?"

Fisher gave a short laugh. "Hardly."

"What do you mean?"

"I'm sick, Larry. Very sick." At Fisher's words, a frown crossed Karis's brow. She tipped her head, listening intently. "My days are numbered. But yours aren't. And you'll have to live with this for the rest of your sorry life: knowing we framed an innocent bystander and destroyed his life. Even though right now you think it won't affect you, one day it will. I can promise you that." She paused. "I'm not sure what you call freedom, Larry, but I don't think it's this."

In the moments that followed, Max held Karis's gaze. She lifted her hands so the gun was close to her face.

"Your patriotism is contagious," Roebuck said. "But I don't think I'll be leaving my safety in anyone else's hands.

Least of all God's." He gave a short laugh. "But it sounds like you've made your peace with him, so you won't mind if I help you along your way."

Frantically, Max shook his head. *Don't go in, Karis!*

"Put down the weapons!"

In a split second, Karis Deen was no longer in the doorway.

Leaping forwards instinctively, Max followed her.

A shot tore through the silence, brutalizing his ears.

Horrified, he watched as Karis's knees buckled and she fell to the floor.

Roebuck stumbled backward, the gun still in his hand.

Fisher quickly moved to stand between Max and Karis, her gun aimed at Max's head.

"Stop right where you are!" she said.

With nothing less than a guttural roar, Max flung himself at the man who had shot Karis; the man whose plan had almost brought down the entire expansion project. His fist ploughed into Roebuck's stomach.

"Max, stop!" He heard Fisher only dimly.

As their bodies hit the floor, Roebuck fought back. He was older, but he was strong.

"Max Burns! Step away!"

But Max saw only red as rage tore through him. He punched with all the might of his anger, and heard a sickening crunch as Roebuck's nose broke.

The two men were locked together as Roebuck's fist collided with Max's jaw. Searing pain shot into his eyes, and he jolted back, bringing the full weight of the older man with him.

Above them, Fisher stood with both hands on her gun. It was pointed at Max's head.

Recoiling, he released his grip on Roebuck's neck, and a second shot rang out.

Through the ringing in his ears, Max became aware of a voice.

He opened his eyes.

It was Tucker Avila.

Fisher lay, motionless, on the floor.

With blood dripping from his chin, Roebuck scrambled on hands and knees toward the corner of the room.

Instinctively, Max got to his feet and, shaking, started walking toward Karis. A dark stain was spreading on the floor by her shoulder.

"See to Agent Deen," Avila barked. He moved swiftly across to Roebuck and cuffed him.

Max sank to his knees at Karis's side.

He wanted to touch her, to stop the bleeding, but he didn't know where it came from.

"How could you do this?!" he said. "How could anyone do this?" He didn't look at Roebuck, though his words were meant for him.

"Karis!" he urged. "Karis! Can you hear me?"

"Sea Bass to Hub: this is Avila. We have two agents down ..."

Chapter Seventy-Three

US Embassy Medical Facility, Clayton, Panama

Max stood near the doorway, a large bunch of long-stemmed, white chrysanthemums in his hand.

In full view of the corridor, Karis was seated on the edge of the hospital bed. Morning sunlight caught her hair while she made conversation with an unseen visitor. She wore her arm and shoulder in a sling.

Max knocked on the doorframe.

Karis stood quickly, seemingly caught off guard. "Max!"

He walked across to the bed and held out the flowers.

"They're beautiful!" she said, taking them from him. "Thank you."

He smiled. "They're from Steven. He said they symbolize strength and longevity."

"Really?"

"I'd have thought you'd know that sort of thing. Being a biologist and all."

Her laugh lit up her face, and she winced, touching her shoulder gingerly.

"Yes," Max continued, "he's really sorry about what happened to you. He sends his best wishes."

She inclined her head to the side, and Max became aware of the man standing at the foot of the bed.

"You know Agent Avila," she said.

"Call me Tucker." Avila shook Max's hand warmly. He wore an aquamarine shirt bearing a pattern of pineapples and surf boards.

"Tucker!" Max said. "I don't know what to say. I am deeply in your debt. Thank you."

"It's all part of the job." Avila grinned.

"Well … indeed. The job," Max echoed. Karis's eyes were on him. "May I ask," he ventured, "how you knew where we were? And that we needed help? Was it some secret agent magic?"

Avila started laughing. "Yeah, I wish!" He gave Karis some kind of significant look. She shrugged, as though to say she had no opinion, and Avila turned back to Max. "I can't give you details, but our colleague was monitoring Karis's biometrics. That's how we knew she'd found Roebuck and Fisher. And that she was in trouble."

"I see. Sort of." Max laughed, self-conscious. He wasn't sure what to say. "Are you … staying on in Panama, then?"

Avila shook his head. "I'm taking off for a couple of weeks' holiday. I just came to say goodbye to Karis." He turned to speak to her directly. "You'd better be in full health for Roebuck's inquiry, Deen. It starts in a couple of months: fraud … murder … You won't wanna miss that one!" He grinned, but then his smile faded. "Did you have any idea Fisher was that sick?"

Karis shook her head. "No, and I can't believe I didn't notice something was off." Her gaze slid across to the window, and she stared for a moment in silence, before looking at Avila. "She didn't have any family," she said, simply.

Avila was silent.

"Shall we get going?" Max prompted, gently.

They turned to him, and Karis nodded.

"Well, I'll be off, then." Avila said, with a cheerful tone. "We'll stay in touch?" He stepped forward and hugged Karis gently. "Gonna miss you, Deen."

"You too, Tuck." Karis now placed the flowers in her restricted hand and then lowered herself into the wheel chair.

As Avila walked away, he tipped an invisible cap at Max. "Look after her!"

Max smiled. He swung Karis's bag onto his shoulder and took the wheelchair handles.

"How's Godfredo doing?" she asked, as they moved toward the door.

"Oh, you know Godfredo: he'll be okay. He's in a detention facility, and I don't think the beds are quite up to his standard, but he's a survivor. He'll probably get a few years in prison for fraud. I saw him a couple of days ago, and he told me Sofia's visited him every day so far."

"No way!" she laughed.

"I know." Max grinned and wheeled the chair down the corridor, toward the elevator.

"Avila just told me Interpol has put out a red alert for Paco, so they'll get him eventually," Karis said. She reached out and pushed the elevator's 'down' button.

Wearily, Max ran a hand through his ever unruly hair. It was hard to believe how close the entire expansion project—and his life—had come to collapsing.

He sighed. Even if he wanted to tell someone the real events of the past few weeks, who would he tell? Who would believe him?

Alan. That's who.

But now he was gone: the man who had nurtured him for so many years. The man who had been there with a kind word and a cold beer, who'd not hesitated to drive through the night to deliver shattering news in the snowy, Swiss mountain village, all those years ago.

The man who embraced life with all its terrible, wonderful stories, and who'd taught him the meaning of love.

"You okay?" Karis's voice was soft.

Max nodded. But the words didn't come. After days of legal bargaining and bureaucracy, he'd been informed he could leave the country to be by Alan's bedside. But by the time that decision was made, it had been too late.

An aching sorrow stole over him.

Karis reached out with her free arm. He took her hand.

In the Embassy hospital foyer, sunlight was reflecting off sparkling floors. The room blazed with the promise of the day to come.

"Max, hold on!" Karis said. "I want to hear this."

Max looked in the direction she was pointing, to see a television screen mounted in the corner of the room, bearing an image of Panama's President Guardia.

The superscript said: *Talks with China and the US.*

Nobody in the foyer was paying any attention to the television.

Max wheeled the chair closer.

"In related news, Panama's President Fernando Guardia held a press conference this morning after talks with US and Chinese officials, where he put an end to rumors that the expansion project will be in any way compromised or delayed by recent events."

There was a cut to President Guardia standing at an official podium.

"Panama has seen many difficult days, and the events of the past week are no exception. However, I'm very pleased to report that with the proposed coordinated financial assistance provided by China and the United States of America, we believe we will be able to complete the expansion project within the expected timescale."

Panama's President waited, smiling, as camera flashes went off. He held up his hand and continued speaking. *"I am also happy to announce that this morning we received confirmation that the chief engineer of the expansion project, Dr. Max Burns, will see the project through with a newly configured consortium ..."*

Karis turned abruptly to look at Max.

"You didn't tell me," she said. "You're staying in Panama?"

"Yes." Max smiled. He knelt in front of the chair so as to look at her directly. "Actually, I was hoping you'd consider staying on with me. I'm sure there'd be a job for you at the Smithsonian Tropical Research Institute," he teased.

She smiled briefly. "Max …" She stopped. "I'm not sure I have what it takes."

He took her hand. "Do you think it's worth a try?" He drew her hand to his lips.

She closed her eyes and took a deep, shuddering breath. As she exhaled, she sat back in the chair.

Slowly, Max wheeled her through the sliding doors and out into sharp, blinding daylight.

Without warning, the chair came to a standstill, and he soon saw that Karis was getting to her feet. She seemed steady. She handed him the flowers.

"Are you sure you're okay?" he asked.

She nodded. "I'm sure. I don't need any help." She gave the wheelchair a gentle push so that it came to rest alongside a bed of red-fruited shrubs by the hospital's sliding doors. She turned away, the wisps of white cigarette smoke from a smattering of people in hospital gowns drifting in her wake.

She fell into step alongside him.

"I called Dalisha last night," Max said. Several cars passed as they stepped onto the sidewalk. "I told her you'd be staying with me for a while. Actually, I wasn't sure what to tell her—"

He didn't finish his sentence because a man was blocking their path.

"Agent Deen?"

The man wore wrap-around sunglasses and an earpiece.

"Agent Deen," he said, again. "Are you ready to go?"

Acknowledgments

The Expansion is a story that landed in my head one day and stubbornly refused to leave. The story was of a scope that I realized would be best tackled by more than one mind, so I approached Libby O'Loghlin, an experienced novelist and substantive editor. Two years later, the magic of collaboration has resulted in The Expansion novel, and a storyworld with characters whose adventures are stubbornly demanding to be continued.

We would like to thank all those who generously gave of their time and expertise to help us enrich and/or hone the manuscript: Jürg Arquint, Timon Birkhofer, Lindsey Grant, Dr. Iris Guery, Sulay Hernandez, Dr. Matthew Larsen, Dr. Roman Müller, Brendan O'Loghlin, Andrew Slater, Brigitte Sommer, Caspar Steiner. We also thank Gareth Howard, Hayley Radford and the Authoright team. And, finally, we thank our families and friends for their enthusiastic support.

About Christoph Martin

Christoph Martin Zollinger is a Swiss entrepreneur whose career spans legal, military, corporate and private enterprise. Christoph graduated with a law degree from the University of Zürich, after which time he went on to live and work in Panama in corporate and private enterprise for more than a decade. In 2012 he returned to Switzerland with his wife and children. He divides his time between his home in Zürich and a tiny Alpine village in Graubünden.

About Libby O'Loghlin

Libby O'Loghlin is an Australian novelist and prize-winning short story writer who has a career in narrative media production, including film and television, as well as print and digital publishing. She has lived in the UK, USA and Malaysia, and she now lives with her family in Switzerland.

www.theexpansionbook.com